Cover design and illustration by Mave Gibson

Library and Archives Canada Cataloguing in Publication

Winkler, Derek, 1971-

Pitouie / Derek Winkler.
ISBN 978-0-9812612-2-5

I. Title.
PS8645.I57255P58 2010   C813'.6   C2010-906228-0

The Workhorsery
132 Heward Avenue
Toronto, ON
M4M 2T7
www.theworkhorsery.ca

10 9 8 7 6 5 4 3 2 1

Mixed Sources
Product group from well-managed forests,
controlled sources and recycled wood or fiber
www.fsc.org   Cert no. SW-COC-000952
© 1996 Forest Stewardship Council
FSC

Pitouie

Derek Winkler

THE
WORKHORSERY

Prologue

Clement Bridgewell, senior vice president of operations, IntraChem Holding Group Plc, was unaccustomed to being shot at. Granted, the bullets in the air did not seem to be aimed specifically at him, but they were travelling in his general direction and coming altogether too close. It was disconcerting.

In his suitcase, which was still in his room, was a half-read paperback spy novel. The protagonist, dejected and haunted by self-doubt, had just had his cover blown and was in the process of fleeing some God-unwelcome Eastern Bloc regime. His controller back at headquarters reported to the chief that the agent had left "in his socks," which was apparently 1960s British spy jargon for "very, very rapidly."

Bridgewell was not wearing socks. He was wearing a fine pair of Italian leather loafers and a lightweight linen suit, minus the jacket and tie, which were also still in his room. He was, however, fleeing a foreign country very, very rapidly. He felt that he was entitled to a bit of exotic jargon.

"Are they far off, Major?" he said.

The major cursed in English and Spanish as the truck hopped across the ruts in the gravel road that plowed its way down the mountain to the airstrip.

"We'll make it," he said, shoving the stick shift down a gear. "The vermin will be too busy looting the palace to secure the airstrip for another half hour at least."

Bridgewell eased one eye around the edge of the canvas top and peered back through the early morning mist and shadow. Dieter Werner from DeutcheSchlamm AG, who was leaving the country "in his pyjamas," elbowed him in the ribs nervously.

"What do you see?"

"Smoke," said Bridgewell. A column of oily black smoke was rising through the red sky above the palace, the residue of the explosion that had awakened him exactly seventeen minutes ago. He didn't know it was exactly seventeen minutes, as his watch was also still in his room.

The explosion happened at dawn, so near that the bomb might have been in his room right next to his watch, his socks, his tie, his electric beard trimmer, and his novel. He had barely slid his feet into his comfortable, handmade Italian leather loafers when the major, pistol in hand and uniform unbuttoned, kicked in his door.

"Los guerrillas," he said, in a sort of contemptuous hiss. He hustled the senior vice president, sans socks, through the palace corridors and into the great hall.

"Wait here," the major said, and ran back toward the guest quarters.

Bridgewell had a few minutes to himself. He spent the time staring at the body on the floor, its face half-turned in a black pool of blood. Bridgewell recognized it as that of the apparently former president. So much for that contract. London would not be pleased.

The major returned, trailing the island's other visitors. Two of them, Werner and Gaston Rostand from Méchant Produit Chimique, Bridgewell had met before. The other three had been strangers to him when they arrived, and they were strangers still. He did not think this was an accidental lapse of courtesy. All took the time to stare at the former president as the major shepherded them across the room, down another hall, out a small side door and into a dusty transport truck. As they bounced through the courtyard and out the main gate, a small group of men with strange hats and automatic rifles opened fire on them.

The gunfire and the shouting foreign voices could still be heard in the distance as they pulled up at the airstrip. The strip was hewn out of the blunt shoreline, almost in the water, the only place on the island flat enough for a runway. The turbo props of the stubby cargo plane were already spinning. The major shoved them up the steps.

"Aren't you coming?" said Bridgewell.

"No, sir," said the major, mirrorshades glinting in the dawn light. "My fate is here. Tell the world how we met our destiny. Tell them Puerto Ombligo is dead."

He snapped a salute, then closed the hatch. A moment later the plane began to move. A moment after that, there was only the red sun on the dark Pacific below.

Chapter 1

*I*t was the backscratcher that did it. If not for the backscratcher, Otis really felt like he could have handled it.

"I'm not going to do this," he said. "It's too dumb."

The backscratcher was about eighteen inches long. The wooden shaft was carved with some kind of pseudo-native pattern to give the impression that this implement came from a remote tribe where the mystic secret of really effective itch relief had been handed down through the centuries. One end bore the avatar of a small hand in ivory, the four fingers crooked and the thumb tucked underneath. The other end was provided with a loop of rawhide cord to keep the device securely attached to the wrist during an intense session.

Which was what was going on now. The Backscratcher was hunched up in his vile orange office chair, rubbing the instrument vigorously up and down his back like a dog humping a really good leg.

"They're all dumb," he said, a semi-orgasmic look on his face. "Never stopped you before."

It was not a face that benefited from a semi-orgasmic look. It was fifty-ish, red and puffy, with a rough patch of hair across the top. The nose was squashed flat, like a boxer's. The body below was also like a boxer's, thirty years past its prime and well marinated in cheap rye.

The Backscratcher kept a bottle of cheap rye in his desk drawer. Together with his wooden prosthesis, Otis supposed it was enough to get him through the day. He wondered if he should try it.

"This is the dumbest one yet," he said. "We have to draw the line somewhere, right? Eventually we have to say, this is too dumb even for us."

The rye, at least, was fitting. All in all, the Backscratcher looked like he should be wearing a trench coat and fedora, working the crime beat on the bad side of town for a trashy tabloid. At the editor-in-chief's desk of *Waste Insight* magazine, he just looked goofy.

"Your problem, kid," he said, eyes squeezed shut with pleasure, "is that you still take this job seriously."

"I don't, Merle," said Otis. "Really. I don't."

"Maybe not," said Merle, opening his eyes and pointing the ivory hand at his head-and-only writer. "But you still feel like you should." He went back to scratching. His eyes closed again.

"Our readers are idiots, Merle. I know. I've met them. I don't feel like I owe them anything much. I'm worried about me. What the fuck am I still doing here? This job has killed my career dead."

Merle snorted.

"Not this shit again. How old are you? Twenty-six? No one has a career at twenty-six."

"I'm thirty-one," said Otis. Merle's brow furrowed under his thatch of hair.

"Damn, where does the time go?" he said. He stopped scratching. Otis was silently grateful.

"The thing about your job," said Merle, sweeping his scepter of friction toward Otis's desk, "is that no one can really tell if you're doing it well or not. And most people don't care. They don't read your stuff to be informed. They read it to feel like they're keeping informed. If they read it at all. Our readers buy our magazine to feel like they've left the door open to becoming informed if the need should ever really come up. I thought you understood this."

"Merle, you're so far past burnout you're carbonized," said Otis. "Did you ever care about this job, way back when the Earth was green? I don't mean this bullshit magazine. I mean the great and noble calling of journalism."

"Maybe. For a while. I forget. Listen. Journalism is not a great and noble calling. It's a fool's errand at best and a cynical con at worst. And we all end up at the cynical con end of the spectrum eventually. You just got here sooner than most. Don't worry. You'll numb to it soon."

"Seven years I've been doing this," said Otis. "Seven years today, actually."

"Happy anniversary," said Merle. Otis snorted.

"When I got here I told myself I'd stick it out for a year or two, pay down my student loans, catch my breath, then go find a real job. What am I still doing here?"

"Collecting a paycheque," said Merle, turning to his keyboard. "Which is more than most people ever get to do by writing. Don't feel bad, kid. I've had those real jobs in this biz. They really aren't any different. Now quit whining and write the damn story."

Otis and Merle formed the entire editorial staff of *Waste Insight; Your Doorway to the Mind of Waste Management*. Once a month they emailed the fruits of their labours to a graphic designer neither of them had ever met, and a new issue would arrive from the printer a couple of weeks later. Together with the publisher, who was also the owner, president, and sales manager, they comprised the complete staff of WI Communications Inc.

"Is our esteemed publisher in today?" said Otis.

"He's got a lunch thing," said Merle, still typing. "Setting up another sponsorship deal."

"Did I ever tell you how much I hate charity golf tournaments?"

"Yes. Write the story."

"What are you working on?"

"The usual. A flattering portrait of the executive vice president of Garbadex and his plans to revolutionize the handling of solid waste in Simcoe County."

"Sounds like cover material."

"Probably. Write the story."

There is a special hell for bright-eyed reporters who don't quite make the big leagues, and it is called trade journalism. *Waste Insight* was the shittiest room in that particular mansion, and Otis was up to his neck in it. They didn't do breaking news or investigative stories at *Waste Insight*. They covered garbage: the collection, transportation, and storage of waste, solid, liquid or gaseous. Their readers consisted exclusively of the mirthless professionals engaged in this inglorious pursuit. No newsstand carried *Waste Insight*, nor did the magazine have any paying subscribers. It was sent free of charge to anyone who might not automatically throw it away as soon as it arrived. The advertisers footed the entire bill.

For this reason, it was pretty much flattering portraits all the way. Otis scanned his eyes over the framed covers of past issues that papered one wall of the office. Each one depicted a silver-haired white guy in a dark suit, gazing into the camera with his best combination of charm and steely resolve on his face. He looked at last month's issue. He had written the cover story. One phone call. Fill in the blanks. Ask for a photo. The cutline read, "Charles Fantino takes FantiCore to new heights!" No one ever took their company to new depths in the pages of *Waste Insight*. If the share price crashed or the police came with warrants for the shredder bins, *WI* would follow the Soviet example and neglect to remember that such a person ever existed. The advertisers preferred it that way.

"Did it ever occur to you that what we really do here amounts to blowjobs for ad dollars?" said Otis.

"Mmm," said Merle.

"I mean, no one here ever just comes out and says it, but everyone seems to understand that if you buy a year's worth of advertising, you get yourself a magazine cover to hang on your office wall."

"Stop stalling and write the story. Then you won't have to think about it anymore."

Otis swivelled his chair back around to his desk. The desk was beige; a steel monstrosity that could have seated three and sheltered them all underneath during an air raid. The chair was beige. The carpet, which had the texture of shredded tires, was a light brown close enough to beige as to make no difference. The walls and acoustic ceiling tiles had once been off-white, but decades of cigarette smoke had yellowed them to the point at which you might as well break down and call them beige too. The room simply wanted to be beige.

The office was on a middle floor of an anonymous concrete cube about halfway between downtown and the suburbs. The publisher lived in the suburbs and commuted in. Otis lived downtown and commuted out. Merle seemed to live at the office. The building was grey. Its windows reflected the featureless slate of the late afternoon, late autumn sky.

Otis didn't have a window. He had a grubby beige computer, a grubby beige phone, and a grubby beige cup of coffee. These were the tools of his trade. As long as he had these, he didn't need to see the world in person.

He prodded the computer. His inbox contained six penis enlargement treatments, five mortgage refinancing offers, and one press release. The press release was the least believable of the messages, but Merle wanted the story, so Otis would write the story. He clicked and read the thing again.

To: owilson@wasteinsightmag.com

From: svache@pitouie.com
Subject: Press Release - Pitouie hosts business
development seminar
For Immediate Release
Attn: Business Editors

The president of the independent corporate freehold of
Federated Pitouie and the chief executive officer of the
Pitouie Development Corporation cordially invites all
interested parties to a seminar and reception. Bask in
the beauty of the southern Pacific Ocean as we discuss
development projects of mutual benefit. Isolation can
be a virtue in sensitive business operations, but in an
increasingly interconnected and carefully monitored
global community, true isolation is becoming a rare
commodity. Come discuss how Pitouie Island can free
your company to operate creatively and without the
restrictions of conventional, regulated international
business. Come and see our flexibility and willingness
to work with you to meet your goals and solve your
waste management problems.

Date: November 30 to December 7
Location: Presidential Palace, Pitouie City, Pitouie

For more information or to make travel arrangements,
contact our public relations representative Sarah
Vache at svache@pitouie.com or visit our website at
www.pitouie.com - 30 -

Otis read through the message several times. Invitations to
business seminars were an occupational hazard he had long since
learned to avoid, but a business seminar on a remote South Pacific
island had rarity value. On top of that, this island seemed to be
soliciting international corporations to descend upon its virgin

shores and rape them until the bones showed through. That would be kinky to watch.

Otis opened a new browser window and punched up pitouie. com. An animation began to play, backed by anthemic music that was probably more impressive when not piped through tinny computer speakers. On the screen, pictures of a green and rocky landscape were sliding back and forth and fading in and out. When the slideshow ended a logo appeared in the centre of the screen: a generic, circular, swirly thing in blue and green. The text underneath read, "Welcome to Pitouie." The music, more like a jingle than an anthem, looped back to the beginning. Otis turned the sound off.

He clicked a button labelled "About Us." The logo and button bar swirled their way to the top of the screen to make room for a block of text. It read:

> The island of Pitouie is an independent corporate freehold in the southern Pacific Ocean approximately halfway between Chile and New Zealand. Although diplomatically in free association with Chile, the island is owned and operated by the Pitouie Development Corporation. Travel to the island is by boat or by chartered flight from Santiago. Please visit our Contact page for more information about making travel arrangements. Please click this link for more information about the people and history of Pitouie.

There were two images. The first was a map of the South Pacific with a yellow star floating in the middle of it. A set of longitude and latitude coordinates were printed neatly across the blank blue virtual sea. The second image was a portrait of an unsmiling man in a severe suit. He had a deeply lined and weather-beaten face, a grizzled beard, close-cropped grey hair, and blank, expressionless eyes. The caption underneath read, "President Don Roderigo Esquival Bolivar San Sierra Lopez."

Otis clicked the "Mission" button. Another block of text faded into view. It read, "The Pitouie Development Corporation strives to achieve growth by synergizing with international corporate partners in a paradigm encompassing mutual benefits." The letters were large and set in the middle of the screen like a Zen koan. Otis thought they must have gotten some professional help with that one.

In the "News" section, he found only the press release he already had. The "Images" button triggered a replay of the slideshow. The "Contact" page was blank except for an email link to info@pitouie.com.

Otis went back to the "About Us" page and clicked the "more information" link. It took him to a long article that seemed to have been copied and pasted from an encyclopedia. Believing in the value of thorough research, Otis began to read.

Pitouie

Pitouie [pit-OO-ee] is an island nation in the southern Pacific Ocean. Although self-governing, it is in free association with Chile. Pitouie is located 1,300 km west and 250 km south of Easter Island. The approximately 1,500 residents of the island are predominately Polynesian and speak a regional dialect of their own, although official government business is usually conducted in Spanish.

Capital: Pitouie City

Government: Corporate freehold

Head of Government: President Don Roderigo Esquival Bolivar San Sierra Lopez

Area: 50 square kilometres

Population: 1,500 (estimated)

Currency: Chilean peso

History: Pitouie was first settled by Polynesian explorers approximately 400–600 CE, according to limited archaeological evidence. This would make the settlement of the island roughly contemporaneous with that of Easter Island and Hawaii. This early settlement did not endure, however, for the island was uninhabited when first encountered by Europeans. There is no evidence to suggest why the colony failed. Even the question of whether the inhabitants died out or simply moved on has not been satisfactorily answered.

The English explorer James Cook encountered the island in 1774, referring to it as Steep Island in his log. As it contained no natural resources that could not be obtained more easily elsewhere, no European power ever claimed the island as a territory, and it continued to stand empty.

The government of Chile laid claim to the island in 1923, naming it Puerto Zepto and installing a skeleton administrative staff on the site that is now Pitouie City. Government geologists spent several years prospecting for minerals, but found nothing valuable enough to justify the expense of extraction. Bird guano harvesting continued for almost a decade, but eventually the Chileans abandoned their outpost.

In 1945, the United States Navy built an airstrip and a harbour on the island in order to use it as a rear area and refuelling station in its war with Japan. By the time construction was completed, however, the war was over. No operations were ever conducted from the outpost, designated McClellan Station, which was abandoned by the American military in 1946.

Given the improvements made by the Americans, the Chileans re-asserted their claim to the island in 1962 with plans to market it as a tourist destination for travellers seeking the ultimate in isolation. The Chilean advance party found the place occupied by Polynesians who had been displaced from their homes during the war and who had been living unnoticed on the island since 1947. However, the Polynesians had no objections to having the Chileans among them, and the Chileans had no objection to sharing their resort with a picturesque group of native fishermen, so no conflicts arose.

The Chileans refurbished some of the military structures left over from the war, repaired the neglected airstrip and harbour, and renamed the island Isla Verde. Despite a considerable marketing effort, the promise of complete isolation failed to draw large crowds. In 1987, the Chileans pulled out again, leaving a few token government representatives. The natives simply went on fishing.

In 2002, the elders of the tribe formally adopted the Chilean governor, Roderigo Lopez, who renounced his Chilean citizenship and began negotiating the island's independence. Two years later, this was achieved with the signing of a contract of free association between Chile and the island, now officially renamed Pitouie.

There was more, but Otis didn't feel any burning desire to read it. Pitouie sounded like a place where failure went to die. Maybe he could retire there in another thirty years or so.

He flicked back to his word processor and read through his day's output. He was writing short news brief stories for the front of the issue; small fecal appetizers for the reader before the featured dish of bullshit. The first one read, "Allomex Industries has introduced a new integrated customer management system at its head office in Duluth. According to the company, the system, installed at an estimated cost of $2.6 million, will allow managers in its branch offices to access customer purchase histories through a web-based interface 'with unprecedented speed and efficiency.'"

Otis wasn't exactly sure what that meant, but he was pretty sure no one at Allomex knew what it meant either. He noticed during his read-through that he had neglected to mention what the company did. He pulled up the press release. It didn't say what the company did either. Otis decided he didn't care and let the story stand.

The next item read, "Vilantra Inc. has appointed Franklin Houlton to the position of executive vice president of integrated development. He was previously the senior vice president of development integration at Mollbol Ltd."

Otis had no idea what an executive vice president of integrated development was supposed to do all day, nor what the difference was between an executive vice president of integrated development and a senior vice president of development integration. Again, he found he didn't care. No matter how much he left out of a story, no matter how opaque the management jargon became, no one ever asked for clarification. Otis liked to imagine it was an Emperor's New Clothes situation, with no one in the crowd willing to call his bluff and risk looking ignorant of the latest management buzzwords. More likely, no one was reading his stuff at all, except maybe to do a quick scan for their own names. Otis often considered writing a computer program that would take random sentences from their archive of 12,942 old stories and recombine them into new stories, just to see if anyone would notice. But this would mean learning to program first, so it was easier to keep writing them himself.

Like in this case. He took a sip of lukewarm beige coffee, poised his fingertips over the grubby keyboard and began the act of composition.

"The island of Federated Pitouie will host a business development seminar on November 30 intended to inform potential investors of the waste management opportunities offered by the small South Pacific nation. The Government of Pitouie, in association with the Pitouie Development Corp., is seeking development copartners open to the advantages of doing business in a remote and autonomous area. Interested parties can find more information on the island's website, located at <http://www.pitouie.com>."

He read it over again. It sounded like a thinly veiled come-on from a prostitute in the classified section of a tabloid newspaper. Good enough. He hit save. 12,943.

"Story's done, Merle," he said. Merle grunted. He left for lunch, secure in the knowledge that he had earned his daily bread. Well, maybe earned wasn't exactly the right word. What was the right word? He didn't really care.

"Here," said Merle. He dropped a small plastic box on Otis's desk. "You want this?"

"What is it?" said Otis.

"An MP3 player, I think. Or a digital voice recorder or something. Just came from the launch event for that new recycling centre. Everybody got one."

"You actually went to that?"

"There was an open bar."

Otis turned the thing over in his hands. It was shaped like a little garbage can with a tiny LCD screen on the back. There was an illegible logo silkscreened on the side, along with the slogan, "Save it!"

"Why is it shaped like a garbage can when they're supposed to be into recycling?" said Otis.

"Probably because no one makes a voice recorder in the shape of a recycling bin," said Merle.

"But they make them in the shape of a garbage can?"

"Evidently."

"You know I don't like to accept trinkets from the people we write about."

"You didn't accept it. I did. Besides, it could be useful. Happy anniversary."

"Thanks."

"You've got a call."

Otis looked down at the blinking phone and grimaced. It was late. Five more minutes and he could have escaped. Public relations flacks from across the nation continued to call him every day, even though he never had any follow-up questions, never needed them to set up a personal interview with the senior vice president of acquisitions and never accepted invitations to attend power breakfasts with their clients. He was privately of the opinion that they continued calling out of sheer bloody-mindedness. He picked up the phone.

"Otis Wilson," he said.

"Mr. Wilson?" said a smooth female voice. Flack. Her first question is going to be, Did you get the press release I sent over?

"This is Sarah Vache of Vache Communications. How are you today?"

Okay, mandatory minimal courtesy didn't really count.

"I'm fine," he said. "How are you?"

"Fine, thank you," said the voice. "Did you receive the press release I sent you earlier today?"

Otis banged his brain against the side of his skull to wake himself up.

"Which one was it?" he asked.

"The one about Pitouie Island."

"Yes," he said. "I have it right here."

"Oh good," said the voice. It was a very pleasant voice. "Do you think your publication will be interested in covering the story?"

Otis didn't tell her the story was already written; a one-paragraph encapsulation of the release that had taken him a tough three minutes to compose.

"We'll probably do something with it," he said.

"Wonderful," said the voice. "Do you have any questions? Is there any more information you need?"

Otis didn't need any more information, but because the voice was so pleasant he quickly scanned the release again and came up with something to say.

"What's a free association?" he said.

"It means that Pitouie is an independent, autonomous state, but Chile represents us in the international community in certain limited areas. We don't have a seat in the United Nations. We don't have foreign embassies. We don't have an army. If we ever need any of those things, Chile lets us borrow theirs."

"Mmm," said Otis. "Pitouie. Is that a Polynesian word? What does it mean?"

"It's not Polynesian, and it doesn't really mean anything. When the island gained autonomy two years ago, nobody could agree on a new name. Eventually they hired a corporate naming consultant. Told him they wanted something that evoked the spirit of contemporary business practice while at the same time paying homage to their Polynesian heritage. The consultant asked where the island was. I told him it's sort of halfway between Pitcairn and Niue. So he came up with..."

"Pitouie," said Otis.

"Yes," she said. Otis could feel her shrug over the phone line. "The islanders all seem to like it."

"You keep using the word 'autonomous,'" said Otis, "But you don't use the word 'sovereign.'"

"According to the strict definition of international law, Pitouie doesn't quite qualify as sovereign, but the Pitouie Development Corporation has title to all the real estate and unrestricted development rights. The Government of Pitouie, under the terms of the Contract of Free Association, has full authority over domestic, civil, and legal matters."

"Is there any conflict between the corporation and the government?" asked Otis.

"Oh no," said Vache. "They're both run by the same man. Our president."

"He's president of the island and the company?"

"Yes. Also chief executive officer and tribal chieftain."

"So he gets to make laws that benefit his own company? The other businesses on the island must love that."

"There are no other businesses on the island," said Sarah Vache. "Just the Pitouie Development Corporation. Every resident of the island is a shareholder. Our town hall meetings are also board meetings."

"Mmm," said Otis. "And the corporation is in the waste management business?"

"That's right," she said.

"People really find it worth their while to go all the way out to the middle of the Pacific just to dump their garbage?"

"Some do. It depends on the garbage."

"Mmm."

"Why do you keep saying 'Mmm?'"

"I learned it from my editor," he said, surprised into honesty. "It acknowledges a reply without agreeing with it, but it still sounds friendly and thoughtful."

"Mmm," she said.

"Nicely done."

"Thank you."

"I'm still not sure I understand about the garbage."

"Well," she said, extra pleasant. "Why don't you come to Pitouie and see for yourself? We have a limited number of positions open at our upcoming conference for members of the media. I would be glad to hold a spot for you."

Otis took a moment to savour the offered bribe. Lots of flacks had tried to buy a good story from him with drinks, meals, T-shirts, once even a weekend skiing trip. He always turned them down. He liked to think it was the difference between being personally corrupt and being part of a corrupt system. Even so, no one had ever offered him a trip to the South Seas before.

He considered selling out, just this once. Then he had a better idea. He could pretend to sell out. He could go to this island in the guise of a well-trained lapdog, then suddenly snap and tear the throat out of his unsuspecting new owner. The outline of the story flashed in his head: the innocent natives, the corrupt government officials, the heartless international corporations. The title: A Paradise Lost. By Otis Wilson. *Waste Insight* wouldn't run it, but he knew someone who would.

He'd have to pitch the story first. What was that guy's name again? He'd have to get time off work. Merle wouldn't be thrilled. He'd have to explain it to Clarisa. She'd never come with him. He'd have to get a passport and probably a bunch of vaccinations against vicious tropical diseases. He'd have to spend days on airplanes and in rat-hole South American airports. All to go to some island no one had ever heard of and watch them hopefully drop the soap in the prison shower of international commerce. It was tiring just to think about it.

"I'm not sure I can fit this into my schedule," he said. It was a line that had gotten him out of many a flack-laden event. He was going to have it carved on his tombstone. "Let me get back to you on that."

"Of course," she said. "Do you have any other questions?"

"While we've been talking, you've kept switching back and forth between 'we' and 'they.' Are you from Pitouie yourself?"

The phone crackled.

"I'm related to the people of the island," she said finally, "but I wasn't born there and I don't spend much time there. It's one of the reasons I handle their media relations."

"I'm sorry if that was too personal a question," said Otis.

"Not at all," she said smoothly. "Thank you for your time. I hope you'll be able to make it to the conference."

"Thank you," said Otis. There was a click, and the pleasant voice was gone.

"Pitouie," he said, and hung up the phone.

Chapter 2

*L*ars Varick stood in the gloom at the end of the runway and listened to the drone of a plane he could not see. The runway was a narrow strip of hard-packed snow lined on each side with oil drums full of rocks. Each drum had a tall pole planted in it, and each pole had an alarmingly dim blue light on the top. It didn't matter. It was a ski plane. Hitting the runway was more or less optional. The double row of landing lights mostly served as an arrow pointing to the nearest heated building.

The drone grew louder. Lars heard a thump and the scrape of skis. The plane was down, evidently. A shape detached itself from the shapeless night and trundled into view. It was an ugly, indestructible little plane with a single propeller to pull it through the air, seats for six and a cargo pod slung underneath. The pilot killed the engine and climbed out while his vehicle was still sliding the last few feet to a halt. He walked over to Lars.

"Varick."

"McMannus."

The pilot produced a small plastic bag and laid it in Lars's hand without ceremony. Lars hefted it appreciatively, slipped it inside his parka and handed over a wad of cash. McMannus nodded. He walked around to the other side of his craft and opened the passenger door. A figure was huddled inside, strapped down tight in the copilot's seat. McMannus unbuckled him, then walked away toward the idling snowmobile. The man eased himself out of the plane as if he were afraid it might wake up startled and suck him back in.

The stranger was a civilian. His face was barely visible under the hood of a brand new and expensive-looking down parka, but he was middle-aged, soft and well rounded. He did not seem thrilled to be there.

"Welcome to PIN-AA, sir," said Lars.

"Yeah, thanks," said the man. "I'm here to see somebody called Woolsey."

"Chief Woolsey is waiting for you. This way please."

Lars led the way to the snowmobile, the stranger stumping and sliding along behind him. The three of them piled into the bus, a beetle-like relic of the fifties. Lars got the beast in gear on the third try, and its broad tracks shoved them the quarter-mile up the rocky access road to the station. The stranger peered out the grubby porthole.

"Not much to see out there," he said.

"You're a little early," said Lars. "Dawn's not for another three weeks. To the left are the storage huts. To the right is the fuel dump. The station is that light up ahead."

Distant Early Warning Line Station PIN-AA was stuck like a thumbtack into an outcropping of rock on the coast of the Arctic Ocean in the Northwest Territories of Canada. It was a train of five prefabricated steel modules like oversized railway boxcars balanced on a thicket of stilts. Standing over the station on a squat tower was a large, white geodesic dome. Inside the dome was a 30-foot wide antenna, rotating once per minute.

"What in God's name are human beings doing up here?" said the man.

"Standing on guard for thee," said McMannus.

Lars had to admit, there wasn't much to see at PIN-AA. Life here was coloured black, white, and green. Black January sky.

White snow on the ground to the horizon in all directions, unseen in the blackness. A green line sweeping the black face of a radar screen twenty-four hours a day, scanning for Russian bombers that weren't coming. Lars had grown to appreciate the sparseness of it, the minimalism. Life here was like a wireframe drawing with nine-tenths of the detail omitted. Existence reduced to a black void and a sweeping green line suited him very well. A thousand miles from anywhere, waiting dispassionately to see if the world would end. Nothing else expected of him. It was a little dull, but satisfying in its own way. Even comforting, sort of. His job was to stare into the empty screen for a third of each day and press a button if anything should ever appear there.

Russia's bombers were obsolete now, replaced by intercontinental ballistic missiles. The missiles were watched for by satellites floating in space, the only lookout even colder and blacker than this place, the most distant outpost of the coldest of wars. The DEW Line was obsolete too, but in the finest military tradition, it soldiered on regardless. From the Aleutian Islands to the east coast of Greenland, men crouched in metal boxes in the middle of an eternal midnight blizzard, just in case.

PIN-AA was an anomaly in this useless chain of apocalyptic heralds. It was the last of the I-class stations. The "I" stood for "intermediate." With flawless military logic, this meant it was the smallest type of outpost. The six big Main stations, spaced every five hundred miles along the Arctic Circle, were teeming urban jungles in comparison. With a crew of fifty, a Main station was a bastion of civilization. They had libraries, movie theatres, bars. Maybe even an occasional woman. Between the Main stations were twenty-three Auxiliary stations, one every hundred miles. An Aux station had a crew of about twenty. They got films to show on nailed-up sheets after the Mains were done with them. The cooks were usually pretty good, and the weekly beer ration could make life fairly pleasant.

Between the Aux stations had stood the I stations: twenty-eight gap-fillers with crew compliments that could be tallied on one hand. They had only simple fluttar radar that would be tripped by low-altitude targets directly overhead. Twenty-seven of the I stations had been closed down and abandoned ten years ago. Because it occupied a particularly favourable site, PIN-AA had been allowed to remain in operation. During the brief summer of 1965, the weedy fluttar antennas had come down, and the mighty white ball had gone up. Lars had arrived eight brief summers later. Most technicians were only expected to pull a two-month stretch at an I station before being allowed to return to humanity. Lars had stayed for two years. The place was home.

He pulled the snowmobile to a stop along side the station and held the small door open for the stranger and McMannus. Then he held the door to the station open for them, only having to kick it twice in the lower right corner to break it loose. The door led to a small room like a combination airlock and closet. Lars and McMannus peeled off toques, mitts, and parkas and hung them on hooks. The stranger did not.

"You can leave your coat here, sir," said Lars. "The base is quite comfortable."

Reluctantly, the man unzipped himself and shrugged the coat off. It wasn't a working coat. It was a garment designed for lounging around ski resorts. Lars took it from him and hung it next to his own parka of olive drab canvas and molting fur trim. Under his designer coat, the stranger was wearing a full three-piece suit complete with tie tack and cufflinks. Lars looked down and saw that the man was also wearing thin patent leather dress shoes, the kind with vent holes around the toes. Brand-new parka and patent leather shoes, thought Lars. Clearly the guy has never been up here before. Someone told him he would need a parka, so he went out and bought a parka. Lars wondered if he were a government official, but government guys didn't dress this well.

Even CIA guys didn't dress this well.

Lars showed him to the door of the station chief's office and knocked. There was a sort of bark from the other side. Lars opened the door and stood aside to let the stranger enter. Then he placed himself in the doorway to await further orders. McMannus stomped off toward the mess and the coffee pot.

The chief's office was cramped, like every room in the base. There was a metal desk, for once devoid of file folders. There was a filing cabinet, where the folders had likely been shoved a few minutes earlier. There were a couple of metal chairs. There was a bookcase filled with technical manuals. The walls were covered in maps of the polar region studded with pushpins.

There were a bottle of Scotch and two glasses on the desk. Lars blinked. He had never seen the chief take a drink. Then again, the chief had never seen him roll a joint, so he supposed they were even. The chief stood behind his desk. He held out his hand to his guest, who shook it perfunctorily. No salutes, Lars noted.

"Thank you for coming," said the chief. "Please sit down."

The man did so, his eyes on the bottle.

"Dismissed," said the chief to Lars. Lars closed the office door and went to find his rolling papers.

The papers were where he had left them, tucked inside the April 1971 issue of Playboy in his footlocker in the sleeping quarters. He plucked them from between the thighs of Miss April, then tossed them and the baggie to Franks. Franks pivoted cleanly into an upright position like someone had pulled a lever under his bunk.

"Thank God," he said. "I don't think I could have handled another straight shift."

His fingers moved with speed and precision. A minute later, the sleeping quarters began to get hazy. A minute after that, the unseen hand released the lever, and Franks relaxed back onto the bunk. He passed the joint to Lars and reached without looking for the turntable. He lifted the arm back to the edge of the record and set the needle in the groove with imperturbable precision. A distorted guitar began to play again.

"Thought you said you were going to lay off after the old man caught you last time," said Lars. He took a toke. It was weak shit, but you took what you could get up here. The thought of facing the long, dark days ahead without the solace of the baggie had been disheartening.

"Nah. I said I was going to lay off smoking at the console. He never would've known otherwise. When was the last time he ever came in here?"

Their quarters took up half of a module. It housed three sets of bunk beds for crew and visitors. In the absence of visitors or extra crew, Lars and Franks had divided the six bunks between them and rotated daily. They did this partly for the sake of variety and partly to put off the day they would have to break down and wash the sheets. The room smelled like a place where men had spent fifteen years wearing a lot of heavy clothing and seldom doing laundry. The permanent fog of smoke didn't improve the atmosphere. It was just as well no visitors ever came by. The station chief had his own quarters at the other end of the module train, next to his office. He never came by either.

"So did the big mystery guest arrive?" said Franks.

"Yep."

"Did the old man say what he's doing here?"

"Nope. 'You're not cleared to know, soldier. Escort him to me and don't ask him any questions.'"

"What a prick."

"Nah, he's all right."

The station chief called everybody soldier, even though they were all civilian contractors. Lars didn't mind. Sterling Woolsey was a retired Canadian Army captain, a trim man on the north

— 26 —

side of sixty who still retained the stiffness and the mustache of his military days. Lars had wondered a bit at the old-timer when he arrived a year ago. The Powers-That-Be usually favoured young men for DEW Line duty and Americans for station chiefs. Then again, it was hard to persuade anyone to accept a post at PIN-AA, so maybe they had been happy to get him. The grapevine considered him impressive. The man had stormed Juno Beach in '44 and taken a bullet during the Battle of the Scheldt. Now he was old and winding down, but he was an okay chief.

PIN-AA currently had a crew of three: Woolsey, Franks, and Lars. Lars was the radician. He maintained the radar and communications equipment. He had learned his trade at an exact recreation of a DEW Line Aux station in an Illinois cornfield. Radio maintenance was routine. He tested all the bits and pieces according to a regular schedule, and if anything looked like it was on the verge of going pop, he yanked it out and slotted in the spare. Once in a while, he would power something down and clean it, digging into the back of a dull green metal cabinet with a non-conductive brush to scrub the crud from between the circuit boards. In his twenty-four years, he had never known less stressful work, and he felt a moderate satisfaction every time he sat down at the scope and watched the green line sweep the screen once a minute, regular and reliable.

They used to have a fourth crew member: a cook named Travis Something. He had been a good cook and a pretty decent guy, but the solitude and the darkness had got him. He became convinced that the seals were out to get him, swore he could hear them moving around under the kitchen module, bumping their heads against the floor looking for air holes. Lars had found him one day crouched on the counter next to the stove, still as a stone and pointing a revolver at the floor, waiting for the first whiskered snout to appear. No one had ever seen that revolver before. The cook was flown out strapped down on a stretcher. PIN-MAIN hadn't got around to sending out a replacement cook yet. The three of them had been living on beans and toast ever since. This also had not improved the atmosphere in the sleeping quarters.

"What are you going to do when you get out of here, Frankie?"

"Ehh. Got a cousin back home who works at a garage. Said he could get me a wrenching job."

Steve Franks was a mechanic from Edmonton. He looked like seven coat hangers caught in a sweater, but he was a demon with a diesel. He maintained the generators that kept the station running and the bulldozer that kept the runway open. His only problem was that he could not sit still for ten minutes without green and leafy assistance, which made manning the scope for eight hours a day pure torture.

Lars took another toke and held the joint back to Franks.

"I got no idea what I'm going to do," he said. "They offered me a new contract at CAM-MAIN, but I said no. Don't think I could handle a crowd that big after this. Might as well go back to civilization. Thing is, I can't go back home either."

He stopped. Should he have said that? What the hell. Frankie wouldn't care.

"I left some things behind that are still there," he said. "Things I wouldn't want to find again. Or, you know, more like, things I wouldn't want to find me again. I, uh, never told that to anyone before."

He noticed he was still holding his arm out. He turned his head to look at Frankie. He was asleep. Lars lay back and finished the spliff himself as the guitar turned itself inside out in the background.

He wasn't feeling keenly inquisitive when he was summoned by loudspeaker back to the chief's office an hour later. He knew from experience that Woolsey wouldn't notice his chemically enhanced condition, but he was slightly concerned about the stranger. However, when the door opened he saw that both men had a certain rosy glow of their own, and he passed without suspicion.

"Varick," said the chief, slapping the stranger on the back. "Escort our guest back to the plane."

Lars threw an unrequired salute and did so, collecting McMannus from the mess on the way. As the plane droned back into the darkness, Lars was already putting the strange visit out of his mind. After two days, he had ceased to think of it.

Then the plane landed again.

It was the same drill. A well-dressed civilian arrived at the base in brand-new cold weather gear, had a private meeting with the chief and flew away an hour later.

The next week, a third stranger arrived. After ensconcing this one in Woolsey's office, Lars went in search of McMannus. He found the pilot in the kitchen, drinking coffee and listening to the weather radio.

"Who are all these assholes?" asked Lars. "Where are they coming from?"

The pilot shrugged.

"Don't know who they are, but they aren't official."

"What does that mean?"

"I mean, they don't work on the line. Line personnel always transfer through a main station. I picked these guys up at the airfield in Inuvik."

"The military isn't sending these guys?"

"Nope."

"Could be Western Electric guys."

Western Electric operated the DEW Line stations under contract to the United States Air Force, which shared its authority over PIN-AA with the Royal Canadian Air Force. Lars wasn't sure which of these had the final authority over him, but since no one had ever tried to exert any authority over him, he wasn't troubled by the ambiguity.

"No, those guys all go by Alaska," said McMannus.

"Then they're government."

"No. This is a special private charter."

"By who?"

"Your chief."

Lars didn't bother to suppress the blink.

"But you can't just bring civilians into a place like this," he said. "This is supposed to be a top secret national defence installation. How did he get clearance for this?"

McMannus checked that no one else was in the mess, then leaned forward and lowered his voice.

"I don't think he did. My flight plans for these little trips all say I'm going to the village of Iglertok. It just so happens that this is the closest airstrip, and as a military contractor, I have clearance to land."

"But these assholes don't have clearance to enter the base."

McMannus shrugged.

"I hand them over to you, an official member of base personnel. If you take them inside, that's your breach of security, not mine."

Lars blinked again.

"You bastard," he said.

"What do you care?" said McMannus. "It's all on the old man if it blows up."

"Risky for you," said Lars. "If anyone finds out, you'll never get another military contract."

The pilot shrugged again.

"Plenty of flying to do up here. Besides, I owe Woolsey a few favours."

"How many more are coming?"

"No idea."

"What are they doing here?"

"Don't know. Don't care."

McMannus drained his cup and stood up.

"It goes without saying," he said, "If you mention this to anyone else, you'll be smoking seal shit until the end of your stay."

"Who would I mention it to?"

"You'd find somebody. You're just itching to get into this, and you don't even know why. I can see it on your face. This is the first interesting thing to happen to you in years. What the fuck you're doing, sitting up here in a little tin box, is beyond me."

He walked out. Lars sat and thought until the loudspeaker summoned him again.

Chapter 3

"This guy is perfect."

"What makes you say that?"

"Did you read what I sent you?"

"Sure. It's garbage."

"Yes, but the thing is, he's actually very sharp. Under other circumstances, he would probably be producing great stuff."

"You talked to him?"

"Yes. He's got just the right mixture of self-hatred and self-pity, with just enough self-respect left to get him started."

"So you invited him. What did he say?"

"He said no, but I think he'll change his mind."

"Why?"

"I think he's about to get dumped by his girlfriend."

"How the hell do you know that?"

"You asked me to check him out. You know I believe in thoroughness."

"Uh-huh. So when will we know for sure?"

"Shouldn't be long now."

"I got invited to a conference in the South Pacific today," said Otis. "On a little tiny island called Pitouie."

"Never heard of it," said Clarisa. "Are you going to go?"

"Nah. Told them I couldn't fit it into my schedule."

Clarisa began to push the remains of the vegetarian bread pudding around her plate more forcefully. Otis made it from his sister's recipe. It tasted like fermented plastic, but his Clarisa liked it. He had overcooked the broccoli again.

"You remember I told you about that guy who lives next door to me?" she said.

"Jimmy something. The pothead."

"James," she corrected. "I told you that last month the smoke rolling out from under his door set off the fire alarm. The smell was unbelievable."

"You used to like it," said Otis, tipping more wine into their glasses.

"It's the incense he uses to try to cover it up," she said. "Smells like every sweat sock in India burning all at once. I told you that the next time he was polluting the whole floor with that crap, I would bang on his door and tell him I prefer the smell of the weed."

"Yeah."

"Well. I did. Thursday night."

"Heh. What happened?"

"He invited me in to finish off the baggie," she said. Then, drawing an irrevocable breath, she added, "I didn't get home until Saturday morning."

"So that's where you were," said Otis. "I called. Crashed on his sofa, huh?"

A longer pause.

"Not on his sofa," she said. She looked at him steadily.

Otis looked at her blankly. It was the only look in his repertoire that matched what was going on in his brain.

"It's for the best," she said. Her voice sounded like high heels on eggshells. Clarisa didn't eat eggs and she didn't wear high heels, but she did a good vocal impression. "We're not going anywhere.

I'm sorry."

"Just like that?" he said. "A couple of bong hits, a one-night stand, and you're ditching me?"

"Two nights," she corrected. "Plus the day in between. Plus the days since then." She glanced around his apartment, and her eyes went from expressionless to sad. "Plus the last year and a half."

Otis didn't moved. He considered the state of his brain. He felt there should be more going on in there. This was the woman he loved, right? Loved as much as he had ever loved anyone. He had cleared a space for her in his life. He was used to the idea of her. He cooked terrible vegetarian food for her. Now she was going. Okay, maybe it wasn't much of a cue for passion, but shouldn't there be something? At least for the sake of form? But there wasn't. Just a sort of dull buzzing of the synapses.

There was a way to salvage this, he knew. She wasn't really going. She was just unhappy for some reason. All he had to do was figure out what was making her unhappy, then say something that would let her know it would be all right. He just needed to say the right thing.

"Are you sure?" he said.

She nodded. She stood up. She was willowy to the point of being spindly and she moved like she was powered by wound-up rubber bands and Otis couldn't remember her ever being more beautiful. She put her hand over his hand where it lay motionless on the table, next to the cheap and mostly empty wine bottle.

"We're stuck," she said. "I'm stuck. You're even more stuck. Your whole life." She shook her head. "I just feel like there should be more. I'm going to go see if I can do something. You should too."

She walked to the door. She walked out. She didn't look back.

Otis sat for a while and examined the buzz in his brain. Maybe there would be a delayed reaction. Was he about to flip over the table, weep uncontrollably, maybe hurl the empty bottle at the door where it would shatter into a thousand razor-sharp splinters symbolic of his broken heart?

Apparently not.

He cleared the table. He did the dishes. He sat down at his computer and loaded an ultra-violent video game. He slaughtered a few dozen mutant invaders. Maybe he could channel his suppressed rage and pain into this harmless escape, thereby releasing himself from the desperate need to go kick down her door. He didn't feel such a need, but it was good to have options.

Maybe he would enter into the game deeply and reach a Zen state of no-mind with which he could achieve a full understanding of his place in the universe. He chased a mutant around a corner and caught a rocket-propelled grenade in the virtual face. The level reset itself. He quit the game.

He punched his way across a few websites, but nobody seemed to have anything very amusing to tell him. For lack of a more interesting destination, he pulled up pitouie.com. The swirly logo and jingly anthem moved him not. He watched the slideshow of palm trees and rocky hills and ocean vistas and smiling natives without sensation. He clicked back to the encyclopedia entry and finished reading it.

Geography: Pitouie is approximately fifty square kilometres in area. It is a volcanic island roughly triangular in shape. The dormant volcano, Mount Pitouie, is located in the southeast of the landmass. The terrain is very steep and rocky, yet the tropical climate and rich volcanic soil produce a thick covering of plant life over most of the island.

Economy: Pitouie has no measurable economy. The residents live on fish, birds, and local root vegetables. There are no natural resources of any value on the island and no industry. There is only one company operating on the island, the recently formed Pitouie Development Corporation, which exists to promote development opportunities to foreign investors. To date, no such investors have been attracted.

An interesting feature of Pitouie Development is that every resident of the island holds a share in the company, and the current head of government is also president and chief executive officer of the business entity. This unique arrangement, according to the Government of Pitouie, comprises an entirely new system of government, which it has dubbed the corporate freehold. However, this term is not widely recognized by political scientists or economists. Until such time as Pitouie generates any revenue, the question is largely one of semantics.

What a useless place, Otis thought. Pathetic. He played the slideshow again. He had been invited. He could go and stand on that beach right there, with all the native losers. He could do that.
He watched TV instead.
Three hours later, it hit him.

The fear came upon him like half a glass of ice water poured into his heart, like a jacket two sizes too tight zipped-up his chest. He felt the need to flee. His heart beat like the organ would break itself free of his rib cage and scuttle away under the sofa. He sat and sweated and hyperventilated and waited to see if he would die.
He didn't. Gradually the adrenaline drained away, leaving him shaky and a bit sick. He got up and began turning on lights. He paced around his apartment and looked at it like it belonged to a stranger. Tiny and kind of dingy. Furnished with odd leftover bits

from the basements of parents and former roommates, bolstered by the occasional discount warehouse heirloom. Ten years he had lived in this place without ever really liking it, but without seeing any particular reason to go anywhere else. He had moved in as a student, and his life had not advanced one pace since. Nowhere to go and no reason to go there.

Well, now he had a reason and a place.

He went to his computer and began composing emails.

To: svache@pitouie.com
From: owilson@wasteinsightmag.com
Subject: Your conference

Hello Sarah. Thank you for your invitation earlier today to the Pitouie business conference. I've spoken with my editor, and we agree that it would make a very interesting story for our readers. I would be glad to attend, if any media spots are still open. Please forward me any travel details or accreditation forms. Looking forward to meeting you. -Otis Wilson.

To: mdonahue@wasteinsightmag.com
From: owilson@wasteinsightmag.com
Subject: Vacation time

Hey Merle. Just to let you know, I'm going to need some vacation time in late November/early December. You and I both know I've never asked for a vacation in the entire time I've worked here, so I'm hoping you'll make it easy on me. Talk to you tomorrow. -Otis

To: cbathis@notthatmagazine.com
From: owilson@wasteinsightmag.com
Subject: Story idea

Hey Chuck, long time no see. Congratulations on making associate editor. I've got a story to pitch to you that's perfect for *Not That Magazine*. Would you be interested in an exclusive feature about an idyllic tropical island that's about to become a waste dump for the highest corporate bidder? It came to me here at *WI*, but of course they're only interested in the pro-business aspect. I know you'd give me a proper forum to bring this outrage to the world's attention. I'll be travelling there in November. The arrangements have all been made. Let's have a drink and I'll give you the details. Say hi to Becky. -Otis

He powered down his computer. He poured himself a drink, then left it on the kitchen counter. He paced some more. He thought of the natives of Pitouie and wondered if they knew what they were about to do to themselves. It didn't matter. They had a champion now. He would protect them. He would spread the pages of a feature magazine article over their heads to ward off the blows of a cruel world. And if he couldn't save them, he would at least document the fall of a noble and righteous people, swallowed up by uncaring civilization. Then he would feel better.

He curled up in his easy chair, stared at the wall and waited for the future to arrive.

Chapter 4

*L*ars crouched outside the chief's office door, attempting to pick the lock. Woolsey was taking a shift on the scope. Franks was baked in his bunk. He had all the time in the world.

Two days had gone by since the chief's last unofficial visitor, and Lars was preparing a dangerous play. If another guest were coming, he would be coming any time now. Lars wanted to know what all these suits were doing up here in the cold and the dark. The more he thought about why he wanted to know, the more he was forced to admit the truth of McMannus's assessment. He was bored out of his gourd, and this was something interesting. There were only so many times you could get high and listen to the same ten albums, and he had passed that point long ago.

Lockpicking is much more of a craft than a science. Lars had some experience with the necessary voodoo, dating back to rougher and younger days. He had taken a certain amount of pride in his technique back then. Any thug could pry open a door with a crowbar and ransack a place. It took a skilled technician to enter the same place in silence, extract one item of maximum value and withdraw without leaving a trace.

He had scavenged the prerequisite instruments from the maintenance locker. The first was a six-inch length of hacksaw blade, filed down to a narrow strip of metal with a tiny hook at the end. The second was a small Allen wrench with the short end filed flat like a screwdriver blade.

Picking a lock with these tools is easy in principle. The method relies on the imperfection of mechanisms; there is always some slack to play with. Lars inserted the flat end of the wrench into the keyhole and held it to one side with his thumb, putting the cylinder inside the lock under tension. Then, with his homemade pick, he felt inside the cylinder for the five tiny metal pins that kept it from rotating further. Each pin was spring-loaded and split in two some arbitrary way along its length. With the hook end of the pick, he would have to jostle each pin up and down until the break lined up with the edge of the cylinder. Then, thanks to imperfect manufacturing, the cylinder would rotate a fraction of a degree, holding that pin open by friction. When he had done all five pins, the cylinder would rotate all the way around, drawing back the deadbolt and opening the lock.

This he was now utterly failing to do. He had been poking around with the pick for five minutes without locating the break point of a single pin. When he had been in his prime, he could open most household locks in under a minute. He wondered if this were some new kind of high security military lock.

Then he wondered something else. He twisted the knob and pulled. The door swung open. The chief had not locked it. Okay then.

He stepped in and closed the door behind him. He was more nervous than he had expected. Maybe it was the awareness that he couldn't just make a run for it if things went bad. It was a particular very bad thing that had caused him to run all the way up here in the first place. From here, there was nowhere else to go.

Better not screw this up then.

He took a long look around the room. He was in here every

day, but he had never looked for one specific thing: a hiding place. The filing cabinet wasn't pushed all the way back against the wall. Good enough.

He unclipped the walkie-talkie from his belt, one of a pair pilfered from the emergency stores. This one he had prepared for duty by unscrewing the cover and disconnecting the speaker wires. Now it could only transmit. He switched it on and checked the frequency setting. Then he wrapped a rubber band around the push-to-talk button, extended the antenna and stood the thing up behind the filing cabinet. He walked around the office and checked that the radio was completely hidden. The batteries would last maybe two days. Maybe less. Until then, the radio would transmit every sound in the room to the matching unit he had stashed in the latrine. If a new guest did not arrive in that time, he would have to sneak back in and change the batteries. He withdrew, leaving the door unlocked behind him.

Two days later, Lars again found himself forming a one-man reception committee at the end of the airstrip. Again, McMannus pried an awkward passenger out of his plane and into the snow. Lars forced himself to smile a big innocent smile, then remembered he was wearing a scarf over his mouth.

"Welcome to Station PIN-AA, sir."

Grunt. Mumble.

"The chief is waiting for you sir. This way."

Lars chauffeured the new mystery guest up the hill to the module train, then escorted him courteously to the chief's office. As soon as the door clicked closed, he rushed to the head, sick that he would find his makeshift bug dead just a few hours too late. He had tested the link the previous day and heard the captain rustling papers and humming to himself with surprising clarity. If he missed his chance now, he might have to make a little detour to the storage sheds on the way back to the plane and extract Woolsey's secrets from the man through more direct means, like high voltage to the testicles.

He locked the bathroom door and stepped quickly to the toilet. He lifted the lid off the tank and fished out the receiver, carefully wrapped in plastic. With a pocket knife, he slit the plastic wrap and fumbled the radio out. He turned the volume knob down to nearly nothing, pressed the "On" button and held the speaker to his ear. He held his breath. Success.

"...unique opportunity," the chief was saying. "The kind that comes along only once in a lifetime. However, being in the position I am, I can hardly take advantage of this situation alone."

"I've come a long way," said the stranger. He sounded tired, but not stupid. "Obviously my people are intrigued. But we need to hear more than a sales pitch."

"I don't have a sales pitch for you," said Woolsey stiffly. "If there is any point of my proposal that is not clear to you, I will explain it."

"Let me make sure we understand each other," said the stranger. "You want to sell us a mining concession."

"Certain mineral exploitation rights, yes," said the chief.

"Uranium."

"Yes."

"Who holds these rights now?"

"The local Inuit who live in Iglertok and the surrounding area. They have a land claims agreement with the federal government."

"And you are acting for them?"

"Yes."

"Why?"

"They trust me. I once cured one of their elders of a gastrointestinal infection with a simple course of penicillin. In thanks, they inducted me into their tribe. They even gave me an Inuit name. Itterk. Literally translated, it means 'Trustworthy

One.' In short, they don't want to deal directly with white society. If you knew their history, you wouldn't blame them."

"So how did these Eskimos figure out they were sitting on all this uranium?" asked the stranger.

"Inuit, please," said Woolsey, laying a respectful emphasis on the word. "They didn't figure it out. I did."

"Really," said the stranger. "How?"

"Before entering the service as a much younger man, I studied to be a geologist," said the chief modestly. "I still take a keen interest in the subject. To pass the days at this outpost, I used to read the geographical surveys of this area. I have them here."

There was the sound of rustling paper.

"Please take these back to show your board," said the chief. The stranger grunted.

"As you can see, the results indicate an intrusive-related uranium deposit, hosted by brecciated or cataclastic granite enriched in fluorite. Uranium mineralization is present within this lens, which is up to seventy-five yards wide. Historical surveys suggest that mineralization extends perhaps one hundred and fifty yards below the surface and at least a thousand yards along the strike. During our brief summers here when the rock is exposed, I have collected quite a few samples myself. Like this one."

There was the sound of a desk drawer opening, then a metal clunk as something was placed on the desk. There was a pause.

"It's a rock," said the stranger.

"Yes," said the chief. "It is fortunate that this base was constructed in expectation of nuclear war. We have certain special equipment here."

There was the sound of another drawer sliding open and a softer clunk as something else was set on the desk, apparently more gently.

"You know what this device is, of course," said the chief.

"Yeah," said the stranger.

There was silence. Then a noise. A slow, constant, clicking noise. Fat electrical pops like a lightning storm in a bottle. The clicks grew more rapid, more insistent, until they blurred together into a threatening buzz of static. They slowed again. Lars recognized the sound. It was a Geiger counter.

He heard the sound of a chair scraping back.

"It's fucking radioactive," said the stranger, sounding farther away. "Are you insane, exposing us to that?"

"Not to worry," said the chief. "You'd have to swallow this for it to do you any real harm. But if it will set your mind at rest, I'll put it away. I keep it in a lead-lined box with my other samples."

"You found that rock?" said the stranger. "Near here? You've got others?"

"Oh yes," said the chief. "Once I found the first of them, I began taking the Geiger counter out with me on my little expeditions. There are unusually high levels of radiation all over this area. There are also unusually high levels of childhood leukemia in Iglertok. I have the medical reports here. I think there can be very little doubt as to what it means. Won't you sit down?"

The stranger sat with a scrape.

"Uranium," he said thoughtfully. There was a pause, more rustling of paper. "Okay. But why all the secrecy? Why am I dealing with a man in a shack in the Arctic instead of with your Minister of Northern Affairs, or whoever?"

"The Canadian government is not yet aware of this deposit," said the chief. "But they will be soon. What I'm about to tell you is very sensitive information given to me by a personal friend in Ottawa. The government is about to introduce a new law nationalizing all uranium deposits in the country as essential to national security. The bill is quite similar to your own Atomic Energy Act of 1946. In anticipation of the bill's passage, the Department of Defence has ordered a geological survey of many Arctic regions, including this one. However, between now and then lies a window of opportunity for you and for me."

"How so?" said the stranger.

"When the act passes into law, the government will be committed to buying any privately owned uranium deposits at a fair market value. If you buy the Iglertok rights now, you can sell them to the government at a considerable profit within a year, without even digging a hole in the ground."

"Only if your locals will sell cheap," said the stranger. "Why wouldn't they wait and sell to the government themselves?"

"The Inuit do not know this bill is being considered," said the chief. "Also, they do not know the fair market value of a uranium deposit. Such things are entirely outside their experience. They will accept your valuation, if I endorse it."

There was another pause. A long pause.

"Why would you do that?" said the stranger. "Why wouldn't you wait for the government offer?"

"This station is going to be closed down in three months," said Woolsey. Lars jerked like he had just grabbed a live circuit. "I'm going to be forced into retirement. I don't relish the prospect of living out the rest of my days on nothing but an army pension. Let me be blunt. I am offering to sell a group of simple, honest people who trust me. For that, I expect your group to compensate me with a large deposit into a Union Bank of Switzerland account. I may find it hard to live with myself in future, but at least I will live well."

"How much time have we got?"

"Not very much. The bill will be public knowledge in a matter of weeks."

There was the sound of scraping chairs.

"I'll take your proposal to my board."

"I'll call someone to show you back to the plane."

Lars started. He snapped the radio off, dropped it back in the toilet tank without wrapping it, banged the lid back on and hurried out just as the chief's voice crackled over the loudspeaker, calling his name.

Chapter 5

*T*he airplane was a twin-engine turbo-prop that took off from a small airfield on the outskirts of Santiago. It was an angular, ugly craft with a good few decades on the clock, but it was spotlessly clean and seemed to be in good repair.

The plane was a flying boxcar. Most of the space was crammed with cargo, but up by the nose, ten jump seats were bolted to the floor with a makeshift aisle up the middle. There were no windows, so as the plane droned over the Pacific, Otis watched his fellow passengers instead.

Six were men, all white, all fifty-ish, all uncomfortable and trying to seem unconcerned. "Cramped?" their bearing seemed to say. "Well, maybe a little. But I've seen tougher times that this, my friend. The Aramco merger negotiations, for instance." They all seemed to be Americans, evenly split between west coast tans and Great Lakes pallors.

These would be the prospective clients, assumed Otis, on their way to the conference. They were all wearing dark business suits in black and grey and blue. Otis was wearing a wrinkled shirt with a slightly frayed collar and a pair of badly scuffed shoes. Never hard to tell the covered from the covering in a group like this.

The final passenger was a woman. She was also wearing a dark grey business suit, but her bearing was infinitely more relaxed. Slowly she worked her way down the aisle toward the back of the plane, smiling at each traveller and making small talk over the burr of the engines. The invisible sign floating over her head read, "Hospitality: Enquire within." She was in her late twenties. Her round face was outlined by shiny black hair pulled back in the tightest of professional pony tails. The slight bronze tint of her skin and burnt almond eyes gave her an exotic appeal even from the far side of the six fidgety businessmen.

Finally she came to Otis, sitting on his own in the back left seat. The empty seats around him were both a buffer and a courtesy, like the unspoken every-second-urinal rule of the public men's room. She sat down across the aisle from him in the back right seat and extended her hand.

"You must be Mr. Wilson," she said. "I'm Sarah Vache. We spoke on the phone."

Otis took the hand. It was warm and dry and strong.

"Of course," he said. "Good to meet you."

"We're so glad you could join us after all," she said, smiling. The smile was also warm and dry and strong. "We're eager for all the media coverage we can get for our new venture."

"Naturally," said Otis. There was no other press on the plane that he could see. He decided this was not the time to point out that *Waste Insight* magazine had a circulation of about three thousand. They should have looked that up before inviting him. "I'm looking forward to seeing your operation. Based on what you told me on the phone, it seems to be a unique situation."

"We believe it is," she said. "In many ways."

"How so?" said Otis, doing his best imitation of a reporter.

"Let's not talk business now," she said. "We'll have a detailed presentation for you tomorrow morning."

"Not until then?" said Otis. "How long is the flight?"

"Eleven and a half hours," she said, unapologetic. "I'm afraid there's no food, no drinks, and no in-flight movie. I suggest sleep. That's what I usually do."

She leaned her head back in her non-reclining seat, folded her hands and closed her eyes. After a few minutes, her breath deepened, and her head rolled slightly to one side.

For a while, Otis sat and watched her sleep. It was soothing and better than most in-flight movies he'd seen. He looked out the window for a while. He looked around the plane. He looked in his bag to see if he had remembered to bring something to read. He had not. Time passed without the soothing balm of fiction. Eventually he too closed his eyes, folded his hands and slipped into unconsciousness in the sky over the ocean.

He woke with a start when Sarah touched his arm. She was standing in the aisle, leaning over him and smiling. There were worse things to see when you opened your eyes, thought Otis.

"We're about to land," she said. "Could you fasten your seat belt?"

She moved up the aisle, pausing at each of the passengers for a few last reassuring words, then she walked to the forward bulkhead, stepped through the open hatch and strapped herself into the copilot's seat.

Otis leaned out and looked up the aisle, through the hatch and out the windscreen of the plane at a blank blue sky. With a lurch, the nose of the plane tipped forward and the windscreen was full of blank, blue ocean. In the middle of the ocean was a grey-green triangle, blurry around the edges and getting bigger very quickly. Pitouie.

The plane shook and bucked and made unhappy noises as it fell out of the sky. Otis leaned back in his seat and decided to pretend he was still asleep. His stomach kept him informed as to developments. The plane levelled out, which was encouraging, then stood itself on one wingtip in a steep banked turn, which was less encouraging. When the plane levelled out again, there was a bang and a jolt so immediate Otis figured they had just crashed. They had not. They had landed.

They were met at the end of the narrow cement runway by a short motorcade of SUVs. A tall, imposing man with a hard face and a spotless uniform stood formally at the head of the column, shimmering slightly in the heat.

"This is Colonel Juan Cortez Garcia," said Sarah, waving an introduction between the gleaming officer and the rumpled suits. "The colonel is head of security on the island."

"Bienvenidos," said Garcia coldly. "Welcome to Pitouie. Please step into the cars. A truck will follow with your luggage."

Amid muttered greetings, the sweaty executives boarded the waiting vehicles. Otis hung back, getting a first look at the landscape.

At ground level, the island was just as grey and green as it had been from the air. The grey was rock, shooting up out of the water at strange, steep angles like the whole place was made of untidy heaps of broken asphalt. Ladled over the heaps and softening their edges was green. Green palm trees with green bark. Green bushes. Green grass waist-high. Wherever a root could get a toehold, wherever a drop of water might flow, something green was making a life for itself. Birds sang. Insects buzzed. Otis sweated. He considered the fact that the next chain of islands was over a thousand miles away in any direction. He thought of ancient Polynesians setting out from perfectly good islands in tiny wooden boats, looking for new islands anyway because there was always another island. The thought made him shiver, even in the heat.

"What do you think?" asked Sarah. She had drawn up beside him in silence, and he started again.

"I think it's amazing that people ever found this place," he said.

"If there's a place, people eventually find it," said Sarah. "It's what people do. This place was found at least three different times."

"I know," said Otis. "By the Polynesians, by the Europeans, and by the Americans."

"You've been doing historical research," she said, mock impressed. "Unusual in a business reporter."

Otis decided not to tell her that his research had consisted of five minutes at pitouie.com.

"I've always been interested in history," he said. This was a blatant lie, but he resolved to be more interested in history in the future.

"Come on," she said. "Dinner will be waiting for us."

They walked to the last car, which set off up a winding gravel road leading from the airstrip to Pitouie City.

Pitouie City was a bit hard to see. It was all spread out over the side of a hill sloping up from a beach and a harbour. Most of the clapboard buildings were half-swallowed by green and growing things. The road wound back and forth between them, taking the path least resistant to gravity and geology. Otis could see people ambling between the buildings as the convoy grumbled past, but in the dimming light he could see few details. One old woman stood solemnly in the doorway of a shack and watched the cars pass like it was a funeral procession.

"Will we be able to see more of the city while we're here?" he said.

"Of course, if you like," said Sarah, less mockingly.

"I'd like to talk to some of the people," said Otis. "What language do they speak?"

"Well, the official language of the island is Spanish, but most of the islanders speak a native dialect. I may be able to find a few who speak English."

"Thank you," said Otis. He decided to say something potentially unwise. "I'm not really here because I want to attend your conference. I came to see the people. I, uh, hope you don't mind."

Sarah looked at him as closely as the failing light would allow.

"No," she said. "I don't mind."

When the motorcade pulled up in the courtyard of the palace, she linked her arm through his and led him inside.

The palace was not an impressive building except in comparison to the rest of the local architecture. It was a flat, four-storey structure that looked like an office block. Cinder blocks showed through the cracks in the stucco. The addition of a Spanish arch here and there could not hide the building's utilitarian design.

"The Americans built it in the forties," said Sarah, as she escorted him through the retrofitted wrought iron gate and across the small courtyard to the big double doors. "This was their command post during the war. That tower on the corner used to be for air traffic control. There's a beautiful view of the airstrip and the harbour. They built those too, and most of the roads. This was going to be a major staging area for the ground assault on the Japanese home islands, but then they decided to nuke them instead, and this place was left to gather dust. It's been cleaned up since then, of course."

They passed down a hall and into a large banquet room. A single long table was elegantly set for ten. The chair at the head of the table was large and imposing in dark, heavily carved wood. Garcia and the six executives stood to one side making small talk.

"I hear you have a band of rebels up in the hills," said one of the suits, waving a glass of something in the general direction of the hills. "Do they give you much trouble?"

Garcia was too dignified to scoff, but he indicated his desire to scoff by stiffening his shoulders a little more and standing even straighter.

"No, Mr. Homme," he said. "They are a pathetic joke, to be pitied more than feared. They are a tiny group of malcontents with no popular support. Sometimes they raid a village for fish. That is all."

"Will we see any on our tour?" asked the executive.

Garcia shrugged.

"Better if you don't," he said. "They are brigands and desperate men. They are no respecters of personal dignity. Better you stay clear of the interior without an escort."

There was general nodding. A savage place. Lawless. Then again, that's why they were here.

"Look at them," said a voice in his ear. Otis turned. One of the executive visitors was standing by his elbow with an amused look on his well-moisturized face. "All huddled together like some mythical multi-headed beast drooling over a secret treasure."

"And if one head is cut off," said Otis, "will two more grow in its place?"

"At least two. Senior vice presidents are a commodity product where we come from. If you'll pardon me, I must join the throng."

"I'm sorry. I didn't get your name."

"Trace. Christopher Trace."

"Otis Wilson."

With a nod, the man went and took his place in the beastly cluster around Garcia. Otis kept his distance. A gong sounded. Garcia excused himself and exited through a door at the far end of the room. A moment later he re-emerged and stood stiffly to attention.

"Honoured guests," he said in a loud, formal voice. "May I present His Excellency, President of Federated Pitouie, President and Chief Executive Officer of the Pitouie Development Corporation, Potent Chieftain, General Don Roderigo Esquival Bolivar San Sierra Lopez."

A figure appeared in the door. He wore an impeccable charcoal suit of silk, a crisp white shirt and a simple striped tie. A single medal gleamed on his chest in the firelight, and a large diamond ring glinted on the pinkie of one hand. His greying beard attested to sixty-odd years, but the eyes in the severe angular face were bright and clever. He stood straight, but held an ornate walking stick in one hand. Wordlessly he took his position at the head of the table before the carved wooden chair. Garcia stood to his right, Sarah to his left. The six suits lined up on either side of the table. Otis took the last seat on the left.

The president sat. Garcia and Sarah sat. The suits and Otis sat. The president moved one finger slightly and tapped a small silver bell. Dinner began.

Dinner was served by a collection of liveried attendants and consisted of food Otis could only guess at. There was a spiky thing that might have been an anemone. It certainly didn't look like a friend. There was some stringy green goo, which was probably seaweed. There were oysters, which Otis couldn't eat because shellfish always made him break out in vomit. Finally there was a main dish, which he thought was salmon but turned out to be whale. After a while he gave up foraging for nourishment across the vast expanse of the table and contented himself with bread rolls and wine.

On the wall behind the almost-throne hung a flag, the greeny-blue swirly logo from the island's website centred on a field of deeper blue. The other walls were hung with thick curtains of dark blue and green. Most of the light in the large space came from three immense candelabra on the table. Four more candelabra stood on small tables in the corners of the room.

Otis looked down. The floor in the dim light seemed at first to be made of tile. Then he saw it was purest linoleum stamped with a tile pattern. Here and there he could see scuff marks where smaller tables had once stood. Otis realized he was sitting in a cafeteria all dressed-up for prom night. He looked up for the disco ball, but he couldn't see the ceiling. He would have taken a bet that the lights were low to hide the foam acoustic tiles above their heads.

He turned his eyes back to his fellow dinner guests, still stuffing the bounty of the sea down their maws. The president held himself upright and aloof on his almost-throne, slowly moving forkfuls of food to his mouth with the deliberation of a man who knows the meal will not end until he says so. He still hadn't spoken. Garcia sat like a waxwork, barely eating, saying nothing. Sarah was relaxed and casual, smiling around the table and chatting amiably with her neighbours. The suits took turns talking to her, but they didn't have anything to say to each other. They had come to compete, Otis realized, not socialize. This was not a crowd that would be playing charades together after dinner.

"Is that your flag?" asked one, pointing with an oyster shell at the blue-green swirly thing.

"Yes, Mr. Coombs," said Sarah. "It's brand new. Do you like it?"

Coombs put his head on one side and assumed an attitude of deepest reflection.

"It's very blue," he said. "What does it represent?"

"The deep blue is the ocean," said Sarah. "The green swirl represents the island. The light blue swirl in the centre represents Lake Pitouie, which you have all come so far to see."

Now all the visitors turned a respectful gaze upon the flag. Coombs nodded, with respect, then said, "I thought the island was a triangle."

"It is," said Sarah. "But our brand activation consultant said that a swirl would be more dynamic and visually impactful."

Coombs nodded again, less respectfully.

"They always say that. Blue-green swirls have been the fashion in corporate logos for the last ten years at least. Damned if I can figure out why."

No one else seemed eager to voice an opinion on the subject, and so the attention of the table returned to the shellfish.

After several hours, the unidentifiable foodstuffs stopped coming. They were sitting around the table with coffee, brandy and cigars when the president finally spoke.

"Gentlemen," he said, rising to his feet. "You are all welcome to Federated Pitouie. I hope you will enjoy your stay on our beautiful and unique island. You have travelled far to avail yourselves of our hospitality and our services, but there will be time enough to discuss business tomorrow. Tonight, you relax in my house. I bid you good evening."

So saying, he turned and walked out of the room, limping slightly. Garcia and Sarah stood as he departed, and, half an awkward second later, so did everyone else.

"It's late and you've all had a long day," said Sarah, just as everyone was moving to sit down again. "Your luggage has been brought up. Let me show you to your rooms."

On the inside, the palace looked like what it was: a dormitory trying to pass for a seat of power and prestige. Works of art and impressive furniture were scattered through the halls, but it all looked picked at random from a collection of movie props or hotel lobbies. Otis decided to give the island a pass on this one. A tiny population living on a flyspeck in the middle of nowhere, just recently out from under the colonial thumb; how much high culture could you expect?

Sarah led the group to the guest quarters on the second floor, installing each suit in his own executive suite with an instruction to ring for the night porter if they needed anything. Again Otis hung to the back of the pack, so again he found himself walking alone with Sarah as she showed him down the hall to the last door on the left.

"This is your room," she said, pushing the door open. "It's just like the others. Wouldn't want you to think we would give you a lesser room just because you're not Fortune 500."

"Never crossed my mind," said Otis. "Thanks."

She paused as if she wanted to say something, or as if she wanted him to say something. Otis felt like a moment was passing that he was meant to seize, but the feeling came too late and the moment passed.

"Goodnight," she said, and walked off down the hall. Otis retreated into his room and closed the door.

It was a hotel room cross-bred with a dorm room. The walls were painted cement blocks, but the furniture was dark, ornate wood and too big for the space. Inoffensive artwork hung on the walls and a thick rug covered the floor. He pushed back the corner with a toe. Linoleum.

A writing desk was shoved up against the wall opposite a ridiculous Arabian Nights bed. A glossy folder of deep blue lay upon it, the blue-green Pitouie logo embossed on the surface like the stationary equivalent of a volcano. Otis flipped it open. Tucked into the left-hand flap was a Letter From the President, welcoming him again to the island. The swirly logo appeared on the letterhead and again on Sarah's business card, clipped to the top of the page.

The right-hand pocket bulged with a thick booklet labelled *The Pitouie Development Corporation LLC Phase II Project Report*. It was an impressive document. Fifty glossy pages at the least. The spine cracked with meaty authority when he opened it. He had seen annual reports from billion-dollar companies that couldn't match these production values. The pages were covered with huge graphs and charts, interspersed with blocks of text in tiny type and more pictures of Pitouie landscapes. He leafed through it without reading more than three words per page, then tossed it back on the desk. Up and down the hallway, he could almost hear the well-engineered thump of his fellow travellers doing the same.

"Well," he said to the booklet, "Now what?"

Chapter 6

*L*ars sat at the radar desk, thinking. The scope was a good place to think. The circular screen was shielded from the light of the room by a goggle-shaped hood. His face was inside the hood, where no one could read his expression or see by his eyes that his mind had cut loose. The green line scanned the circumference of the black screen once per minute, steady as a second hand. Despite the hood, the lights were kept low. The equipment emitted a relaxing hum. Even the chair was comfortable.

He had lain in his bunk most of the night before, thinking. Thinking of the station and how it would be swallowed up unremembered by the white and the black. Thinking maybe he could make a plaque or something. Here lies PIN-AA, 1957–1973. It was good for nothing, but it was there. Thinking of what the hell he could do with himself after the station shut down. Thinking of certain old acquaintances down south who were probably still thinking of him, and not fondly.

Most of all, he had lain there thinking of Woolsey and his plan. Wondering how in the name of the frozen earth he could expect to pull it off. Did he really have the core indifference it would take to throw a whole village full of people to the dogs like that? Back in the old days, Lars had known lots of guys who could've done it as a routine matter of business, even a few who would have seen the opportunity as a rare treat. Guys like that had a certain stance.

You could see it a mile away if you knew what to look for. It was the stance of a weasel, up on its hind legs and scanning for its next mouse.

The chief did not have that stance. Woolsey was a former military officer. Not a career for the selfish. He took a walk up a Normandy beach that killed every tenth man and earned a Military Cross on his stroll through Belgium. Now, almost thirty years out of uniform, he was serving in the least comfortable billet the military had to offer. This man had saved a life in the village he now hoped to sell.

Lars reached a conclusion. The chief must be desperate. A desperate man would be eager for help. Or, if not eager, open to persuasion.

When Franks relieved him at the scope three hours later, red-eyed and dreamy, Lars went to the chief's office, took a deep breath and knocked.

"Come in," said Woolsey.

Lars opened the door and took one step inside.

"Could I speak to you for a moment, Chief, on a private matter?"

The chief's eyes flicked up from his papers flicked back down.

"Very well, Varick."

Lars closed the door and locked it. Now the chief looked up. He laid down his pen and gazed at Lars expectantly. Lars unclipped the soggy walkie-talkie from his belt and laid it wordlessly on the desk. Then he went to the filing cabinet, knelt beside it and drew out the hidden twin. He brought this to the desk and laid it along side the first, still saying nothing. He took a step back and waited.

The chief picked up the radio that had been stashed behind the cabinet and fingered the rubber band wound around it. He set it down. He leaned back in his chair. He gave Lars a long, appraising look.

"What do you want?" he said.

"I want in," said Lars. "I think you could use my help."

"In on what?"

"Your plan to sell a uranium deposit out from under the natives of Iglertok."

"Why should I?"

"Because if you don't, I'll make sure Iglertok knows all about it."

Another pause. Another long, slow look. Lars could feel his molecules being counted. He watched scenarios flicker behind the chief's eyes, like a computer crunching chess moves. Then there was only a faint smile.

"You would go there? Tell them Sterling Woolsey is keeping a secret from them? Tell them they will all become rich if only they stop me?"

"Uh, yes."

"Go ahead."

Lars continued to maintain a level gaze for a few more seconds, then conceded defeat.

"Really?" he said.

"Yes, really," said the chief. "Take the snowmobile. I'll get Franks to cover your shift if you're not back in time."

Lars stood up and walked to the door. He paused with his hand on the knob.

"How do I get there?"

"Follow the coast west for twenty miles. Just keep the sea on your right. You'll get there."

Lars opened the door and took the snowmobile to Iglertok.

It was a two-hour trip, creeping along the edge of the Arctic Ocean in the dark. The bus had feeble headlights that mostly showed Lars a windscreen full of swirling snow. The coast was rocky and undulating, and it didn't take long for him to completely lose his bearings. For all he knew, he was already a mile out to sea on an ice floe. He puttered along with one hand on the emergency break, expecting every crunch to be the sound of the tracks falling through the ice toward a permanent parking space on the ocean floor.

He knew he had arrived at the village of Iglertok when he came within a foot of bulldozing a small, snow-encrusted shack. It wasn't his fault. Iglertok was running dark. There wasn't a light lit that Lars could see. There were no street signs to mark the city limits. There were no streets, only pathways through the snow stomped flat by feet both human and canine. Iglertok was a haphazard cluster of shacks made of corrugated metal and plywood. None of them looked as well constructed as your average tree house. None of them looked like they would provide adequate shelter from a gentle summer rain, never mind a killing Arctic snowstorm. Yet, here they stood. Lars supposed survival trumped style.

He shuddered and jerked the snowmobile cautiously toward what he estimated to be the centre of the village, then he got out. The sound of an unfamiliar engine had drawn a small welcoming committee. Two figures stood before one of the shacks, decked out in fur-trimmed sealskin parkas and boots like a postcard in a hotel gift shop. Lars held up a hand and approached them.

"Hello," he said. If no one here spoke English, he was pretty much screwed. He had never even seen an English-Inuktitut dictionary.

"Hello," said one villager. His voice sounded like his tongue was made of blubber. He was a large man in late middle age, with cheekbones sharp enough to show through his leathery skin in the gleam of the headlights. The other figure was a young woman, as far as Lars could tell. She looked at him calmly, but didn't speak.

Lars pressed on.

"I come from the DEW Line station, over there," he said, waving an arm in the direction of his track marks. "I have something to tell the village. I need to speak to your elders."

"You can tell me," said the man. "I'll tell the others."

Lars considered holding out for an audience with someone more venerable. He was expecting a real tribal elder: someone ancient and solemn, with a stillness at their core and a deep wisdom in their eyes. He was expecting some ceremony. He wasn't expecting to tell his tale to the first guy he met on the street.

"It's kind of important," said Lars.

"Okay," said the man.

Well, what the hell, thought Lars. There couldn't be more than a hundred people living here. He imagined the news would travel fast enough.

He opened his mouth, then closed it again. He had never dropped the dime on a man before. His record on that score was unblemished and important to him. Still, Woolsey had told him to come, had practically dared him, so he technically wasn't transgressing the code. Even so, it made him uncertain. He opened his mouth again.

"Sterling Woolsey is trying to steal from you," he said.

The man considered this for a moment, then nodded.

"Who's that?" he said.

"The chief of my station."

More consideration. Lars tried again.

"Your elders gave him an Inuit name. Trustworthy One."

The man adjusted the hood of his parka.

"That's not an Inuit name," he said.

"They called him 'Itterk.'"

"Asshole."

"What?"

"Means asshole."

Now Lars was well and truly lost, but he kept the sea on his right and plowed on.

"There's uranium under your village," he said. "Very valuable rock. My chief is trying to steal it from you."

"We haven't seen him," said the man. Lars tried to think of a good way to put the concept of fraudulent mineral exploitation into single syllables.

"No," he said. "He's going to get some other men to come here and take it."

"We haven't seen them either."

"They won't be here until spring."

"Okay. We'll watch for them. Make sure they don't take too many rocks."

Lars wasn't sure if his job was done or not. He looked around the village. A few sealskin forms were trudging here and there, taking no interest. Dogs whined in the darkness. The girl continued to watch him in silence.

"Will you tell the other villagers what I said?" asked Lars.

"Okay."

Lars looked around one more time. There didn't seem to be any help coming.

"Okay," he said. He waved. The man waved back. The girl did not. Lars got in the snowmobile and crawled back to the station.

Lars and the chief faced each other across the desk. The bottle of Scotch and two glasses were between them, but neither were drinking. Lars felt like he was in a parking lot after the bar had closed, just waiting for the fight to start. Much too late to back out now.

"So how did it go?" said Woolsey.

"I don't think they understood what I was trying to tell them," said Lars. "They just sort of stood around and looked at me."

"They either didn't care or didn't believe you."

"Guess not."

"They're right not to."

Lars slumped in his chair and waited for his chief to lift the veil. Woolsey eventually took pity on him.

"What exactly do you think is about to happen here?" said the chief.

"You're going to sell the rights to the local uranium deposit to some mining company dirt cheap. Then they're going to flip it to the government for an easy profit when that new law goes through. You'll get paid off, but the local Inuit won't. At least, not as much as they could be."

Woolsey lifted his glass, took a sip and set it down with a click.

"The local Inuit won't get paid at all," he said. "And neither will the buyers. Only I will be paid. And you, if you help me."

"Are you saying the government won't pay for the uranium?"

"They will not pay."

"Why not?"

"Because there is no uranium out there, kid. Just a lot of worthless rocks."

Now Lars lifted his glass, sipped, and set it down.

"All these guys you've been bringing up here," said Lars. "They're all mining guys?"

The chief nodded. "From some of the biggest extraction concerns in North America."

"And you've given them all the same presentation you gave the last guy?"

The chief nodded.

"So all that stuff about being an amateur geologist, about saving the village elder and earning their trust?"

"Is a fabrication," said the chief amicably. "I've never even been to Iglertok. The local Inuit do have treaty rights to the minerals around here, but there's nothing worth mining. And, of course, I'm not empowered to act on their behalf. They don't know me from Adam."

"But the radioactive sample?" said Lars. "The reports you had?"

"The reports are forgeries," said Woolsey. "It's a skill I picked up in Antwerp. The rock I won in a bar bet from a man I once met in Nevada. He said it came from the Trinity test site. You don't have to believe that if you don't want to, but it is certainly a bit warm. Reads even warmer if you tamper with your Geiger counter a bit."

It seemed like a good moment for another drink. They drank.

"This is a con," said Lars.

"Yes it is," said Woolsey.

"You're not abusing the trust of the Inuit. You're abusing the trust of the miners."

"Exactly. I play for them the role of an old man down on his luck with a map to buried treasure to sell. I tell them the fools standing on the land don't know what the treasure is worth. Throw them a few coins, and they'll let you have it. Throw me a few more coins, and I'll give you the map. This is a very old game. It's called the Spanish Prisoner. It's another thing I learned in Antwerp, and now I'm going to teach it to you. How do you begin?"

"You invite four potential investors up here..." said Lars.

"Six," interrupted the chief. "Two are yet to come."

"...And then you sell the fake concession to whoever offers you the best bribe."

"Why would I do that?" said Woolsey. "I sell to all of them. Six copies of the same bill of goods."

Lars looked at him, mentally agape.

"They're going to be pissed," he said. Woolsey chuckled.

"They will blame each other before they think of blaming me. They will presume industrial espionage and the treachery of their competitors, because men as smart as themselves could never be taken in by an old man in a shack. The legal battle will drag on for years before they even think to check that the merchandise is as advertised. And I will be long gone by then. I will tell you frankly that Woolsey is not my real name. The military has no record of my real name. I haven't used my real name since I was seventeen."

"You joined the army using a false name?" said Lars.

"I, ah, fell in with the army," said the chief. "I never formally joined, as such."

He reached for the bottle and refilled their glasses. He looked up to see Lars watching him skeptically. He sighed in resignation and sat back in his chair with the drink.

"Have a drink, kid. Have I got a story to tell you."

Lars took a drink.

"There I was in Antwerp," said Woolsey. "Year of Our Lord 1945. The British had liberated the city the month before, and I was in town with a few associates plying my trade."

"The Spanish Prisoner?" said Lars.

"Among others," said the chief. "We worked mostly with art. The Nazis had looted artwork from all over Europe, and now they were on the run and leaving their booty behind them, scattered all over the place. No one knew who was the rightful owner of what, or even if they were still alive. Antwerp had been a rich city. Now it was full of orphaned art. It was a good time for me. I was a different grand master every week."

He twisted his glass on the metal desktop.

"We did well for a while, but we stayed too long. We got complacent. Stopped taking the proper precautions. Somebody took an interest. One day, three of my associates just disappeared. With 45 million civilians dead in the war, who'd notice three more refugees?"

He took a long drink, then continued.

"So, as I said, there I was in Antwerp, on the run. I found shelter in an army camp by volunteering to help in the hospital. There I found a young Canadian officer who was dying of tuberculosis. It was an object lesson in the indifference of the world to the fates of men. This soldier had survived Normandy and the bloody sweep up the coast. He had been decorated for courage under fire. Honoured by his people. He had made it through the war, and now he was drowning in his own blood anyway. I came close to weeping for him. And then, the night he died, I stole his uniform and his identification and snuck out of town in the dark. I walked to the frontier and presented myself as a straggler separated from his unit. There were many soldiers in that situation. We were all ganged together and stuck in a corner while the paperwork got sorted out. My paperwork eventually went through, and I found myself on a troop ship to Canada. Once I got here, I found other identities, but ever since I've always called myself a veteran. It's the only tribute I can offer to the man who saved my life."

Lars sat and listened to all this unblinkingly. He rolled the story around in his mind.

"Bullshit," he said.

The chief sat passively.

"It takes years to die from tuberculosis. The army would've never sent that guy overseas. Probably would've never even let him join up."

The chief tilted his head slightly and smiled a very little.

"Not bad, kid. Guess all that weed hasn't totally fried your brain yet."

It occurred to Lars that he was out of his league.

"I came to you because I thought you would be nervous about your big score. I thought I could bully you into letting me in. But you're not, and I can't, so why did you tell me all this?"

The chief smiled faintly again.

"Why did you want in?"

"I'm bored."

"So am I. That's why I'm going to let you in. I am going to retire. This is my last game. I'd like to pass on a few traditions of the trade before I go. And you seem to have some potential. The radios.

Actually going to Iglertok. You've got some intelligence and some nerve. Both could be useful."

"How?" said Lars.

Woolsey drained his glass.

"I'll let you know," he said.

Chapter 7

*O*tis sat over breakfast, still wondering what to do next. It was Time to Get the Story, that much was clear. It wasn't something he'd ever done before. The stories he'd covered, in his own half-assed way, had always come to him ready to go. He tried to think back to his formal training in the journalistic arts. Where did one begin?

A grim realization crept over him. He would have to talk to people. He suppressed a shudder, but could not deny the reality of his situation. If he was going to do this one right, he was doomed to attempt dialogue. With live human beings. In person. Now that the moment had arrived, he missed the prepackaged comfort of a badly written press release. Talk to people. Mmm.

Breakfast was served in the same banquet hall as dinner. The long table, pushed against one wall, now supported a neat row of chafing dishes. In these Otis was heartened to find edible breakfast foods: eggs, bacon, sausage, toast. There was a bowl of fruit and large metal pots of coffee and tea. There was no seafood of any kind.

Small round tables were scattered across the floor in place of the formal oaken slab, each aligned precisely with its designated scuff mark. The curtains were drawn back, allowing mellow sunlight to illuminate the acoustic tile ceiling. Except for himself, the room was empty.

As Otis continued to ponder his options, Christopher Trace walked in. He nodded pleasantly, then got himself a cup of coffee and a frugal slice of toast. He looked around the dining hall, unable to hide its cafeterian roots in the morning light, and winced. He walked to the wall of windows, opened one that turned out to be a door, and stepped into a small garden Otis had failed to notice. Senior vice presidents: one. Keen-eyed reporters: zero.

Otis mused on the value of pre-broken ice. Trace had been the only person on the island other than Sarah to speak directly to him since his arrival. Trace also had an appealing bitterness. Otis saw himself befriending a world-weary and vaguely self-loathing man of affairs and converting him into an inside source at the conference table. He needed that angle for the story. He needed one tight-laced professional negotiator to have a sudden crisis of conscience and seek absolution from a handy reporter. Otis wondered how many drinks that would take and whether or not breakfast would be a good time to open the confessional bar.

He walked back to the buffet and refilled his coffee cup, slowly counting to ten. Then he put his free hand casually into his pocket and strolled casually into the garden. Whoever had planted the garden had probably based the layout on a picture book of English country houses, but that book had gone back to the library years ago, and the garden had gone feral. A perfunctory gravel walkway still divided the garden from the bush, but inside the charmed circle order had long ago given way to chaos. Trace was sitting at a small table under a large umbrella, observing the entropy.

"Good morning, Mr. Trace."

"Ah, Mr. Wilson. Good morning."

"Do you mind if I join you?"

"Please do."

"I was hoping we could continue our conversation from last night," said Otis, scraping back a wrought iron chair and sitting down. "I'd like to hear your views on Pitouie's business model. I think they may be different from those of your fellow guests."

"I expect they may," said Trace. "You are a reporter? Who do you represent?"

"*Waste Insight* magazine."

The smooth face didn't flicker.

"I see," said Trace. He sipped his coffee. "What do you want to know?"

"First of all, what company are you with?"

"None of them. I'm an independent consultant. I'm here to evaluate the Pitouie proposal and proceed with contract negotiations on behalf of my clients if my evaluation is favourable."

"Who are your clients?"

"I'm not entirely sure. The animal in question is all teeth, no head. It's a consortium of investors in control of a holding company. The company has interests in a number of waste management concerns that could use the services of this island. I represent a pool of interests, none of whom I have met in person."

"But someone must sign your paycheque."

"I was retained by a lawyer in Gibraltar who is the nominal chairman of the board of this consortium. He is forbidden by law from disclosing the identities of owners of the company without their permission."

"Why are your clients interested in Pitouie?"

"This island could potentially solve a lot of problems for them. They're middlemen, naturally. They charge large sums of money to take hazardous waste off of somebody's hands and deposit it someplace else. When they took up this trade years ago, you could dump pretty much anything pretty much anywhere, as long as no one was looking directly at you. Now, every ounce and every drop is tracked by computers and regulators and bloggers and activists and class-action lawyers. You can't simply misplace certain substances any more. People notice. You have to find somewhere willing to give you a receipt."

"Somewhere like this?"

"Exactly. A deep hole in the ground with a kind old man standing next to it who will sign a document saying that these materials are now under his care and everything is just fine. Then everybody can stop thinking about it."

"So, if it's such a great idea, why do you need to evaluate it?"

"Due diligence. Nailing down the details. Checking the fine print. For me, it also means a free trip to a tropical island. Plus, I'm charging my clients $600 per hour to sit here in the shade and talk to you."

"Nice. When my story comes out, I'll probably get $600 total for it."

"You should have been a plumber. There's always money for people willing to wade through shit so others needn't spoil their shoes."

"What will your clients dump here if they win the contract?"

"You know, they showed me a shortlist once. Lots of Latinate chemical names and diagrams of molecules. Can't remember any of it now."

"Does the environmental impact on the island concern you? What about the health of the natives?"

"Those are problems for the authorities here to mitigate."

"Even if the substances are poisons?"

"Poison is a byproduct of civilization. If you don't want the poison, you can't have the polis. Maybe we could all live as fishermen on little islands like this, but I doubt many would want to."

Good pull quote, thought Otis.

"How will you make your decision?"

"Well, there'll be the usual dog and pony show. I understand our hosts plan to truck us all into the jungle today to examine their facility. Think I'll claim a shellfish allergy and duck out of that one. Then there will be expert testimony from some scientists, probably. None of us will have any questions for them other than, 'In your opinion, is this a safe operation?' That's so we can stand up in court someday and say, 'The scientists told us it was safe.' Then there'll be another sales pitch from the charming Ms. Vache. After that, they'll give us a day or so to consider our positions before the real negotiations begin."

"What will your position be?"

"Prone on the beach if I can possibly manage it."

"You don't sound very interested."

"I'm not. This will all be window dressing. Show biz. Irrelevant."

"So what is relevant?"

"The money, of course. How much do we pay, and what do we get for it? Not to mention the delicate issue of how big a bribe to offer."

"Bribe? Who?"

"President Lopez, most likely. No one else around here to bribe, really. Don't make that face, Mr. Wilson. This is how business is done in most parts of the world. The formal contract is just a spreadsheet. Any MBA student could run the numbers and work out an acceptable margin. But negotiating an extra-contractual demonstration of sincerity and friendship with a foreign leader, that takes a deft touch. That's why my clients have sent me. It's sort of a specialty."

"Interesting work?"

"Like any line of business, it starts to get tedious when you've done it enough. This is my last at-bat, in fact. After this, I'm officially retired."

"What will you do with yourself?"

"Something unofficial. I see Ms. Vache is approaching. If you will excuse me, I'll go hide in the bushes until she leaves."

Trace stood up and walked away with the air of a man who had nothing in particular to do that day. Otis reached into his pocket and switched off the voice recorder. Sarah stopped at his table.

"Sleep well?" she asked.

"Sure," he said. "You?"

"Oh yes. Have you finished eating?"

"Oh yes."

"Good. The tour up to the crater is about to begin. Shall we?"

"Crater?" asked Otis as he stood up, trying to make it sound like a casual after-breakfast request. Tennis? Croquet? Crater?

Sarah arched an eyebrow at him.

"I thought you had done research," she said. "The island is a volcano. Dormant for hundreds of years, but still technically active. You could say it's the core of our business proposition, so we're taking our prospective clients to see it. It's also very beautiful. So, shall we?"

She slipped an arm under his elbow and led him out.

They crept up the side of the volcano along a rutted gravel road that switched back and forth across the cracked face of rock. The convoy of four-by-fours with their cargo of suits picked its way slowly up the grade in low gear. The whole island was jagged and mountainous, but it had taken them only a few hours to bash their way free of the jungle and reach the base of the cone itself. Now that the ascent had begun in earnest, even four-wheel drive was reaching its limits. Finally the vehicles ground to a halt, and their passengers tumbled out.

"From here we walk," said Sarah to the small crowd with an apologetic smile. "It's less than a kilometre to the top."

The executives, decked out for the rugged occasion in khaki pants and orthopedic walking shoes, made hearty noises and set off after her. Otis did a quick head count. Trace was not among them. The road narrowed to a trail, but it was still easy going, and all the hikers made it up without popping a heart valve, including Otis.

They arrived at a wooden viewing platform at the rim of the crater. Otis, bringing up the rear, edged his way to the railing and looked down. He almost wished he were the gasping type so he could express his admiration in the traditional way. Instead he just stood and looked.

The crater was an almost perfectly circular bowl. The wall of grey glassy rock leading up to the outside edge of the rim was too sheer for even the most tenacious plants to get a grip. The crater itself was not so steep and full of vegetation from rim to rim; a hidden forest at the peak of a mountain. And at the very centre of the forest, at the lowest point of the crater, was a small lake of shocking iridescent blue.

"Told you," said Sarah in his ear. She moved to the front of the pack and turned to face the onlookers, who turned to face her with the look of people who would like very much to get on to the important part.

"Gentlemen," she said in a formal, as-you-can-see-on-page-thirty-seven-paragraph-five voice. "Before you is Lake Pitouie. Three hundred feet of water on top of an active magma fountain. Under that placid surface is a crack in the earth leading straight down to the planet's molten core. Liquid rock at 1,300 degrees Celsius. What goes into that hole, gentlemen, never comes out. Watch."

She pointed across the crater to a nearby spot on the rim. Through the heat haze, Otis could make out a chain of men descending into the bowl two-by-two, each pair lugging a 50-gallon steel drum on a kind of sling. Carefully they wound their way down to the edge of the lake, humping and bumping the barrels along. The workers were dressed in ragged, faded clothing, their faces downcast, their necks shining with sweat. The line of men stretched back over the rim and disappeared.

As each pair made it to the shore, they gave a sort of coordinated shrug, and the drum rolled off the sling and into the water. Each barrel bobbed for a moment, then sank without complaint. The men doubled back up the trail, returning with more barrels to sweep under the delicate blue rug of the lake.

"Our current client is small and can offer us only a limited volume of product," said Sarah. "They were an ideal customer during the pilot phase of our project. Now this contract is coming to an end, and we are prepared for the first time to offer this unique secure waste management facility to the high-volume international market."

She swept an arm theatrically toward the lake.

"Your excess industrial materials will find a private and permanent home here, and will never be subject to any form of national or international inspection or oversight. Our president guarantees it."

"Not much throughput," said an executive. "They couldn't possibly manage the volume we would send them."

"This is only a pilot project, Mr. Laurier," said Sarah. "We're not running at anything near our full capacity. We have only a few dozen transportation associates on-stream here. When we move to full production, we will have approximately five hundred. That should provide adequate bandwidth for even the most high-volume clients."

Laurier grunted.

"Still not exactly nine nines," he said.

"I know you've all read the briefing materials prepared by our geologists," Sarah continued smoothly. "We have an expert standing by at the palace to answer any technical questions you may have. After that, our president invites each of you to join him for a personal consultation. And now, if you would follow me back to the cars, we should return to town in time for a late lunch. Gentlemen, please."

She held her arms wide and herded them like chickens gently toward the trailhead. One remained behind, leaning heavily on the railing of the viewing platform with both hands. He wasn't technically standing next to Otis. If they'd been standing at a bar, there'd have been a stool or two between them.

The man looked mostly like the rest of the executives: silver-haired, well-tended skin, expensive shoes, flawless teeth. The only thing that set him apart was the look in his eyes. They looked simultaneously distant and intent, and strangest of all was the unmistakable hint of deep personal satisfaction at the corners. They were fixed on the impossible lake below, and on the barrels going quietly to their rest there.

"It's perfect," he murmured.

"Is it?" said Otis.

The man's eyes flicked over him, saw nothing alarming, returned to their contemplation of the lake.

"Of course it is," he said. "Have you ever seen anything so beautiful?"

Otis took another look.

"No, I guess not."

"You could dump anything here," said the man, barely breathing. "No one would care. Think what we could do with this place."

"The islanders might care," said Otis, mentally shifting over a barstool.

"They wouldn't know what we were bringing. No one would know. Besides, look who's carrying the payload."

Payload. Interesting word. None of the other potential clients had used it. They stuck to words like "product" and "deliverables." "Payload" was a new one. Otis filed it away.

"It's Mr. Homme, isn't it?" he said.

"Yes."

"I haven't introduced myself. Otis Wilson. *Waste Insight* magazine."

The eyes snapped back for a quick reappraisal, still saw nothing alarming.

"No comment," he said. He took one last, lingering look at the lake, the way a lonely man might watch a beautiful woman pulling away on a train, then turned and followed the others. Otis stayed long enough to watch one last barrel disappear beneath the perfect blue surface with a distant splash. Then he also turned and walked away.

The expert wasn't actually smoking a pipe, but Otis would have been willing to bet he had one in his pocket. The expert was a professor of vulcanology from the University of Chile. He had the full academic rumple. Baggy pants, tweed jacket, crooked tie. His horn-rimmed glasses kept slipping down his nose as he spoke, revealing a pair of mild, distracted eyes.

He stood in front of a projection screen in the dining hall of the palace. The curtains were drawn, and the light was dim. Once again, the tables had been scuffed aside, leaving only the chairs. The assembled visitors only filled about half of them, making the room look like a badly attended continuing education lecture. The professor probably felt right at home.

For close to an hour, he had stood before the screen, flicking his way through illegible slides and gabbling in a low monotone about deformation monitoring and magnetic anomaly patterns and stratigraphic analyses. Otis sat at the back, recording all of it and understanding none of it. Finally the slides ran out.

"Thank you for your attention, gentlemen," he said. He paused for undramatic effect. "Are there any questions?"

Through the gloom came the sound of stiffly shifting bodies. Someone cleared his throat.

"Doctor Sandoval," said Coombs. "In your expert scientific opinion, is it safe to dispose of chemical by-products in Lake

Pitouie?"

The sound of shifting stopped. The sound of intent interest took its place. Otis looked around the room for Trace, but he wasn't there. The expert ran a hand through his professorial hair.

"Oh yes, I think so," he said.

"Thank you, Doctor," said Coombs. And with those magic words of release, all the watchers rose from their chairs and made their way into the light.

Doctor Sandoval remained by his slide projector, looking lost. Otis lingered at the back. He felt like he should go question the authority, press him to justify his position. But Trace had been right. He didn't know enough science to ask a single intelligent question or make use of the answer. When had he gotten so dumb?

The professor was watching him now, still uncertain. Otis thought they must look like the last two wallflowers at the school dance. Well, what the hell? He squared his shoulders and prepared to ask for the pleasure.

Sarah appeared out of the murk at his side.

"Did you enjoy the presentation?" she said.

"Very informative."

"Doctor Sandoval is very highly thought of in his field. It took a lot of persuasion to get him here."

"How much time has he spent looking at your volcano?"

She shrugged.

"Seen one volcano, seen them all."

Hey, he thought, I could ask the expert that question. I could also ask what form the persuasion took. That would be good to know.

There was a rattling sound to his left. A waiter was drawing back the curtains. The room slowly filled with the last of the afternoon's sunlight. When Otis looked back, the professor was gone. He turned to Sarah again.

"I noticed Mr. Trace wasn't here," he said.

"He's in his room," she said. "Apparently he's not feeling well. Too much sun and shellfish, I think."

She linked an arm through his and guided him toward the garden door. Through the glass, Otis squinted down the rocky green slope on which the improbable city was built. The greenery was so thick that only rooftops could be seen, like slightly flatter rocks amid the bushes. He turned back to the empty room. Sarah stood in the shadow of the curtains, and his eyes took their time adjusting. Just as she was becoming visible, she opened the door and stepped out into the garden. Otis followed her out and commenced once more to squint. He steeled himself as he squinted. Having missed his chance with the expert, he felt a sudden obligation to take another stab at Getting the Story.

"Do you think the president would consent to an interview?"

"I thought you would ask. He's very busy of course, but he may be able to give you a few minutes."

"That would be very generous of him. When would be convenient?"

"Are you ready now?"

No.

"Yes."

"Come with me."

The president's office was a long, narrow room done up in Colonial Impressive. Whereas the hallways and guest rooms looked like they'd been furnished by looting the contents of a generic hotel chain, the Presidential Sanctum seemed to have picked up its décor from a jumble sale at an old English explorers' club. It was all plush leather furniture, slightly battered, and exotic souvenirs, slightly disturbing. Stuffed birds. Lots of books bound in more shabby leather. Maps in ornate frames. A massive desk, pristine except for a gold pen and pencil set. It was perfect. All that was missing was a president.

Otis stood in the middle of the room where Sarah had left him twenty minutes ago. He was uncertain of the proper protocol. Should he sit down? Where? By the desk, or in one of the big wingbacks by the cold stone fireplace? Would that be rude? Probably. He continued to stand.

He was nervous. No point in denying it. He had never interviewed a president before. Not of a whole country. Senior vice presidents were more his line. Much less intimidating.

He checked his equipment again. Notepad containing a dozen scribbled questions. Two pens. Voice recorder. Tie. That was it, and they'd had to make a detour to his room to get the tie. Maybe he should have gone into television. All the extra gear might have made him feel more substantial.

He panned his eyes around the room again. This was where the private consultations would take place between the president and the executives. This was where the deal would be done, and the bribe would be agreed. Those would be conversations worth hearing to an intrepid reporter.

Otis turned the voice recorder over in his fingers a few times. It could hold almost forty hours of sound. It had a voice activation function and a fresh battery. He could accidentally leave it behind and get a complete record of the whole sordid sequence of events that was about to unfold in this room. That would be good.

He looked around again, calculating. He could even stash the recorder out of sight before the president got here. In the spiky mouth of that stuffed fish, for instance. Might even act as an amplifier.

Drab practicality intruded on his machinations. How would he get the thing back? He couldn't count on ever being in this room again. What if someone found it? How many laws would he be breaking? As many as the president wanted, he supposed. Better not to think about possible punishments. All in all, it was an idea best filed under "Interesting but Unwise."

The door opened behind him with a ceremonial creak. Otis turned, ready to bow or something.

"Sorry," said Sarah. "It turns out the president has other business at the moment. We'll have to reschedule this."

She ushered him out.

"Do you still want to see the town?" she said.

"Sure."

"The president will be spending the next few days conducting one-on-one negotiations with our potential clients."

"Auctioning off your volcano."

"Well, yes. That is sort of the point."

"One-on-one negotiations."

"Yes. So?"

"So it's an auction where no one knows what anyone else is bidding. He'll play them against each other to squeeze the last dollar out of the lucky winner."

She shrugged.

"The financial negotiations aren't my department."

"Mmm."

"The point is, I won't be needed around here for a while, so if you'd like..."

Otis felt this was a point that needed confirmation.

"You'd show me around?"

"Sure. It's cooler in the evening anyway. Come on."

Garcia sat in his office in the basement of the palace and pondered. In all the time he had held the role of security chief on this island, he had never been called upon to put any security into place. Until ten minutes ago.

The reporter is a special case, the president had said. Watch

— 83 —

him for me.

Watch him?

Watch everything he does. Everyone he talks to. He thinks he can investigate the island. Find out everything he finds out.

How can I do that? I can't follow him around all day.

Find a way. This is of vital importance.

Nothing to do but salute. And ponder.

He weighed the pros and cons of his situation. On the negative side, his security detail consisted of himself and ten empty uniforms, filled by whoever was nearby and not busy when a show of special impressiveness was needed. On the positive side, he had The Book.

He opened a desk drawer, slipped a hand under the jumble of file folders and drew out a battered paperback. He ran a finger down its spine lovingly. It had been his guide and teacher ever since he had first discovered it twenty years ago.

He pored over its pages again, reading the notes he had pencilled in the margins all those years ago, remembering. When he came to the end, he closed the book and slid it to the corner of his desk with a respectful hand. He got out a pad of paper and a pen and placed them in readiness. He closed his eyes and took a deep breath. He held it. He let it out, using the muscles of his stomach to force out every last little bit of air at the bottom of his lungs. He took another deep breath, filling his lungs from the bottom to the top until they could hold no more. He held it. He let it out. He let his thoughts go with it. He opened his eyes. He was ready to begin.

He thought new thoughts. Thoughts of childhood. Long summer days at the vineyard in the Maipo Valley. Running over the low hills, slipping between the vines, cool and slick. His father, strong and wise under a straw hat as he tended the grapes. His mother, beautiful and kind as she beamed at them from the doorway of the little house.

Then a drought. Or maybe a disease. The grapes withered. The rich earth gave no bounty. Their plates were empty. His proud father put his hat in his hand and moved the family up the river to the city in search of work. He was a strong man, and he found small jobs unloading cargo or moving boxes, but it was never enough. Life became hard and grim, and his mother became sad and did not beam. He played in the street with the neighbourhood children, but they played rough, and their games usually ended in black eyes and bloody noses, and of these Garcia took his share.

Then his parents died. How did that happen? Did his mother waste away after his father was killed by a falling shipping container? No. Were they run down in the street by a huge, shiny car that didn't even stop? Maybe. Maybe better if he found them beaten to death in their shabby apartment by thieves who had found nothing worth stealing.

With no other relations, he lived on the streets of Santiago. He learned to take what he needed, and he learned to fight to keep what he had. He became hard and cold, and childhood fell away.

At sixteen, the army. He was under the legal age, but no one seemed to care. He learned discipline. He learned order. He even learned comradeship, to a point. There was always a part of himself that he held away from others.

He served under the command of Colonel Carlos Francisco Franco. (That was a terrible name. Maybe he had a different name.) His unit patrolled the borders and the empty spaces. There were skirmishes with bandits and smugglers. He learned to kill. He learned to rape. (To rape? Really? Well, yes. He learned to take what he wanted and to deal with those who stood in his way.) He grew from a hard boy to a hard man, but he became an effective man.

He rose in the ranks. Colonel Franco took notice and began to use him for special missions. From the Colonel he learned leadership and command. He learned the source of power and the ways of its use. He ran a network of spies and informants across the mountains and valleys, keeping tabs on the bandits and smugglers. He learned the value of information and the ways to make a man provide it.

Then, scandal. He found that the Colonel was taking bribes from the bandits and smugglers without telling him. He demanded his share. The Colonel sneered at him. He threatened to expose the truth. The Colonel said he would make sure they both went down together. He shot the Colonel in the heart and took his rank. He learned about corruption and betrayal, and how to deal with it.

Then, a new administration in Santiago. New leaders looking to bury old embarrassments. He was posted to this invisible island where no eye would ever stray across him again. It was a downfall, but it was better than a firing squad, and there was potential even here.

Garcia looked down at the pad where he had doodled as he dreamed. Among the squiggles and shapes, he saw a circle within a circle, like the crater within the island or the island within the ocean. He closed his eyes and breathed again. A good beginning.

Propelling himself out of his swivel chair, he crossed the room in two long strides and opened a tall cabinet that stood against one wall. Inside were his uniforms, dress and field. There were several peaked caps and several pairs of well-polished leather boots. There were belts and holsters and epaulettes. There was even a riding crop. It had been left in one of the rooms by a former occupant who probably didn't care that there were no horses on the island. It was made of black leather and had a small metal skull embedded in the end of the grip. It had come with a matching blindfold, handcuffs, and a ball-gag.

He took the sleeve of a dress jacket between his fingers and felt the weave. He caressed it. Unquestioned authority, he thought to himself. I am an unbending man of power. I am an omniscient keeper of secrets. My fingers stretch out into the night, unseen.

There was a mirror on the inside of the cabinet door. Garcia gazed at his own face and looked for the secret policeman within. I am hard, he thought. I am cruel and unrelenting. I am merciless. I act swiftly to eliminate those who question my will.

He stared at himself in the mirror for a long time, repeating these words silently. Then, symbolically, he drew the pair of mirrored sunglasses from his breast pocket and slowly lowered them over his eyes. In the mirror, he could now see a reflection of his reflection, distorted and endlessly regressing in the curved lenses.

Ceremonially, and aloud, he spoke.

"What is my motivation?"

It took him until nearly dawn, but he worked it out in the end. He knew what to do.

Otis and Sarah strolled side by side down the road to the town, as if taking a quiet walk on a tropical island was something they did every day at this hour.

"Most of the larger buildings date back to the war," said Sarah. "They've all been adapted to new uses. A school, a medical centre, a community hall."

Otis looked at the slightly shabby structures. Most were clapboard or cheap aluminum siding on wooden frames. Some were concrete blocked and bunker-like. It looked like a tornado had ripped the buildings from a midwestern US Army base circa 1940 and scattered them across this hill. Each building was placed wherever the ground was flat enough to take it, without regard to any other building in town. The residents had imposed their own kind of order by twisting a few dirt and gravel roads back and forth between the buildings until they wound past every doorstep. It was city planning by Salvador Dali.

Otis watched a couple of children burst out of the jungle, laugh their way across the road on bare feet and plunge again into the green.

"How many people live here?" he asked.

"About 1,500 on the whole island," said Sarah. "We haven't done an exact count in a few years."

"So where is everybody?"

She shrugged. Otis tried not to notice the way her shoulders moved under the thin fabric of her shirt. She had swept off her executive suit jacket as soon as they hit the outside air and departed her shoes soon after, leaving the little bundle of formality under a bush at the edge of the garden. Her plain white shirt was sheer and open to the third button. It was, Otis admitted to himself, a distraction.

"Working?" she suggested.

"Hauling barrels?"

"Some of them."

"Those were all men. Where are the women? The rest of the children?"

"Look, this is a very isolated place, in case you hadn't noticed. They don't get many visitors here. They're shy and a little nervous."

Otis saw an old woman standing in the doorway of one shack, half in shadow. It was the same woman who had watched them roll into town yesterday, standing in the same door, watching them with the same grave expression.

"Can't imagine why. Can I meet some of them?"

"Of course. But not right now, okay? I'll arrange something for you."

"Sure."

They walked on in silence for a while, eventually coming to the bottom of the hill and the beginning of the ocean. Between the two was a narrow and very rocky beach.

"Come on," she said. "Let's sit on the rocks and watch the waves for a while. You can ask me questions."

They made their way across the scree to a large, low rock by the water's edge. Sarah sat down and dug her toes into the coarse sand. Otis did not. The sky was orange, and the shadows were slanted.

"Come on," said Sarah. "Talk to me."

Otis mentally chewed his lip for a few seconds.

"How much say do the people of this island have about what goes on here?"

"A lot. The presidency is mostly a corporate position. Civic rule is based on old tribal customs."

"But the president is head of the tribe as well, isn't he?"

"He's a tribal elder. One of a small group."

"But he's the only one who lives in a palace," said Otis. Sarah said nothing. "He's the first and only president this island has had since gaining independence, right?"

She nodded.

"I wonder how long he plans to keep the job," said Otis. "I wonder how he would react if someone were to try to take it away from him. These rebels up in the jungle..."

"You don't need to worry about them. They're really nothing."

"This bottomless-pit-for-rent thing," said Otis, "It was the president's idea, wasn't it?"

She nodded.

"I wonder what the other elders think about the plan."

"Look," she said. "This is a poor island. There's no economy. There's no industry. There's not even any tourism. We've got no valuable natural resources. All we've got is fresh seafood and a big hole in the ground."

She brushed a strand of hair from her cheek.

"You want to know what the elders think about the plan? They think it's better than poverty and starvation. The world has a habit of exploiting places like this for all they've got and then throwing away the husk. These people have just found a way to choose the manner of their exploitation. I hope it works out for them."

She fell silent again, and they sat there for a while watching the sunset.

"Wait a second," said Otis. "You hope it works out for them? I thought you were one of them."

"I am," she said. "But I didn't grow up with them. To tell the truth, it would drive me crazy to live here all the time. The rest of these people don't have a choice."

"For what it's worth," said Otis, "I hope it works out for you too."

She snorted, but there was a smile inside it.

"Thank you, Mr. Hard-Bitten Reporter with the Tender Heart."

He stubbed the toe of his sensible black leather Oxford into the sand.

"You know," he said. "When I was at journalism school, I met people who burned to be reporters, to root out corruption and injustice and bring it to light. I was never like that. To be honest, I'm not really a reporter at all, hard-bitten or tender. I'm more of a typist."

"I thought you were the associate editor of *Waste Insight* magazine," she said.

Now it was his turn to snort.

"Want to hear a joke?" he said.

"Sure."

"A guy dies and goes to hell. The devil tells him he gets to choose how he'll spend eternity. He opens a door and shows the guy a room full of people being roasted on spits. The guy shakes his head. The devil opens another door and shows him a room full of people being whipped by huge demons. The guy shakes his head. The devil opens a third door and shows him a room full of people standing knee-deep in shit, drinking coffee and smoking cigarettes. The guy nods. The devil shows him in and hands him a cup. Just as the guy is about to take his first sip, the devil says..."

"Break's over. Everyone back on your heads," said Sarah.

"Yeah," he said. "Well, that's sort of what my first day on the job was like."

"Fun. So how did you get into that?"

He snorted again.

"The editor called the school and said they had an opening. Asked if there were any promising students who might be interested. What he meant was, who would be willing to work cheap. Graduation was just a couple of weeks away. One of my professors told me about the job and said I should I apply."

"That was nice."

"I thought so at the time. Now I think she must have hated me. I used to argue with her in class all the time, and I used to win too. She didn't like that. I think setting me up with a degrading dead-end job was her way of sabotaging my career before it even got started."

"Mmm," she said.

"Seven years I've been there."

"You could have left. Found something else."

"Yeah. I could have, but I didn't."

"Why not?"

"I don't know."

"Well, I hope it works out for you, too."

"Thanks."

Chapter 8

A week went by. Two more visitors arrived and departed. Lars was not invited to sit in on the meetings. He supposed Woolsey didn't want his investors to know he had a partner on the base.

Lars and the chief barely spoke. There didn't seem to be any great transfer of grifter's lore to a new generation going on. Maybe he was supposed to learn by example, but the chief didn't do anything that was exemplary.

Then, after a week, Woolsey walked into the radar room while Lars was sitting at the scope.

"Report," he said.

"Condition green," said Lars. "The scope is clear." It always was.

"Very well," said the chief. "Report to my office when you are relieved."

"Okay," said Lars, not taking his face from the goggles. He heard the chief walk out.

"We have a problem," said the chief, as Lars stood before his desk an hour later. "It's a problem that I anticipated, but still hoped to avoid. I have a solution ready. This is where you come in."

"Go on," said Lars.

"Several of our prospective customers have decided to be cagey. They want to send their own surveyors up here to examine the ground."

"Do you plan to buy them off?"

"Varick," said the chief. "I do not buy people off."

"Sorry."

"I'm going to deceive them."

"How?"

"We're going to salt the mine," said the chief. "We're going to plant some radioactive material out there in the snow and let them find it. That is to say, you are."

Lars pictured himself, alone in the dark, hiding radioactive rocks under snowmen like a mutant Easter Bunny. It wasn't an image he liked.

"Will that be enough?" he said. "I mean, these will be professionals. Won't they know?"

"Not if we do it right. In case you haven't been outside lately, Varick, it's currently late January on the coast of the Arctic Ocean. It is minus forty-three degrees out there. It's pitch black. The rock surface is under yards of ice and snow. Plus, these people will be dependent on us for shelter, supplies, transportation, and directions, and we won't make it comfortable for them. How long do you thing some geologist from Texas or California is going to want to spend out there? We just need to give them an excuse to jump to an early conclusion. We'll lead them to the water and let the weather make them drink."

Lars considered this. It could work. He'd been up here two years now, and he still didn't like going outside, even in summer. It could work. He just hated it.

"I've given them a tight deadline," said the chief. "They can't wait for spring, and they don't have time to drill core samples. They just want to wave a Geiger counter over a wider area."

"How many of those rocks do you have?" said Lars.

"Just the one," said the chief. "But we won't be using rocks."

"What will we be using?"

"Come with me."

Woolsey led him to the airlock and began to pull on his parka. Obediently, Lars followed suit. The chief picked up a flashlight the size of a prison spotlight clamped to the battery from a Buick and stepped out into the gloom. Lars followed.

It was windy. That is to say, it was just about possible to remain upright and moving forward. The fine ice crystals swirled around their feet in a frenzy to find the seams in their clothing as they crunched along. As always, the shock of the cold was startling. Breathing hurt as the lungs began to freeze, and it took only seconds for an exposed face to begin feeling stiff and wooden. There was a reason Lars didn't like going outside. People died out here. The planet just snuffed them out.

They followed a rope through the darkness. The rope was strung at waist height between stakes driven into the snow. In the fall, it stood at shoulder height. Before spring the accumulated snow would bring the rope down to their knees. Ropes like this ran between the command unit and all the outlying structures: the radar dome, the fuel dump, the airstrip, and the storage huts. Lars wasn't sure which lifeline they were following. The chief's flashlight beam illuminated a circle of bright white snow, a disembodied length of rope, the occasional stake, and nothing else. The darkness was complete and oppressive. It was hell.

They came to a metal storage warehouse the size of a small barn. The chief trudged to the door pulled it open with a metal shriek that made the wind sound cheerful. They entered. The chief closed the door behind them with a bang that sounded much too final to Lars. The unit wasn't insulated. It was just as cold inside, if less windy. It was also unpowered, so they could only see by the flashlight beam as it wandered over shelves full of spare parts and anonymous boxes. At the very back of the unit, the chief stopped and began examining labels.

"Hold this," he said to Lars, passing him the flashlight. Then he carefully slid one of the boxes off its shelf and laid it gently on the floor. Lars could see the label on the side. It read, "Septic tank repair kit." Below that was a stencilled army inventory number.

"Do we have a septic tank?" said Lars.

"No. Hold the light steady."

The chief opened the box, reached in and lifted out a large metal toolbox held shut by a padlock. He unzipped his parka slightly and, to Lars's astonishment, took a key on a string from around his neck. The key opened the lock, and the chief opened the toolbox. The box contained another box.

"This box is lined with lead," said the chief. "Inside the box is approximately four hundred grams of weapons-grade plutonium. I want you to go out and spread it around a bit."

Lars regarded the toolbox with the kind of caution that only a box of plutonium can inspire.

"You've got to be kidding," he said. "Where would you get something like that?"

"I'm just about to tell you," said Woolsey. "But I'm warning you right now, you aren't going to believe it."

"Okay."

"It came from the bottom of the St. Lawrence River on October 15, 1950. It's been waiting all these years for just the right occasion."

Woolsey lovingly adjusted the toolbox so it aligned precisely with the row of shelves.

"Uh-huh," said Lars. "Go on."

"Aren't you going to tell me that I must be shitting you?"

"No. Go on."

"Okay. Here's something very few people know. Back in 1950, Strategic Air Command stashed eleven A-bombs on the base at

Goose Bay, Newfoundland. Just sort of put a few aside for a rainy day. Model Mark IV, the Fat Man design. Nagasaki specials. A classic of annihilation. For some reason, nobody seemed to feel any urge to inform the Canadian public about this little stockpile.

"So one murky night in the fall of that year, something happens that almost nobody will ever find out about. A B-29 takes off from Goose Bay heading back to the States, carrying one of these bombs. As the plane is passing over Quebec, the bomb falls out. No one seems to know exactly how that happened. There was a world-class hush-up. Nevertheless, there is now an atomic weapon at the bottom of the St. Lawrence and they have to get it out.

"So SAC calls up the Canadian Defence Department. The government calls the Royal Navy and tells them to go out and pick up the damn bomb. The navy can't get the necessary gear there fast enough, so they call a private salvage contractor. The contractor goes out on the river in the middle of the night and fishes out the bomb. Then he says he's going to keep it until he gets paid."

"Now we've hit the part I don't believe," said Lars.

"Told you," said Woolsey. The old man crouched down in the dark and spread his hands out over the box as if it were a crackling wood stove.

"Be careful," said Lars. Woolsey smiled up at him.

"Concerned for my well-being? An excellent trait in a partner. Want to hear the rest?"

"Why not?"

"Good answer. Turns out the government was a little late in paying off this salvage company's last contract. The feds said they didn't owe anything at all, since the last job was done in such a half-assed way. Between you and me, that was indeed the case. That particular salvage company was run by a rip-off artist of the highest calibre."

"Let me guess," said Lars. Woolsey smiled again.

"Good guess," he said. "But no, it wasn't me. It was a business associate of mine. Not the most law-abiding man I ever knew, but very innovative in his trade practices. For example, in this case he decided to short-circuit years of legal wrangling by holding that Fat Man hostage. Just for a few hours."

"He wasn't worried about the Americans storming in and killing him?"

"You tend not to storm very much when atomic weapons are involved."

"If he made such a hash of his last contract, how did he get this one?"

"It was an emergency, and he was the only man around who could get the job done. So anyway, there he sat on his boat in the middle of the river in the middle of the night with his very own independent atomic capability and a few hours to kill. Naturally, he poked around the thing a bit."

"He poked around with an atomic bomb?"

"It didn't require much ingenuity. There was this big friendly panel marked 'Access.' He popped that off, and the plutonium core slid right out and landed on his big toe. Rolled off away under the workbench."

"Not sure I believe that, either."

"Okay, so maybe it didn't actually hit his toe. I wasn't there. Don't you have any appreciation for a good story?"

"So then what? He just picked up this lump of plutonium and stuck it in his pocket?"

"He only took half. Those old bombs used a solid sphere of plutonium as their core, and the sphere was split into two halves. One half he stuck back in the bomb, the other half he decided to keep as payment for services rendered. He gave it to me for safekeeping on the dock, just before he was arrested."

"So why aren't you in jail?"

"They couldn't find me. I'm very good at not being found."

"Why aren't you covered in tumours or something?"

"A sub-critical chunk of plutonium isn't that dangerous. You wouldn't want to hide it under your pillow, but brief exposure isn't going to have any measurable effect."

"But you keep it in a lead box."

"Twenty-three years I've been saving this. I'm not stupid."

"You were planning that far ahead?"

"That far and farther. Do you think a man of my ability ends up in a wasteland like this by accident? It took some pretty deft footwork to get this job."

The chief closed and locked the toolbox, then handed it to Lars. He carefully resealed the septic tank repair kit and put it back in its place. Then he took the flashlight from Lars's unresisting mitten and stepped to the door of the hut.

"Come on," he said. "Work to do."

The chief led him through the frozen night to the workshops, another metal door at the end of another intermittent rope. He unlocked the door and ushered Lars inside with a leather mitten. Lars hefted the toolbox against his leg and sidestepped through from the black of the sky to the black of the building. The door squealed shut behind him with another demonic shriek.

"Hang on," said Woolsey. There was the clunk of a switch and a buzz as the overhead lights warmed up. After a few splutters, electricity overcame resistance, and the bulbs popped into life all at once. Lars squinted. He blinked. He looked again.

"Franks is going to be pissed," he said.

The mechanic's collection of chaotically organized tools had been swept to the sides of the room in heaps. The middle of the space was filled with a makeshift tent formed from the large sheets of transparent plastic they kept on hand for emergency waterproofing. The sheets hung from a beam of the ceiling like the canopy of a four-poster bed. More plastic covered the floor. Duct tape held all the seams shut except for a waist-high slit directly in front of them. Lars turned to Woolsey and waited.

"What?" said the chief. "Never seen a field-expedient clean room before?"

"You did this?"

"Yep."

"You didn't make me do this?"

"You were on the scope. We're short on time as it is. Got to get this all taken down and cleared away before Franks gets off his shift. He would be, as you say, pissed."

"What's it for?"

"Put this on."

The chief pulled a folded wedge of plastic off a workbench and shook it. Arms and legs flopped out. It was a radiation suit.

"You gotta be kidding," said Lars.

"Can't grind plutonium without protection, kid."

Lars stared from the suit to the tent to the toolbox. It was getting very heavy. He put it down.

"Why," he said, mouth dry, "are we grinding plutonium?"

"You think maybe we should just drop this whole lump in the snow someplace? That wouldn't convince anyone. We need to salt a much wider area. For that, we need powdered plutonium. For that, we grind. Or rather, you grind."

The chief thrust the suit into Lars's hands.

"It fits right over your parka. Put it on. I'll tape up the seams for you."

Lars stood and stared some more.

"If you want to back out, you can always go back to your bunk and stare at Miss April."

Lars turned the suit over and found the thick plastic zipper that ran from the crotch to the neck.

"Fuck," he said. He tugged the zipper open. The chief smiled.

Franks's bench grinder was set up like an altar in the middle of the field-expedient clean room. Lars stood before it like a petitioner uncertain of which deity he was about to address. In his right hand was a dull grey hemisphere of very heavy metal. By his left foot, the power cord ran under layers of plastic and tape to a socket in the wall.

"Ready?" said the chief, standing conspicuously outside the plastic shrine of dubious sanctity.

"No," said Lars. "This is stupid. The powder is just going to fly everywhere."

"The plastic will catch it. That's the whole point. There's a broom to your left. You can sweep the dust up when you're done. So, ready?"

Lars lifted the lump of plutonium to his eyes and scanned it for mystic runes of warning. There were none. He shrugged and hit the switch. The grinder spun up with an innocent hum. He reached through the suit's plastic faceplate and adjusted his respirator one more time. He began to grind.

The first grinding wheel lasted about an hour before it was reduced to a smooth disk of metal. The hemisphere of plutonium was now an irregular polygon about two-thirds of its original size. The plastic walls of the tent, the floor, and much of Lars himself were covered with a fine grey powder.

"There are spare wheels by the broom," said Woolsey.

"This is the dumbest thing I've ever done," said Lars. "And I've done some dumb things."

"I can't understand a thing you're saying through that mask, so I'll just assume you're telling me how well everything is going."

Lars didn't even bother to glare. He went to find a fresh

grinding wheel. Woolsey parked himself on a stool and leaned a casual elbow on the workbench.

"You know," he said, "Disposal of radioactive material has a fascinating history of unexpected consequences."

"Yeah?" said Lars through his respirator. He fiddled at the grinder with a tiny wrench and a plastic mitten.

"For example, there's a facility in Washington State that used to be a main site for processing atomic weapons material in the forties and fifties."

"So?" said Lars.

"When the place was decommissioned a few years ago, the army sent in a crew of contractors to clean the place up. As you can imagine, there were all kinds of nasty bits and pieces lying around there. Things like cesium and strontium, two of the principal byproducts of the enrichment process. Or so I've been told. I'm not a nuclear engineer myself."

"No shit," said Lars. He tried for the twenty-sixth time to wipe the sweat from his face and put yet another smudge on the faceplate of his hood.

"Now, as I understand it, the crew didn't consider some of this stuff to be especially dangerous compared to the other materials piled up around the place. Like strontium salts, for instance. Just not that scary. So, in the finest tradition of military contractors, they made a big pile of it out in a field, built a box around it and called it a day. Out of sight, out of mind, right?"

"Sure," said Lars, tightening the last bolt. He tossed the expended wheel into a corner.

"Watch the plastic," said the chief. "Anyway, this would have been a perfectly good plan except for the rabbits."

"Rabbits?"

"The field had a sizeable population of jackrabbits. Turns out that rabbits think strontium salts are delicious. They kept burrowing into the storage site to lick the pile of radioactive waste. Then, as is the way with all of us, the rabbits shit out whatever they didn't need. And it turns out rabbits don't need strontium."

"Huh."

"Now rabbits breed like rabbits, and more rabbits means more rabbit droppings. And each one of those droppings was a little concentrated nugget of strontium. When an environmental inspector went back to the site a few years later, that field was practically glowing with radioactive bunny poo."

"Huh."

"The army had to send in another clean-up crew. Those guys are still there, picking up hot rabbit shit on their hands and knees. I often wonder if they sent the same crew that dumped the strontium there in the first place."

Lars walked to the plastic wall and spoke very distinctly.

"Why are you telling me this?"

Woolsey smiled.

"To make you feel better. You think this is bad? You could be grinding up a nice big ball of frozen shit. Now get back to work."

It took two more hours and two more wheels to reduce the lump of plutonium to a nubbin that Lars could no longer keep a grip on. After it flew out of his fingers into the plastic wall for the third time, the chief signalled him to cut the power.

"Guess that's all we're going to get. Sweep up. We don't have much time left. Don't forget yourself."

When Lars had swept up all the powder he could find, it filled the small lead liner of the toolbox about halfway. He dropped in the last nugget of metal and slammed the lid with one foot.

"Over here," said the chief. Lars turned. A deeply unpleasant blast of icy water hit him in the chest. Woolsey waved the fire hose over Lars's body through a slit in the tent and smiled again.

"Turn around. Hold out your arms. Good. Now come get the

hose. Wash down the grinder and the plastic. Be thorough."

Lars was as thorough as he felt able, which might not have been as thorough as maximally possible.

"Good," said the chief. "Start tearing down the plastic."

By the time they had the tent and the radiation suit stuffed into three plastic garbage bags, it was very near the shift change. The chief hosed down the workshop floor once more, then headed for the door.

"A good night's work," he said. "Take the toolbox to your quarters. Guard it with your life."

"From who? Rabbits?"

The chief smiled again. Lots of smiles tonight. They made their way through the swirling whiteness to the command unit. Franks had not noticed their absence.

"You seem down, man," said Franks. "Something up?"

He passed Lars the joint without looking at him, laying flat on his back in his bunk du jour. Melodic distortion played in the background again. Lars rolled the joint between his fingers a few times, then passed it back. He wasn't in the mood to be mellow.

"Not really," said Lars. Well, what could he say? I've got half a kilo of plutonium hidden under my bunk and I can feel my sperm count dropping just lying here?

"What do you think is going on with all these visitors we've been getting lately?" Lars asked. Franks snorted.

"Usual military bullshit," he said. "Somebody's writing a report. Somebody's making an inspection tour. Somebody's trying to get their name seen by the right people. It's nothing for us to worry about."

"I think they're civilians, not military," said Lars.

"Well then it's the usual political bullshit. It all smells the same. The left asshole doesn't know what the right asshole is doing."

This metaphor probably made more sense from inside the baggie.

"I'm going to be gone for a day," said Lars. "The chief is sending me out to inspect the eastern relay station. You'll have to cover my shift."

"Didn't even know we had an eastern relay station," said Franks. "No wonder you're all uptight."

"What do you mean?"

"A whole day outside. Got to be your idea of hell. I never met anyone who hates the cold more than you. Sometimes I wonder what you're doing up here."

"Yeah, me too."

Chapter 9

Garcia sat behind his desk and regarded the two men impassively. The two men stood to something near attention and stared at the wall behind Garcia's head. Excellent. They already had some training. He was careful not to let his satisfaction show. Better for subordinates never to be too certain of where they stand. In security, insecurity was an excellent motivator. He assumed.

Garcia stood up. Still saying nothing, he walked around his desk, behind the men and across the room to the large wardrobe. The two men did not move their eyes from the wall. Excellent. Garcia reached into the wardrobe and, with a small shiver, drew out the riding crop. He took a moment to admire the object. It had a certain menace that a regular equestrian riding crop would lack.

Garcia moved across the office floor, his footsteps making no sound on the thick carpet, the silence only broken by the snap of the crop against the side of his boot. He took up a position behind and between the two men, out of their sight but close enough to murmur in their ears.

He bent his head to the man on his left and murmured in his ear.

"Name?"

The man opened his mouth to speak. Garcia bent his head again and shouted in his ear.

"Your name is gone. From now on, you will answer to the codename Rose. Do you understand?"

The man fidgeted.

"Sir," he said. "Isn't that a girl's name, sir?"

The man on the right snorted and grinned. Garcia flicked him on the ear with the tip of the riding crop. He stopped grinning.

"Name?"

The man opened his mouth. Garcia flicked him with the crop again. The man closed his mouth.

"You will now answer to the codename Krantz. You may find these names amusing, but there is method in them. These are the names of secret operatives. Men whose true identities must be kept dark, even from their superiors, if they are to be effective. You will both address me as Claudius. Do you understand?"

"Yes, sir," said the men, nearly in unison.

"How long have you been a palace guard, Agent Rose?"

"About a week, sir."

"Agent Krantz?"

"Two days, sir."

"Now you are agents of the Pitouie Intelligence Service. You will take your orders directly from me and from me only. For reasons of cover, you are still officially palace guards, but you have been released from your duties."

Garcia moved back around the desk and sat down. He laid the riding crop precisely across the surface in front of him.

"I have been given a special mission by the president," he said. "A secret mission. You two will assist me. You will be my field agents. I am your controller. Do you understand?"

"Yes, sir."

Garcia looked at his field agents. They were thickset young men of about twenty years. Agent Rose had a head like a potato and a body like a sack of potatoes. Agent Krantz was not so attractive.

"Do you know why I have selected you for this mission, men?"

"No, sir."

Because you're big enough to be intimidating and because you were hanging around the palace when I went looking for recruits, Garcia didn't say.

"Because you've got what it takes," he said. "The steel. The backbone." He flexed the riding crop between his hands, backbone-like. "Because you can get the job done. Do you understand?"

Agent Krantz cast a dubious sidelong glance at his cohort. Agent Rose looked back and shrugged.

"What do we need to do, sir?" said Rose.

Garcia favoured them with the cold, thin smile he had been practicing. He reached into a desk drawer and withdrew The Book.

"Sit down," he said. "I'll tell you."

Otis froze as he stepped out of his room. There was an islander down the hall. A waiter pushing a small trolley with a coffee pot on it. Otis watched from a distance as the man stopped before one of the doors and knocked. The door opened, and Otis heard the grumbling of one of his fellow guests as the waiter rolled the trolley inside.

Otis took the chance to move into a better position. The waiter would most likely bring the trolley back to the service elevator at the other end of the hall. Moving on the balls of his feet, hopefully like a jungle cat moving upwind of its prey, he slipped down the hallway, past the door and around the corner to the elevator. When the waiter reappeared a minute later pushing the empty trolley, Otis was leaning casually against the wall by the call button.

"Hello," he said, casually.

The waiter bobbed his head and smiled, but said nothing.

"Do you speak English?"

Bob. Smile.

"Can I ask you a question?"

Slight frown. No bob. Otis pressed on regardless.

"What do you think of your government's plan to allow foreign companies to dump industrial waste on your island?"

The man cleared his throat.

"The president has assured us that this is a safe and effective way to bring new prosperity and growth to Pitouie. I will be happy to live on the new and prosperous Federated Pitouie."

Otis regarded the waiter.

"Did it take you long to memorize that?"

Bob. Smile.

"Thank you for your time."

Otis thumbed off the recorder in his pocket and went down to breakfast, defeated.

"Agent Rose, report. What is the subject doing now?"

"Rose here, Claudius. The subject is currently lurking."

"Say again, Rose. The subject is lurking?"

"Affirmative, Claudius. The subject is lurking behind a hedge. He is in the garden. He seems to be waiting for someone."

"Is there anyone else around?"

"Agent Krantz is pretending to trim a different hedge on the other side of the garden. Other than that, we are alone. Wait. The subject is on the move. A guest has just entered from the dining hall. The subject is moving to intercept."

"Which guest?"

"Unknown. The guest is between the ages of forty-five and fifty-five, with greyish hair, nice teeth, and a dark suit."

"Could be any of them. I'll have photographs for you to look at during your debriefing."

"If you think it'll help, Claudius. Wait. The subject has made contact with the guest."

"What's he saying?"

"The subject has introduced himself. Now he is asking for an interview."

"How is the guest reacting?"

"Like the subject has very bad breath."

"Maintain surveillance."

"Affirmative."

"Good morning," said Otis. "It's Mr. Hyslop, isn't it?"

The man would have started had he been willing to expend the energy. The only reaction he was prepared to extend on credit without security was a slight puckering of the brow.

"My name is Otis Wilson," said Otis in his best biz press bland. "I'm doing a story about the island for *Waste Insight* magazine."

The pucker deepened slightly.

"Never heard of it," said Hyslop. Otis smiled a little more blandly and carried on.

"Do you mind if I ask you a few questions?"

"Better if you contact our media relations department. They'll have answers to all your questions on file."

"But my questions are about your impressions of Pitouie. Since you haven't made your report yet, how can your media relations department have them on file?"

Hyslop rolled that one around for a while.

"You'll have to wait until I have made my report," he said. "Then they will."

Otis knew the thought that had caused the pause. It didn't matter what this man's report would eventually say; his media department already had answers ready for any reporter who might ask. The man had been about to explain this, but had caught himself. We must all observe the decencies.

"Who do you represent?" said Otis.

Now Hyslop started.

"Why do you ask?"

"I can't ask your media department my questions unless I know who you work for."

Hyslop looked as though his fingers itched for a cell phone. Back home he had people for this. People he could call. Here, all of a sudden, he didn't. The man had gone cold handset and was feeling withdrawal. Tough, thought Otis. No shirt, no shoes, no service. That was the policy at this beauty spot.

"I'm not prepared to speak to the press," said Hyslop. "Better if I consult my legal department before making any kind of public statement."

"I don't need a formal statement," said Otis. "I'm only looking for your impressions." He was just screwing around now. Short of a power drill to the kneecap, this guy clearly wasn't going to give him anything. Never go on the record. Don't give them ammunition to use against you later. Better never to be known than to be known as an embarrassment. Sound corporate advice that had saved many a mediocre career. The subject in question had taken it to heart.

"I really don't have anything to say," he said. "Excuse me."

Hyslop walked away. Otis shoved the recorder back into his pocket. Another one down. He pulled out a small notepad and consulted his list. Homme had given him a "No comment" at the crater. Laurier had offered a "Piss off" when he approached him at breakfast. Hyslop had used more words to say the same thing just now. If he kept up this rate of success, he would be done by lunch. The suits had all taken a vow of silence. Except Trace. Trace liked to talk. Apparently thought of himself as a free-thinking speaker of ugly truths. Someone like that was very good to know. But Trace had vanished. Plus, he still had to interview at least one average ordinary islander. He looked around the garden again.

"Claudius, I've been spotted. The subject is coming right at me. What do I do?"

"Keep calm, Krantz. Remember what I told you. Improvise. If that fails, play dumb. Pretend you don't speak much English. Keep the channel open."

There was a crackle of static. Garcia placed the walkie-talkie on his desk and stared down at it intently. His agent was experiencing his first exposure to the unpredictability of field work. He owed the man his attention. Garcia heard the voice of the reporter Wilson over the radio link.

"Good morning."

"Sir," said Krantz. Good. Nothing compromising yet.

"Can I ask you a question?"

"Sir?"

"What do you think of your government's plan to allow foreign companies to dump toxic chemicals in Lake Pitouie?"

Garcia held his breath.

"I, uh, I don't know, sir."

Garcia clenched a fist. Not that dumb, idiot.

"Did you know that the government wants to turn your island into a chemical dumping ground?" said the reporter.

"Uh, no," said Krantz.

"Well, now that you do know, do you think it's a good idea or a bad idea?"

The voice of Agent Rose broke in.

"The president has assured us that this is a safe and effective way to bring new prosperity and growth to Pitouie. I will be happy to live on the new and prosperous Federated Pitouie," he said.

"Uh, yeah," said Krantz. "That's what I think too."

Garcia exhaled. He made a note to think up a commendation to give to Rose in recognition of unexpected mental capacity.

"I see," said the reporter. "Thank you."

There was more crackling.

"The subject has left the garden," said Rose.

"Well done," said Garcia. "Maintain surveillance. Try to keep your distance this time."

"Yes, sir."

Thwack.

"So Wanda says, can't you just issue us another invoice number? And I say, no we can't because we've switched to a new invoicing system that uses a different numbering format and the old system has been taken off-line. So Wanda says, whose dumb idea was it to deactivate the old system while there were still invoices outstanding? And I say, I know and I told them this would happen, but they said the old system had to be gone by the end of the quarter or they'd have to show the operating expenses in next year's annual report and someone was under pressure to improve the bottom line so a lot of legacy systems were just being declared redundant and shut down."

"Mmm," said Otis. "Can we talk about the island for a minute, Mr. Penner?"

They were standing on a concrete platform around back of the palace. Faded and much-chipped paint indicated that it used to be a helicopter landing pad. Now it was Federated Pitouie's infinite one-hole golf course.

Thwack. Another ball hooked out over the jungle and vanished. Penner fished a fresh victim from the bucket with the head of his five-iron.

"I am talking about the island," he said. "What we're standing on is the same type of hole in reality that that orphaned invoice went into. That invoice can't be paid. It can't be reconciled. It can't even be voided. But it's still a legal document and can't be ignored either. Our industrial by-products are like that invoice."

"So what happened to that invoice?"

"Eventually Wanda brought it over to me by taxi, and I printed a lower-case B at the end of the old invoice number with a felt tip pen. She re-submitted using this semi-authorized number, and the system took it right in. No complaints. That's what this island is, Mr. Wilson. It's a felt tip pen that will allow us to get troubling invoices off our books."

Thwack.

"Are you concerned that the rebels on the mountain might interfere with your business operations, should you win the contract?"

"Oh, no. The president has assured me that they won't be a problem."

"You've already met with the president?"

"Yes, I have. A very shrewd man, I thought."

"What did you discuss?"

"A wide range of topics."

"Did he say how the rebels will be prevented from becoming a problem?"

"I believe he means to buy them."

"Buy them?"

"Yes. With all this new money at his disposal, purchasing the cooperation of a few starving troublemakers should pose no difficulties."

"He wants to use your money to bribe the rebels?"

"Well, he doesn't have any of his own."

"So, his assurance that the rebels will be no problem depends on you fixing his problem for him."

Thwack.

"Er, yes."

"He is a shrewd man. But this brings us to another issue, Mr. Penner."

"What's that?"

"Bribery."

"Oh?"

"I have heard allegations that this conference is just a thinly disguised bidding war to see which of you can offer the president the biggest personal consideration. Can you comment on that?"

"In negotiations of this kind, it is often vital to display creativity," said Penner. "As I did with the felt tip pen. As the president will with his rebels. We must sometimes be unorthodox to be effective. Other than that, I have no comment."

Thwack.

"Claudius? Rose here."

"Report."

"The subject has gone back inside. Should we pursue?"

"Can you maintain surveillance without compromising your cover?"

"I believe so, sir. Agent Krantz and I have disguised ourselves."

"Excellent initiative, Rose. What are your disguises?"

"Well sir, we've disguised ourselves as islanders wearing different shirts."

"I see. Where did you get the shirts?"

"Well sir, we didn't want to leave our posts, so Agent Krantz and I just exchanged shirts."

"Ah. Proceed at your own discretion, Rose."

"Sir."

Otis found Coombs in the palace library. It was a small room full of dented shelves and worn leather-ish armchairs. The shelves carried what appeared to be the entire inventory of a Chilean used bookstore. Thrashed paperbacks were stacked cover to cover with massive leather-bound tomes. A selection of magazines was non-piled on an end table. Coombs was treading slowly up and down before the shelves with his head canted over at a spine-stretching angle.

"Good afternoon, Mr. Coombs."

The head canted back in the opposite direction, over-compensated, readjusted and finally came to bear on Otis.

"Yes?" he said.

"Can I ask you a few questions about your impressions of the island?"

Coombs rolled his head around a few more times like it hadn't quite settled on top of his neck.

"Why not?" he said. "If it'll pass a little time. All this stuff is in Spanish."

Otis thumbed the voice recorder.

"Are you here on behalf of anyone in particular?"

"Diox Petrochemical."

"What do you think of the island?"

"It's ideal for the purpose."

"Of hazardous waste disposal?"

Coombs curled one edge of one lip.

"Are you going to play the environmental angle?"

"I can't ignore it."

"Everyone else will. I've been to some of the most polluted places on the planet. Hell, I've made some of them happen. Sumgayit. Vapi. Dzerzhinsk. Tons of material leaching into the ground over the course of decades. Heavy metals, cyanide, pesticides, PCBs, chlorine, aluminum, detergents. Even the people who live there don't really care. At least, not enough to make it stop. The merchandise we're going to bring here is like a teaspoon of baby shampoo in comparison. It won't be so bad."

"I saw those barrels going into the crater. I can't help but think that eventually it will all glom together into something very nasty."

"You're a writer. Did you bring a laptop computer with you?"

"Yes."

"Laptops are full of very nasty compounds, and most of them get thrown away in just three or four years. In China, whole villages of little old ladies are employed to strip motherboards because the components contain rare metals that are worth a few yuan per kilo. I've been there. They sit in a circle around a pile of computer parts like they were making a quilt. They sit there with soldering irons and tweezers, plucking individual resistors and capacitors and integrated circuits like lice from a head of hair, all day every day. They get paid virtually nothing, as you might expect, and it's terrible for their health, but it's the only work they've got."

"Mmm."

"Going to stop using your laptop?"

"Probably not, but I might buy a less toxic model next time."

"A few percentage points either way makes no difference. Until they invent edible microchips, the final phase in the life cycle of a computer will still involve a circle of little old ladies in China, making themselves sick so you can write."

"But you'll be the one making a profit off of it."

Coombs shrugged and began running his finger along the shelf of spines again.

"Somebody will."

"Hello again, Mr. Laurier."

"I thought I told you to piss off."

"Yes, you did. But I thought I might convince you to talk to me if I tried a different approach."

"Doubtful."

"You haven't heard my proposal yet."

"I can't think of anything you could propose that would

convince me to talk to a reporter while I'm in the middle of a business negotiation."

"There you have it, Mr. Laurier."

"What?"

"A business negotiation. That's what I propose."

There was a snort through the speaker.

"Chequebook journalism? You think you can buy an interview from me?"

"Not with money, of course not."

"Then what?"

"Take a look at this."

Garcia leaned forward over the radio on his desk. It didn't help him see anything. He should've given Krantz a camera. One of those really impressive cameras with a telephoto lens like an artillery piece. Crouching behind a hedge in the garden holding his walkie-talkie out wasn't really providing enough coverage.

"So, what is it?"

"A radio receiver. Also a digital recorder. Listen."

The voice of Sarah Vache reached his ear, tinny and very faint, saying something about the president being occupied with business.

"Why is it shaped like a garbage can?"

"It's more covert that way."

"I...see."

"It's not what you can see, Mr. Laurier. It's what you can hear. The transmitter that goes along with this garbage can is currently hidden in the president's office. I had occasion to place it there earlier today while I was waiting to interview him. I believe that's where your negotiations are taking place?"

Garcia stared at his own clunky apparatus in astonishment. He tingled. He felt like a poet on the verge of inspiration. Why hadn't he thought of that? Vast new vistas of possibility were unfolding in his mind. He breathed slowly and carefully so as not to disturb the vision.

"You bugged the president's office?"

"Yes I did."

"You'll be able to hear all the negotiations. Every promise every one of those rat bastards makes."

"Yes I will."

"And if I give you an interview, you'll tell me what they say?"

"No I won't."

Garcia could almost hear the executive blink.

"Why not?"

"I won't help you bribe a government official. That would bother me. However, I wouldn't have any problem telling your competitors everything that you say in that room."

There was a long, crackly silence.

"It seems I underestimated you, Mr. Wilson."

You're not the only one, thought Garcia. He would never have credited the insubstantial reporter with such a dangerous, audacious gambit. The man had clearly broken out an emergency set of cojones.

"Not at all, Mr. Laurier. It was my mistake to approach you empty-handed. I've recently been reminded of the need to be creative and unorthodox. This has given me a better understanding of the situation."

"What do you want to know?"

Garcia switched the walkie-talkie to another frequency and whispered loudly into it.

"Agent Rose."

"Sir?"

"After dark, get a few trustworthy friends together and bring them to me. We need to widen the operation."

"So, what do you want to know?" repeated Laurier.

"Just want to hear your story," said Otis.

"You want to hear a story? I'll tell you a story."

Laurier sat down and motioned Otis to a chair. He looked up and pursed his lips as though he were reading an old file in the cloudless sky.

"When Incidental Chemicals got started back in the late thirties, no one gave a shit about the environment. They gave a shit about blowing up Nazis. We made shit that blew the shit out of a whole lot of Nazis, and everyone who wasn't a Nazi was happy, and the shit that was left over after we made the other shit, we just poured down the sewer.

"When the bottom fell out of the blowing-up-Nazis market in '45, we diversified into other types of shit. Some of it sold well, some of it didn't, but in all cases we kept dumping our leftover shit straight down the sewer. We did that all through the fifties, and no one gave a damn at all.

"Then in the sixties, people got all Save-the-Earth, and they made us stop pouring shit into the sewers. But they still wanted the other shit we were making. So we started putting the leftover shit in barrels and dropping them down the nearest hole. Out first hole was right behind our first factory. Pretty soon, every factory we had had a hole behind it, slowly filling up with barrels of shit. When the holes were full, we'd cover them over with dirt and dig another one a little farther away. Pretty soon, we had holes full of shit all over the damn place.

"In the seventies, the government told us we couldn't dig any more holes on US soil. But everyone still wanted to buy our increasingly wide range of fantastically useful shit. We just had to find some other way to get rid of our leftover shit barrels. We tried a little of this, a little of that, but we were producing too much shit for a piecemeal approach. We needed an organization to take these shit barrels off our hands. After a lengthy tendering process, we gave the contract to the mob. Oh, don't look so shocked. They trucked our barrels to the nearest ocean, put them on boats, sailed out a couple of hundred miles, and then accidentally dropped them overboard in the middle of the night. That worked well through most of the eighties. Then the mob sort of fell apart, and we couldn't rely on them to handle our volume. Since then we've divided the work between a number of Eastern European contractors. Through most of the nineties, we were using Russians to dump our shit off the coast of Somalia, but we had to stop doing that because the Russians kept getting boarded by pirates. These pirates, I swear to God, took our shit hostage and tried to ransom it back to us. It was nuts.

"So now we're here. That's the story. People back home still want the good shit, but every year these barrels of leftover shit have to travel a little further before they can disappear. This island is about as far as they can go. After this, we'll have to start shooting them into space or something."

"Couldn't you find a way to make your good shit without making the leftover shit?" said Otis.

"Get serious, kid," said Laurier, and walked away.

"And that's your idea of a business negotiation?"

"Yes, Mr. Homme," said Otis. "It seems straightforward enough to me."

Homme had found himself a perch on a small balcony off the hallway of the guest quarters. It offered a prime view of the volcano. Homme was gazing up at it with the same meditative expression he had worn at the crater's edge the previous day.

"Straightforward," he said. "Okay. Let's talk about something straightforward. Have you ever been to Easter Island?"

"No," said Otis.

"Neither have I. We passed it on the way here. Well, sort of. We came within five hundred miles of it, which is a pretty near-miss by Easter Island standards. I was sorry we didn't stop there. I've always wanted to see it."

"Yeah," said Otis. "The big stone heads."

"The moai," sighed Homme. "The only thing most people know about the place. They're strictly for the tourists these days. Not what I'm interested in."

"So, what are you interested in?"

"The things that aren't there anymore."

"Like what?"

"The trees, and because of the trees, the civilization."

"What's so special about the trees on Easter Island?"

"There aren't any. I just told you. Not one on the whole island. Just some scrub brush. Place used to be covered in them. Palms so big you couldn't put your arms around them. The islanders cut them all down. Every single one. Centuries ago."

"Why?"

"They were so damn useful," said Homme. "They built homes and boats and tools. They were essential in the raising of those stupid stone heads. They made civilization possible."

"Mmm."

"Easter Island once had a stable, flourishing society. Maybe 30,000 people living under the rule of a divinely chosen king. This worked great for generation after generation, dating back to around the year 1000. Then they started running out of trees."

"So?"

"Turns out Easter Island has a very fragile ecosystem. Self-contained, you know. They passed a tipping point without even noticing and kept on going without looking back. The effects began to domino. Fewer trees meant the wind and rain washed the soil into the ocean. Crops began to fail. The people said the king had lost the favour of the gods. Society broke down into endless clan-based civil war and a ruthless struggle for fewer and fewer resources. All of this on an island only about three times the size of this one. Anyway, trees were being cut down faster than ever, just to keep the other guys from getting them. Inevitably, they got to the very last tree on the whole island. Then they cut that down too."

"Why?"

"What else could they do? Imagine you were the one, the islander standing beside the very last tree in the whole world, as far as you know, holding your stone axe and watching ten other guys with axes closing in from all sides. Now, are you going to have a sudden environmental epiphany and try to save that tree, or are you going to grab it first so your clan will have one more boat than the next clan over?"

"I don't know."

"Well, that guy did know. He took the last tree. Not that it really mattered at that point. They were doomed long before they got to that last tree. But the symbolism of it appeals to me. That last tree represents the end of building, the end of fishing, the end of farming. They ate their last chickens. Then they ate all the rats. Then they started eating each other. The island was ruled by warlords who ran the place like a death cult. The population had already dropped to a fraction of its peak by the time the first outsiders turned up in the 1700s. Maybe a couple of thousand, tops. The Dutch got there first. They wrote that the place was a hellhole with the last few miserable survivors huddled amidst the pieces of their toppled statues. Peruvian slavers and smallpox didn't do much to help. By the time the Chileans took over in the late 1800s, there were only 111 islanders left. They turned the place into a sheep farm. And that's pretty much the way things are today, hundreds more years later. No real recovery. Just a handful of miserable survivors huddled among pointless stone heads that hold no meaning for them anymore."

"Remind me why you want to go there?" said Otis.

"To remind myself that it's possible," said Homme.

"What's possible?"

"For a civilization to wipe itself out. The fate of the Easter Islanders is the fate that waits for all of us. A man in my position needs to remember that, especially at a time and place like this. Here on this island, I'm a man with a stone axe standing next to a tree. It may not be the last tree, but there are certainly fewer of them than there were before. We are coming to the tipping point. We may even have passed it already. All I know is that this island is full of men with axes."

"So, will you swing your axe?"

"As hard as I can, and without hesitation."

"And if this is the tipping point?"

"Then it will only be a matter of time before this planet gets a well-deserved break from the effects of our existence."

"That doesn't bother you?"

"Not at all," said Homme. "Nothing lasts forever. We've all got to go sometime. This is as good a time as any. That's what most casual environmentalists don't seem to understand. The Earth takes care of itself. If humanity grows too burdensome, the planet will arrange for us to go. But the planet will be just fine without us. The planet takes the long view. I sometimes wonder why environmentalists don't find more comfort in that fact."

Otis paused to consider his next question.

"You aren't crazy or anything, are you?"

"I assure you, I'm the sanest man here."

Garcia's exaltation had lasted a good hour. Then he had spent another hour planning operational details. Now he was getting bored. He stood in front of the mirror, practicing his thin, cold smile and testing various poses with the riding crop. The radio was hanging by its strap from a coat hook.

"What's he doing now, Rose?" he said.

"Still walking up and down the road," said his agent. Rose sounded bored too.

"Where are you now?"

"I'm in the medical building. Krantz is in the community centre. Between us, we can see the full length of the road."

"Very well. Maintain—"

"Wait," interrupted Rose. "The subject has stopped. He is approaching a house. He's gone inside."

"Which house is it?"

"Sir, it's the one she lives in."

Garcia dropped his crop.

"Stay where you are until further orders."

"Yes, sir."

Garcia rushed out of his office and pounded up the stairs to the ground floor. It took him a harried three minutes to track down Sarah Vache in the small palace library.

"Your pet reporter is down in the city interviewing someone," he barked. "I suggest you go put a leash on him."

Her face darkened a little.

"It's not so serious," she said. "They all know what to say."

Garcia lowered his voice to an intense hiss that he was really quite proud of.

"He's talking to her."

Her face darkened more. She nodded and walked out, moving fast.

Otis had been wandering around the quote-unquote city for hours when he heard the singing. Up and down the palace road twice, from the gates to the harbour and back, he hadn't been able to get closer than ten paces from any of the islanders without them turning away and swiftly melting from view. He was discouraged. He was unwelcome. But he had just about formed a daring resolution that would make tomorrow different. Be creative? Be unorthodox? Fine.

Then he heard the singing. It was coming from inside a small house. The door stood open, and the voice floated out from the darkness within. It was a thick, muttering sort of singing in the most foreign language he had ever heard. It sounded solemn and sad and old. It was a woman's voice.

He walked softly up to the open door and tried to sneak a look inside without looking like he was staring into a stranger's house. He could see nothing. The singing went on. Otis wondered whether to knock or cough or just walk away. The singer clearly had something on her mind besides houseguests. He took a step back from the door. The singing stopped.

"Come in," said a soft voice. Otis took a step forward, then hesitated again.

"I don't mean to intrude," he said.

"Come in," repeated the voice. "Have some tea."

Ah, thought Otis. An old lady. He could hardly refuse, and he was getting tired. Maybe she would answer his questions. She might even be a tribal elder. He stepped through the door. He wondered if he should bow.

"Sit down," said the voice. There was no light in the single room except for the sunlight that fell in a thin streak across the bare wooden floor. As his eyes adjusted, he made out a small wooden stool and the outline of his hostess. It was the old woman who had watched him into town. He sat.

She lifted a kettle off of a small oil stove and poured some brownish liquid into a cup. As she leaned forward to hand it to him, Otis saw that she wasn't so old. Maybe making her way toward sixty. She had a shawl draped over her shoulders, and her long hair flowed loosely over it in skeins of black and grey. Otis caught a flash of a sad and striking face in the sunlight, then she withdrew again into the shadow.

"Thank you," said Otis. He took a sip. It tasted like something that had been fished out of Lake Pitouie in a barrel. He took another sip anyway.

"What were you singing?" he said.

"A song from my childhood. It reminds me of being young and happy."

"Aren't you happy now?"

She sat very still and watched him.

"You've come from a long way away," she said.

"Yes."

"Why?"

"To write a story about the island and the people who live here."

"The people are the important part. The island is just a place for the people to be. Remember that in your story."

Otis nodded. He eased the recorder out of his pocket and fumbled with the buttons. This was genuine ancient tribal wisdom. Real A-list material.

"What do you think of the president's plan to let outsiders dump their waste on your island?" he said.

"The president has assured us that this is a safe and effective way to bring new prosperity and growth to Pitouie. I will be happy to live on the new and prosperous Federated Pitouie."

So much for ancient tribal wisdom.

"He blames himself," said the woman. "But he shouldn't."

"Who?" said Otis.

"You are staying at the palace?"

"Yes."

"Tell him, if you can. He didn't know. His heart was always weak. It was the strain of the journey. The strangeness of the place. His heart gave out. It wasn't his fault. I can't tell him. He doesn't talk to me. No one will talk to me about him. They think it is a kindness, but they don't know. Only I know."

Otis stared into the shadows again. He wasn't sure if the woman had lapsed back into ancient tribal wisdom or early-onset dementia. He leaned forward and tried to think of something reassuring to say. The light in the doorway flickered.

"There you are," said Sarah, just slightly too brightly. "I've been looking for you everywhere."

Otis stood up, just slightly too quickly.

"Oh, hello," he said. For some reason, he felt like he had been caught at something illicit.

"It's starting to get dark. I'm going down to the beach. Do you want to come?"

"Sure," he said. He turned back to the woman.

"Thank you for the tea," he said, setting the cup awkwardly on the stool. "It was nice to meet you."

The woman began to sing again, very softly. Sarah led him out. They began a slow stroll through the twilight in the direction of the shore.

"How did you end up in there?" she said.

"I heard her singing. She sounded so sad. Then she asked me in for tea. I couldn't really say no. Who is she?"

"Oh, nobody in particular. She's really very sweet, but if we had cats on the island, she'd be the old lady with thirty cats."

"Mmm. Besides, I wanted to get out of sight for a while. I think I'm being followed."

"What?"

"These two guys have been following me around all day."

"They're probably just curious about you. None of our other visitors have bothered to leave the palace."

"Probably."

Garcia assembled them in the basement. It was a storage room, scattered with boxes and mops and dust. It lacked dramatic atmosphere, but at least it was underground.

His six recruits stood before him. The recruits were, as far as he could tell, just a random sampling of islanders. Rose and Krantz had gathered up whoever they could find who didn't mind staying up past sunset. It didn't matter. He would impart unto them the necessary skills. He signalled Rose with the tip of his riding crop. Rose locked the door.

"Ladies and gentlemen," Garcia said. "Thank you for coming. I have an important assignment for you. This order comes directly from the president. I have the utmost faith that you will not fail to rise to the task."

He swept the group with a piercing eye. They shuffled a bit and glanced sideways at each other. The piercing eye might need more practice.

"As some of you may know, there is a reporter on the island. There is a chance that he intends to disturb the negotiations. We cannot allow that to happen. You are going to prevent it from happening."

A tentative hand went up from amidst the mops.

"How?"

"You are going to gather intelligence on our guests. You will watch them night and day. You will follow them. You will note who they talk to and what they say. All this you will report to me. You are now agents of the Pitouie Intelligence Service, and I am your chief. You will refer to me as Claudius."

More shuffling. More glances. Rose growled down the line, which fell still. Garcia was impressed. Rose clearly had sergeant potential.

"You are uncertain," said Garcia. "This is natural. You have never undertaken work of this nature before. Do not worry. I will not send you into the field unprepared. Your training begins now."

Garcia walked up and down the line of recruits, snapping the crop against the side of one polished boot. It was time to teach them the wisdom of The Book.

"The first and most essential skill of an agent is concentration. You must maintain a strong and undeviating attention to the work. When an agent's attention is distracted, he ceases to function as an agent. Every day you are distracted by stimuli competing for attention. An agent must learn to direct his attention. You must force concentration on an object until genuine interest begins to appear. Do not try to ignore distractions. Focus on the object until the distracting elements disappear."

Garcia stabbed at a recruit with the riding crop.

"You."

"Me, sir?"

"Yes. Tomorrow you will take a book from the library. You will take it to a place where many people are holding conversations all around you. You will read the book. Concentrate. Focus until the distracting conversations disappear. Then come tell me what the book was about. I will want details."

"Yes, sir."

Garcia went back to his pacing, his half-closed eyes on the ceiling. He was enjoying this. He was passing on the traditions of his trade, just as they had been passed on to him.

"The agent must train himself to analyze his own motives and to detect the motives of other people," he said. "You must continually work on the skill of determining other people's characters, professions, and habits from their appearances. This is observation."

The crop struck out at the next recruit.

"You."

"Sir?"

"Tomorrow you will follow one of the guests. Pick any one. It doesn't matter. Observe him. Observe his dress, his manner, his interactions with others. Determine his character by analyzing these observations. Then bring your report to me."

"Yes, sir."

They were watching him now. They were interested. Such was the power of The Book.

"An agent must have faith in the cover story he is using. If you do not, no one else will. You must invent reasons in your head to make your cover story seem realistic to you. You must know the background, every detail of your false life. This is the only way to convince another. This is scenic faith."

Another stab.

"You."

"Yes, sir?"

"In the morning, you will invent a cover story to explain why you were so late getting home tonight. You will be able to explain exactly where you were and what you were doing during every moment of your absence. You will know every detail. Then you will come and try to convince me that you believe it."

"Yes, sir."

Garcia walked on.

"You must have at your command many moods and feelings to match the cover you are using. To be convincing, try to remember a specific experience from your own life that made you feel a certain way, and base your performance on a recreation of that feeling. This is emotional control."

The crop shot out and tapped the last two recruits.

"You and you."

"Yes, sir?"

"Tomorrow you will recall experiences from your past. You, a happy memory, and you, a sad memory. Relive them in every detail. Remember how you felt. Feel that way again. Then come to me and show me how you feel. You must convince me that you are truly happy, and truly sad."

"Yes, sir."

Garcia was winding up. He walked slowly back to the middle of the room and ran his eyes over them again, more paternally this time. He softened his voice and leaned in to impart the greatest secret.

"Every operation is the product of imagination. You must use imagination to associate disparate objects, to unite, separate, modify, and recombine them. This is how raw data is converted into intelligence. The bolder your imagination, the more power you have as an agent. This is not something that can be taught. This is something you must create for yourself out of your own life. You will learn this in time, as I have."

He looked each one in the eye and saw that they believed it. His work here was done, for now. He turned his back on them and retuned the steel in his voice.

"Dismissed."

It was cool on the beach after the sun went down, but the humidity remained, transmuted into grim clamminess. Sarah took a box of matches from her pocket and shook it festively.

"Grab some driftwood," she said. "We'll make a fire."

Otis wandered around her in a circle and came back with a small armful of polished and twisted branches.

"How does driftwood like this end up here?" he said. "This isn't palm wood, is it?"

"We fly it in from Vancouver Island and scatter it around to impress the guests," she said. "It's the little touches. All part of the service."

"Are you serious?"

"What do you think?"

The wood caught easily, and soon they were sitting on the sand with a small fire and the swell of the ocean before them. They were alone, at least within the circle of firelight. Sounds came from the darkness now and then, but Otis couldn't tell if they were people, birds or bears.

She shifted on the sand and rubbed her arms. Otis considered trying to slip an arm around her shoulder, just for warmth, but she was just far enough away to make it awkward. He sat still.

"So, um," she said. "Got a girlfriend back home or anything?"

Well, that was unexpected. Hopeful, but unexpected.

"No," he said, neutrally.

"Really?"

"I did, but I don't anymore."

"What happened?"

"She said she wanted to try and do something."

"Mmm. How long were you together?"

"Almost two years."

"And how long since it ended?"

"Couple of months now."

"Do you miss her?"

He checked.

"Not really. She feels like a character in a novel I once read. Ever been in love with a fictional person?"

"No."

"I have. You live to turn pages. The rest of life is unreal in comparison. Then you get to the end, and you feel sad because you won't have that person in your life anymore. Doesn't matter that it was only words."

"You could always read it again."

"It's not the same. It's like running into your high school crush ten years later when she's married with two kids. Nostalgia is all you can hope for."

"Too bad."

She inched a little closer to him on the sand until their hips were touching, their backs flat against the side of the rock. Entirely without fuss, she took his hand. Otis turned his head. She was watching him and smiling just a bit.

Well, what the hell. He leaned over and kissed her. She kissed him back, but didn't exactly melt into a puddle. He pulled away.

"Sorry," he said. "Inappropriate."

"No," she said softly. "It's fine."

She leaned her head on his shoulder. Otis wondered if he should tell her about his daring plans for tomorrow. Would she be impressed? Would she try to stop him? Would she maybe help him? He allowed himself a moment of fantasy: Two against the world. At least, two against an island. Really, just two against six businessmen and a president. Still; two. That was the main thing. Inside the little circle of firelight, it might as well be just the two of them, alone on a tropical island. Otis felt her hair against his cheek and decided that was fine with him.

The fantasy receded a little. He thought over his daring plan again. He could tell her everything, right now. He didn't. They sat and looked into the darkness.

Chapter 10

*T*he next morning, Lars set off to salt the mine. He was wearing two full sets of thermal underwear under two pairs of wool pants and two wool sweaters. All this was under a heavy pair of ski pants and his parka. He was wearing so many socks his boots barely fit on his feet. He was wearing gloves inside his mitts. He was wearing a toque underneath his hood. He had a long wool scarf wrapped around his face. He wore goggles over his eyes. He was still freezing.

He was wearing one other item of clothing over top of everything: another thick plastic anti-radiation suit liberated from the emergency stores. The suit included plastic booties for his feet, plastic mittens for his hands and a plastic hood for his head. The joints were sealed air tight with tape. He wore a respirator under his scarf. He felt like an alien invader.

He was riding the station's backup snowmobile, a thing like a squat motorcycle, open to the air and exposed in every way. It was not a form of transportation he enjoyed at the best of times, and he enjoyed it even less with Woolsey's glow-in-the-dark toolbox strapped to the seat behind him.

"Ride east for a while, then head south," the chief had said. "Here's a map. Here's a compass. Once you get about twenty miles away from the base, start spreading the powder. Zig-zag back and forth. Just stop every hundred yards or so, and toss a handful up into the air. I'd stand with my back to the wind, if I were you.

"Remind me," Lars had said. "Why aren't you me?"

"Rank has its privileges, kid. I'm old, and you wanted in."

"Why can't I take the bus? With the roof and the heater?"

"I'll need it tomorrow to shuttle our guests out to the site."

"I'll be back by tonight."

"Good. See you then."

Two hours later he was closing in on his target. The map was in a clear plastic pouch taped to his thigh. It wasn't a very useful guide. There were no landmarks once he turned away from the coast. He navigated by his compass, his watch, and the speedometer. Due east at 15 mph for 60 minutes, then due south at 15 mph for another hour.

He stopped. He held the illuminated dial of the watch, taped around the outside of his Michelin Man wrist, to his face. Close enough, damn it.

He took a look around, but there was nothing to see. Just blackness in all directions except for the wedge of flat, white snow glowing in the snowmobile headlight. This posed a problem. If he rode the machine criss-cross over a couple of acres of terrain, he would never find the exact path back to the station. If he were off by a few hundred yards, he could sail right past it in the dark.

He turned the snowmobile in a tight circle and lined it up exactly with the tread tracks that had brought him here. He shut off the engine to save fuel, but left the headlight on as a beacon to guide him back. He would do the spreading on foot.

Satisfied with his precautions, he got the rest of his gear unpacked. Across his back, he slung a World War One issue Lee Enfield rifle, in case of polar bears. On his feet, he strapped a small pair of snowshoes, in case of drifts. With his left hand, he picked up the flashlight and with his right hand, he hoisted the toolbox. He was ready.

He picked a direction at random and marched one hundred paces into the darkness. He checked that the snowmobile headlight was still visible. He opened the toolbox. Inside were the small lead box and a long wooden spoon purloined from the mess. Gingerly, as though he were performing surgery on a kitten, he lifted the lid of the box. He dipped the spoon inside and felt it dig into the coarse, sugary substance.

He checked that his back was to the wind. He checked that the respirator was snug against his face. He held his breath for good measure. He eased the spoon out. Holding the bowl back with the barest tip of one mitten, he cocked his wrist. He thought of the money. He let fly. The coarse black powder disappeared into the air.

He waited. He exhaled. He inhaled. That was that. Not so bad. He packed up his box and spoon and stood up. He picked another direction at random and began to march. After he had flicked two more spoonfuls of powder mashed-potato-like into the wind, he began to hum.

After thirty-five spoonfuls, the box was getting lighter. He checked his headlight beacon. It glinted in the distance, barely visible. Lars checked his watch. Two hours he had been out here playing in the snow. The sweat trapped under his plastic suit squished as he moved. Fuck it. Good enough for government work.

He shuffled his way back to the snowmobile. It was further than it looked and he was tired by the time he got there. He didn't relish the windy ride back to the base. He realized as he was strapping down his gear that Woolsey had never mentioned how much money he expected to bring in with this game, nor what kind of a cut Lars could expect. They would have to discuss that when he got back.

Lars threw a stiff leg over the cold plastic seat of the machine. He turned the key and pressed the start button. The starter motor whined and chugged. The headlight dimmed, flickered and went out. The starter motor stopped chugging. Lars sat there on a dead machine in the dark and listened to the wind blow.

Okay. Don't panic. You've run down the battery, but it can't be completely dead already. Just give it a few minutes and try again. He sat and shivered. Now that he had stopped moving, his sweaty clothes were already feeling chilled and clammy against his skin. He thumbed the start button again. The engine grunted once. He pushed the button again. Nothing.

Okay. Don't panic. You can use the battery from the flashlight to jump start the engine. Easy. He unstrapped the lamp with its bulky Buick battery from the rear seat and flicked the switch. The bulb burst into light with reassuring intensity. There was no problem here.

He got off the snowmobile and lifted the hood, revealing 350ccs of inert metal. The dead battery was bolted into a plastic box in a corner of the engine compartment. It looked smaller than the one in his hand. He scoffed. What kind of engineer would design a snowmobile with such a puny power supply? Didn't he realize that lives would depend on this thing? Lars looked at the lamp. This battery wouldn't fit in the little plastic box. He would need jumper cables. He inspected the cubby holes and storage compartments built into the snowmobile. It didn't take long. He had no jumper cables.

Well, maybe he could undo the battery wires and pull out enough slack to hook them to the flashlight. If he had to creep home with the hood up and the flashlight balanced on top of the engine block, he would. He went back to the engine and played the beam over the wires. They were attached to the dead battery with nuts and bolts. He reached in with one hand to test the tightness, but couldn't get a grip through his second, third and fourth skins. With some fumbling he managed to untape one wrist and peel off his extra insulation. He reached with his bare fingers and tried the nuts again. They were tight. They were also corroded. He twisted harder, but the cold metal only dug into his flesh. He gritted his teeth and squeezed until his fingers bled, but the bolt would not budge. He needed a wrench.

He searched the cubby holes and storage compartments again. He had no wrench.

Lars took stock of his situation. His base was twenty miles away. It was somewhere in that direction. He could try walking back. It would be a pleasant eight-hour stroll in minus 40 degree weather with no food, water or shelter, and no light once this useless flashlight died. Still, given the alternative, he supposed the exercise would be good for his health.

He moved to strap the snowshoes back onto his sore feet but couldn't. His legs were shaking too hard. His hands were also shaking, which didn't make the job any easier. He surveyed the rest of his body. It was shaking. Would that be fear or hypothermia?

He sat down again and tried to remember his emergency training. Hypothermia. Defined as a drop in core body temperature to below 95 degrees. In mild cases, symptoms include shivering and hyperglycemia, whatever that was. In moderate cases, symptoms include violent shivering, stumbling, and mild confusion, not to mention pale skin and blue extremities. In severe cases, symptoms include difficulty speaking, pronounced mental confusion, amnesia, and loss of motor function. Most fun of all were paradoxical undressing, during which a freezing victim helps the process along by stripping down just for the hell of it, and terminal burrowing, during which a victim digs a nice hole in which to lie down and die.

He considered this last option. Supposedly, freezing to death wasn't that bad. After a while, the pain of the cold went away, and you just drifted off. Easy. Still not very appealing. This had all seemed so much less unpleasant in that Illinois corn field.

Treatment options. Well, there was only one really: Warm the bastard up again. Dry clothes. Blankets. Hot water bottles. Apply with aggression depending on the severity of the case, to be determined by the administration of a rectal thermometer.

Lars considered the contents of the storage cubbies. He had no dry clothes. He had no blankets. He had no water bottles and no way to heat the water anyway. He didn't even have a rectal thermometer.

He did have a rifle. There was at least one action he could take.

Carefully, methodically, he checked the ancient weapon. The Enfield rifle was still used in the far north because it was utterly reliable down to temperatures of minus 60. Reliability was such a comfort. Slowly, deliberately, he chambered a round. He took five unsteady paces into the darkness, then he turned, raised the gun and put a bullet through the treacherous machine. The report was swallowed up instantly by the snow.

The snow. There was something he would need for the snow. Back at the snowmobile. He trudged back the five paces. There they were. Snowshoes. Very good for snow. He reached down for them. He stood up.

The dizziness came upon him like a bottle to the back of the head. He saw stars. He wobbled for a moment, then slowly, gently, softly fell over. When his temple hit the gas tank, it felt like the caress of an old, old lover. See, he thought, this is why I don't like going outside.

He woke up. That was unexpected. There was a dim light. He was inside something. Getting more specific than that was beyond him for the moment. It didn't seem like a very pressing issue anyway.

There was movement. A face eased into view. A dark oval with high, severe cheekbones. Eyes dark and soft under a fringe of straight black hair. No other details to report at this time.

He decided to experiment with his mouth.

"Hello," he said.

The face smiled. Experiment successful.

"Hello," said a woman's voice. The lips on the face seemed to move at about the same time. He concluded that his ears still worked and that the face could speak. Additional: the face was evidently female. The face was becoming a more agreeable companion by the minute. Time to broaden the scope of his investigation.

"Where am I?"

"Iglertok," she said.

"How did I get here?"

"Big Joe found you. He was hunting."

"When?"

"Two days ago."

He nodded wisely. Neck still worked.

"Who are you?" he said.

"Agatha."

"Why does my foot hurt, Agatha?"

"Frostbite. You lost your little toe."

"How did that happen?"

"Big Joe cut it off with bolt cutters. It was all black. You nearly died. But you'll be okay now."

It was a long speech. A lot of data to process. He nodded again. He passed out.

He woke up. The face was still there, but farther away. It was attached to a slender female body in a long, heavy shirt. The body was sitting in a chair next to his cot.

"Hello," said Agatha.

"Hello."

She handed him a plastic mug with some thin soup in it.

"Eat," she said.

He tried to push himself up into a sitting position with his elbows. As soon as his head left the horizontal, it split open and let some of his brains leak out.

"Ow," he said.

Agatha slid an arm around his back and eased him upright. She had a firm, careful grip.

"You hurt your head," she said. "That's why you sleep so much. Eat. You'll feel better."

He put his free hand to his temple. His head was wrapped in bandages and very sore. He drank some soup. It was barely warm and didn't taste like anything in particular. It was wonderful. It took him a few minutes to get it all down. Agatha handed him some bannock bread and another mug with tea in it. She also handed him a couple of small white pills.

"Aspirin," she said.

"Agatha, I love you."

She smiled.

"I've seen you before," he said.

"Yes. You came to the village to say men would steal our rocks."

Feeling an unaccustomed interest in life, he took a good look around for the first time. He was in a small room with clapboard walls, a plywood floor, and a sheet metal ceiling. A stove made from an old oil drum burned in the corner. There was a table with an oil lamp on it. There was a chair. There was a battered trunk. There was a rancid smell. That was all there was.

"What's that smell?" he said.

"Seal oil," she said.

"Do you live here, Agatha?"

She nodded.

"Alone?"

She nodded again, eyes down.

"Big Joe said for me to look after you."

"Thank you," he said. She smiled. A thought struck him.

"Am I in your bed? I'm sorry. Where have you been sleeping all this time?"

"With you," she said. "To keep you warm at night."

Now Lars took a good look at Agatha for the first time. It was a thing worth doing. She was beautiful and young and alive. Lars was suddenly aware of his nakedness under the blankets.

"I'm sorry to cause you so much trouble," he said.

"It's okay," she said. Then, as naturally as breathing, she slipped off her coarse shirt and slid under the blankets with him. She rested her head on his chest. After a moment, he put his arms around her. She sighed. They slept.

When he woke for the third time, the first thing he was aware of was the girl's naked body warm against his. The second thing was the chain of events that had got his bare ass out there.

He heaved himself upright. He head split open again. He ignored it. Agatha was awake and watching him with concern in her soft, dark eyes.

"I need to talk to Big Joe," he said. "It's important."

"He's sick," said Agatha. "He got sick the day after he brought you in."

His heart thumped. Don't panic. It could be just a cold. Deer fever maybe.

"Do you have my clothes?" he said. "Do you have the plastic suit I was wearing?"

She pointed into a dim corner of the room where his six layers of clothing were folded and piled next to her own. He swung his legs out of the cot and tottered over to them. The radiation suit was there. He flailed his way into one pair of long johns, one pair of pants and one sweater. Then, with distaste, he pulled the plastic suit on over top.

— 142 —

"What's it for?" said Agatha.

"Protection," said Lars. He pulled his boots on over the little plastic slippers and reached for his parka.

"Which way is Big Joe's" he asked.

She stepped out of the cot and began to dress. She moved easily and without wasted effort.

"I'll show you."

A few minutes later she cracked open her plain wooden door and Lars stepped out into the village of Iglertok for the second time. It still wasn't an inspiring sight, this cluster of half-buried shacks shuddering in the light of Agatha's dim and flickering lantern. None had windows that might leak a little friendly illumination. They were made of trash, but they were sealed up tight.

Agatha seized his hand and led him past three or four of these huddled boxes to another shack as insubstantial as the rest.

"This is Big Joe's," she said.

"Wait here," he said. "Please."

He pushed open the door and stepped inside. It was like Agatha's, but messier.

There was a hacking cough. Lars turned to the figure on the cot, huddled under a blanket. The light was dim and Lars could barely make him out. He lifted the lamp from the table and turned the wick up until a slightly less feeble light fell on the form of his saviour.

Big Joe was a man of about fifty. He was thickset and had a face like a walrus. His eyes were turned to the wall. Lars recognized him as the man he had met on his last visit. His heart thumped again.

"Big Joe?" Lars said. The man grunted and coughed again.

"My name is Lars. You brought me in out of the snow. You saved my life. Thank you."

There was another grunt.

"Agatha told me you were sick."

The man on the cot looked offended at the implication.

"Are you throwing up?" said Lars. The man nodded.

"Headache? The runs?" More nods.

Lars reached out and ran a hand gently through the man's hair. A few strands came away between his fingers.

"There was a toolbox on my snowmobile. Did you open it?" The man nodded.

"Needed a wrench."

"I know. Rest. I'll be back."

He went outside. Agatha was waiting for him.

"Is there a radio in the village?" he said. "We need to get him to a hospital right away."

Her look went from solemn to frightened. A stab of pain went through him that had nothing to do with his head or his foot.

"This way," she said, setting off. He limped along behind her, determined to fix this.

The radio was in another ramshackle shack at the edge of the settlement. It was a Heathkit ham set possibly designed by Marconi himself, but it worked. Lars dialled up the station frequency, clamped the headphones over his plastic hood and keyed the mic.

"Station PIN-AA, come in."

No response. He fiddled with the knobs and tried again.

"Station PIN-AA, come in."

"This is PIN-AA," said a voice. "Who the hell is this?"

"Franks? Is that you?"

"Lars? Where the fuck are you? Thought you were dead."

"Never mind. Put the chief on."

"Can't. He's not here."

"Well, go get him."

"No, I mean he's gone. He left yesterday with McMannus while I was on shift. Just after his visitors left. Didn't leave any orders. Didn't say a fucking word."

Bastard. Franks went on.

"I'm all on my own here. I haven't left the scope room in thirty hours. Haven't slept or eaten for thirty hours. I radioed PIN-MAIN to report the both of you missing. Military police are on the way."

"Good," said Lars. "Call them again. Tell them Pinnacle Broken Arrow at Iglertok."

"Pinnacle Broken Arrow? Are you high? That's a—"

"I know what it is. Tell them at least one man needs emergency evac. Maybe more. Tell them it's bad. Tell them to bring everything they've got."

"Where are you, man?"

"Iglertok, asshole. Where do you think?"

"Roger that. PIN-AA out."

Chapter 11

*T*he door to Garcia's office in the basement of the palace banged open, and Sarah Vache rushed in.

"He's gone," she said.

"Who's gone?"

"Otis Wilson. He's wandered off into the jungle by himself. He's gone to find the guerrillas in the mountains. He wants to interview them."

Garcia rolled his eyes behind his mirrorshades.

"So what's the problem?" he said. "We both know how that will go."

"But what if he gets lost?" she said. "What if he gets hurt?" There was a pleading note in her voice he had never heard before. Were he lost in the woods, Garcia doubted the cool and efficient woman would be so worried for him.

"Why did you let him go in the first place?"

"He sneaked away early this morning. He didn't tell me he was going. He left me a note."

Garcia held out a hand.

"Let me read it."

"Um, no," she said, flushing. "It's personal."

Garcia withdrew his hand and looked at her in amusement. She stared back at him with a look that was halfway between defiance and indifference.

"What do you expect me to do?" he said.

"Find him," she said urgently. "You are the security chief."

"I am the head of the island's security force, true," he said. "I am also the entirety of the island's security force." He made a retroactive command decision that intelligence agents were not the same as security officers. "In case you hadn't noticed, we have more than one guest on the island at present. I'm needed here. I don't have the manpower to search the whole island, beating the bushes with sticks."

"Then get some help," she said, incredulous. "Find him."

"This is a very delicate time," said Garcia. "Without a directive from the president, I cannot leave our other guests."

Her look modulated to a spot on the dial between defiance and contempt.

"Fine," she said. She walked out. Garcia watched her go, then reached again for The Book.

The president sat at his desk and regarded Garcia blandly over folded hands. The security chief stood before the desk, not quite at attention but far from at ease.

"I gather our friend the reporter has wandered off the beaten path," said the president.

"So I have been informed, sir," said Garcia. This? He had been called here for this?

"As head of security, his safety is your responsibility," said the president. "I instructed you to watch him. How did this happen?"

Now Garcia pulled himself to full attention and directed his gaze to a spot on the wall above the president's head.

"There was no way to prevent it," he said. "We do not keep the guests on a leash. We do not even lock their doors at night."

"No. We rely on giving them the strong impression that their lives may come to a quick and bloody end if they venture into the interior alone. That has always been sufficient in the past."

"Yes, sir."

"But not in this case, apparently. Why not, would you say?"

"Sir, he is a reporter. Perhaps he felt it was his job to see for himself."

"A reporter?" said the president. "He's a hack from a tiny industry magazine, not a war correspondent. Perhaps you did not make your impression forcefully enough. Why did I appoint you chief of security?"

Garcia's eyes snapped down from empty space and locked on those of his commander.

"You know exactly why you made me security chief," he said. "You also know exactly what my responsibilities are. Babysitting is not among them."

The president held his gaze for a moment, then nodded.

"Nevertheless," he said. "The man must be found. I'm giving the assignment to you."

"But the others," said Garcia. "The preparations. The plans."

"Our friend the reporter is also part of my plans. We need him back here."

"Sir, I don't have the manpower to mount an effective search of the whole island."

"Use the palace guards. Recruit whatever personnel you need. This is a top priority."

"Very well, sir," said Garcia. He saluted and left.

The trail was clear and easy going. It began at the beach and appeared to head straight up the mountain. It looked to Otis, who was no woodsman, reasonably well used. He had no idea where it was going other than up, but up was where the rebels were hiding, so up was good enough.

He pulled the voice recorder from his pocket, pressed record and held the microphone ceremoniously before his mouth.

"Field notes, Pitouie Island. I have slipped out of the government compound and into the jungle. It is said that a guerrilla force hides in the hills. I intend to find them."

He looked around for a few telling details.

"The jungle is very green and, uh, hot," he said to the recorder. He looked around again. "Remember to bulk this section up later."

For the first few hours, he strode between the trees quickly and with firmness of purpose. A few hours after the first few hours, he eased himself to the ground by the side of the track and pulled out the recorder again.

"I probably should have brought some water," he said. "Maybe some food too. A map would have been good. Also a compass and a pair of shoes that aren't black leather Oxfords. I wonder if the rebels know I'm here yet? They could be watching me right now, invisible and silent among the trees. At least they're not laughing out loud. Yet."

More than a few hours after that, as the sunlight began to slant across the shoulder of the crater and the shadows of the trees grew longer, he curled up with his back to a boulder and cursed the unreliability of the modern guerrilla. His cursing was muffled by the wad of leaves he was chewing. Their taste was not helping his attitude, but thanks to their moisture he could at least still speak. He spit the sour wad into a bush and spoke to the recorder.

"I mean, I've been stomping around in their jungle all day," he said, "and no one even comes to take a look? I could be anybody. Don't these guys patrol their territory? You can't just sit around camp all day smoking cigars and writing manifestos. There are practicalities to consider."

The sun snuck behind the mountain as he crouched there, and suddenly it was dark. He thumbed the recorder again.

"For instance, when you might need to spend the night in the woods, bring a flashlight. Or some matches. Also bring a tent and a sleeping bag—"

An unidentifiable something made an unidentifiable noise in the not-distant-enough distance. Otis held the recorder closer to his lips and spoke more quietly.

"—and a field guide to the local dangerous animals. Gotta admit, I really didn't plan this phase of the operation very well."

The night wasn't as unpleasant as it could have been. No dangerous animals happened by, and the temperature didn't get low enough to count as cold. The worst he could say as a molten metal sunrise spread across the ocean below him was that his boulder was hardly orthopedic, and that humid days often became clammy nights.

"Field notes, Pitouie Island, day two," he recorded. "More things I should have brought: change of clothes, toothbrush. Hope the rebels aren't offended by morning breath. Wonder if they offer an all-day breakfast?"

He stood, joints cracking, and turned his face again to the summit and the trail leading there. He walked on.

Some time in the late afternoon, slightly dizzy from hunger and sick of leaves, Otis paused to file another report.

"I begin to consider the possibility that I have made a serious miscalculation. Why is this island so empty? Okay, rebels need to hide, but I haven't seen even a hint of any kind of human out here."

He peered up and down the trail for the hundredth time and sighed. Might as well record all of it, for posterity if nothing else.

"If I don't meet someone soon, this could be really bad. My feet have gone from blistered to bleeding. I've spent the last three hours trying to remember the difference between sunstroke and heatstroke. All I can remember so far is that you're supposed to wear a hat. I'm not even sure I could make it back to the city if I turned around now. To walk into a jungle looking for dangerous rebels and die because you couldn't find them; that would be really embarrassing in an obituary."

He walked on. He plucked a huge palm frond from the general green of the ground and wrapped it around his head like a bonnet, holding it below his chin with one cramped hand. He couldn't tell if it was helping. After another hour, life got more encouraging. The trail turned away from the peak of the island and sloped back down to the coast. The walking was easier downhill and the ocean didn't seem far away. He blearily recalled from his copious research that the crater was off-centre: much closer to one coast than the other. Half-stumbling, half-sliding as the trail grew steeper, he fetched up on the shoreline just as the sun was about to touch the sea again.

He glared up the trail, now winding along side the scraggy tree line. There were some odd angular shapes in the distance. He blinked a few times, shook his head and squinted. Yes, it was. It was a village.

Garcia stood in the palace courtyard and pondered again. The middle-aged executives who came to the island had always been happy to stay on his carefully marked nature trail. A pair of mirrored sunglasses, a stiff back, and a smoothly delivered warning had always been more than sufficient to tame them.

"Oh," he would say, his tone finely balanced between pity and cruelty. "There is a small band of rebels in the jungle. They are starving, powerless, hiding like whipped dogs. They pose no threat to us here, but you, sir, would be wise to stay clear of the interior without an escort."

They would nod easily, as if dodging guerrilla soldiers was something they did twice a week after squash practice, but they would never stray out of eyesight.

Until now.

He weighed the pros and cons of this new situation. On the

negative side, he had a reporter wandering the island off the leash and lost in the bush. On the plus side, now he had the palace guard under his exclusive command.

Garcia reviewed his troops. Slowly he walked up and down the line of seven men, his hands clasped behind his back, his eyes scanning over every inch of each of them before moving on.

The guards stood convincingly to attention. Each was dressed in a uniform that was almost identical to those of the palace waiters, but with more brocade and brass buttons. Each wore a peaked cap on his head, highly polished boots on his feet and an empty holster on his belt. They were local boys taking their turn at a civic duty and getting away from the fishing boats for a while. Palace guard was not a demanding job. Once each recruit had mastered the skill of standing upright on either the left or the right side of a door, his training was deemed sufficient. They would not require the wisdom of The Book.

Garcia completed his inspection and walked back to the centre of the courtyard. He turned and addressed them, thus:

"Men, one of our guests is lost somewhere on the island. The president has assigned us the vital task of finding him. As you know, this island is approximately fifty square kilometres in size. Each of you will search a grid square approximately seven square kilometres in size. Maps and a photograph of the subject have already been distributed to you. A boat will take three of you to the north shore to begin your search there. The rest of you will fan out from the city. If you find the subject, detain him and escort him unharmed to the palace. If you do not find him within your search area within twenty-four hours, return to the palace and report. Good hunting. Dismissed."

The guards looked at each other. They examined each other's maps and tried to estimate how many footsteps it would take to criss-cross seven square kilometres thoroughly enough to find a single man. They looked at each other's shiny patent leather boots and imagined them scrambling over boulders and fallen trees. They looked at each other's fussy, close-fitting uniforms and wondered what it would be like to tramp through the bush in them for a day and a night. They looked at their tiny ceremonial rucksacks and lamented the few mouthfuls of food and water crammed into them. Then, under Garcia's glare, they heaved a collective sigh, squared their collective shoulders and more-or-less marched out the gate.

Garcia watched them go. They were good, honest lads who would give this pointless task a good, honest try. He would be able to look the president in the eye and say he had done all he could do. Besides, pointless tasks were a military tradition. This would build loyalty and camaraderie in his force.

He nodded curtly to Rose and Krantz, who were practicing their lurking in a corner of the courtyard. The agents approached with trepidation. Garcia maintained an intimidating silence for a while, then began the debriefing.

"You were under orders to keep the subject under constant surveillance," he said. "How did he manage to evade you?"

Rose and Krantz bobbled their heads at each other in the international gesture meaning "you tell him." Finally Rose cleared his throat.

"You told us to stay where we were until further orders," he said. "But then you didn't give us any more orders. So we stayed where we were until it got dark, then we went to get people for the meeting."

Garcia made a show of pinching the bridge of his nose.

"At the medical building," he said.

"I was at the community centre, sir," said Krantz.

Garcia fixed him with his best steely look. Krantz bowed his head.

"Very well," said Garcia. "I have a new assignment for you."

They stood a little straighter.

"Relocate the subject before the palace guards find him."

They slumped again.

"If he is not a total fool, he will not strike out randomly into the jungle," said Garcia. "I have recently come to believe that he is not a total fool. There is only one clear trail across the island other than the one that leads to the crater, which he has already seen. You will follow that trail. If he keeps to it, there's only one place he's likely to get to. If he makes it there, he's likely to stay a while to investigate. But I doubt he's ever spent a night outdoors in his life, and he may not make it that far, in which case he will be lying under a tree somewhere waiting to die. In either case, find him. Bring him back. Carry him if you have to."

His agents saluted and prepared to return to the field.

The light barely qualified as dim by the time Otis shuffled into the little cluster of huts. The village consisted of a dozen tiny structures, haphazardly assembled from corrugated sheet metal and remnants of plywood. Some of the roofs were patched with bunches of leaves. It didn't look as if any of them would stand up to a light breeze. One stiff gust could probably push them all into an evenly spread layer of detritus. From a distance, it looked like this had already happened.

Then again, he had spent last night huddled up to a rock, so he wasn't in a very good position to sneer at someone else's domestic arrangements. He walked on. There were a few narrow boats pulled well up on the beach. Otis allowed himself to leap to the conclusion that it was a fishing village. He thought of fish, fried, baked or raw, and looked around for somewhere he might be able to get some. He turned in place until he had done one slow revolution. No sign of movement. No lights. No sound. Nobody home. Nobody here at all. He pulled out the recorder. He spat out some leaves.

"This just isn't fair," he said. "Two days in the bush almost starving to death, then a heroic entrance to a remote native village. I really feel like I'm entitled to some awe and worship here. In the movies, guys like me get offered a place of honour at the tribal counsel and the companionship of the chief's daughter. All I want is some fish. These bastards are slacking off."

With as much righteous fury as he could manage in his weakened state, he marched up to the door of the nearest hut and kicked it. It was a good, solid kick. Straight from the hip to the sole of the foot. Straight from every cop show he had ever seen. The door failed to fly open in a spray of splinters. Otis failed to keep his balance and flopped gracelessly onto the sand. He brought the recorder to his mouth again.

"On the plus side, at least nobody saw that."

He flailed his way back to his feet and took a closer look at the door. It was a chunk of plywood, held on one edge by two flimsy aluminum hinges and on the opposite edge by a flimsy aluminum latch. He placed the tip of one finger on the latch and pushed. It flipped open and the door creaked toward him an inch. Okay then.

The inside of the hut was pitch black. He slid one cautious foot out onto the floor. It seemed strangely smooth. He slid one hand along the wall next to the door jam for guidance. It was also smooth and cool. His fingers found a familiar thing, but his brain refused to accept that such a thing would be on the wall of a native hut. His fingers, not waiting for further instructions, flipped the switch anyway. The hut was filled with light. Otis stood in the doorway and stared, thinking maybe he was passed out on the sand and dreaming this.

He was in a gleaming white cube, like a hut-sized shower stall. The walls, the floor and the ceiling were all made of smooth, seamless plastic. The light came from a single fluorescent bulb housed in a strangely elegant bubble in the ceiling. He turned around and walked out.

Ten paces outside, he looked back. It was a shack. Plywood and corrugated metal and rough-hewn palm logs. He walked back and peered through the doorway again. The dilapidated exterior was a shell, hiding the white plastic cube from view. He looked at the door. On the inside, the plywood was backed by a slab of plastic that fitted closely into the door jam like an airlock. A question sprang to mind, and he asked it aloud.

"What the fuck?"

When the shack made no reply, he shrugged and went inside.

There were a small table, a couple of chairs, and a cot arranged neatly along the side walls. A cabinet stood against the back wall, and a chemical toilet squatted in the corner. He went to the cabinet and pulled open its double doors. Inside were a microwave oven, a toaster, a coffee maker, and a can opener. Below these were a case of bottled water and a collection of food in cans.

His hand shaking slightly, he pulled one of the small plastic bottles out of the cabinet and cracked the seal. He poured a little water into his hand and patted it cautiously to his lips. He had seen that in a movie. You wander out of the desert, almost dead from thirst. You stumble upon a well and drink deeply of its waters. Your stomach twists itself with cramps until it ruptures. You die in agony. That would not be good. He patted a few more drops to his lips. After a while, he poured out a little more and tilted it onto his tongue. He spent the better part of an hour taking tiny sips of water and gradually beginning to feel human again.

When the bottle was half empty, he went back to the cabinet and began to rummage through the cans. He didn't know who had built this place or why, where they had gone or when they might be back. Right now he didn't care. He had found the can he wanted. Tuna.

He ate. He shook for a while. He slept.

When he woke up, the sun was high and someone was watching him.

There was an eye at the crack of the door. Otis had not pulled the door closed before collapsing onto the cot the previous night. Partly he had been too tired to take the four steps to the door, and partly he had feared getting himself locked in like a mouse in a live-capture trap. Better to leave himself a clear escape route.

His escape route was now blocked by a narrow sliver of face wedged in the crack between the door and the wall. Though he couldn't see it, Otis was willing to bet there was some sort of body backing that face up. Statistics dictated that it was probably a bigger body than his. In retrospect, he could have given this escape plan a little more thought too.

He turned his attention to the eye again. It was dark brown, framed above by the brim of a camouflage cap and below by a checked bandana pulled up across the nose and mouth. With the door on one side and the wall on the other, the eye seemed to hang there like a biological security camera.

Otis had not moved from his semi-fetal pose on the cot. He had merely opened his own eyes and found another gazing at him fixedly.

Camo. Bandana. Guerrilla. Must be some kind of patrol or foraging party. About damn time. So, now what? If he were a grizzled correspondent out of one of those seventies movies, he would allow himself to be taken captive, endure a certain amount of torture and abuse, then eventually earn the respect of the rebel leader with his courage and sincerity, and be permitted to document the actions of the group in the interest of history. That sounded like a pretty good plan, except for the torture and abuse part. Mindful of his recent lapses in advance planning, Otis lay still and tried to think of a way to skip that stage.

The eye vanished from the door. There was the sound of receding footsteps crunching across the sand. Otis sat up.

"Uh," he said authoritatively, "Hey! Wait!"

He burst out of the hut into intense sunlight. Squinting around, he just glimpsed a camo-wearing figure, complete with bandana and backpack, slipping into the shadow of the trees. Without pausing to plan, Otis bolted after it.

He took ten steps into the jungle and stopped. There was no sign of the rebel. He looked around the ground desperately, seeking a footprint or a bent twig or a handy spray-painted arrow that would tell him which way to go. There was no such thing. The only human he had seen in three days had melted into nothingness. The bastard.

Otis allowed himself to feel cheated and hostile for a minute. Then he remembered that breakfast awaited him back at the shack, and his priorities shifted.

After stuffing himself with canned ham and instant coffee, Otis began a survey of the village. More precisely, he walked from hut to hut, throwing open doors and becoming more and more puzzled. Every single half-assed hut concealed an improbable white plastic cube, each one equally well provisioned. He rummaged through them and made himself a small pile of water and ready-to-eat food on the beach. He found a first aid kit and bandaged his feet. He found a flashlight and took that too, along with a blanket. He even found a hat. It was a floppy straw hat and probably looked stupid, but no one was around to see so he jammed it on his head anyway. A day earlier, he would have felt uneasy about looting the homes of humble native fisherman probably only one bad catch away from starvation. Now he was of the opinion that these humble native fisherman would just have to tough it out until the next catch of canned tuna and Spam came in. That is, if they ever came back. He would wait and see.

When the sun went down, Otis built himself a fire on the beach, spitefully refusing the hospitality of the plastic boxes. He sat on the sand, huddled in his blanket, turned his back on the offending fabrications and gazed out to sea. He pulled out the recorder.

"I mean, come on," he said to the device. "A fake village? Crappy huts that look like space station modules on the inside? No people anywhere? What the hell is this? It's like a tropical island theme park, that's what it's like. I mean, I found one hut full of ripped-up, worn-out clothing all neatly folded and vacuum-sealed in plastic bags. Something deeply weird is going on here. Damned if I know what."

"I know," said a voice behind him.

Otis spun on the sand, tangling one arm in the blanket over his shoulders. The guerrilla stood silently on the beach about ten paces away, dressed as before in green-grey camouflage gear, a checked bandana tied across his face. In the gloom, Otis couldn't make out much more. He couldn't see a gun, but that was slim comfort. If it came down to hand-to-hand combat, he doubted his knowledge of classic Kung-Fu movies would avail him much against a hardened mountain fighter. He sat still and said nothing.

The rebel did not approach. He squatted on his heels and regarded Otis with an air of bland competence, like a man who expects no great difficulties.

"Corruption," said the figure at last. "That is what is going on here. That you ask this question thinking yourself alone tells me all I need know of you. You are not one of them. Therefore, you are not my enemy. I have watched you. You are a stranger here, but you are not one of those who come here looking for a hole to shit in. Who are you?"

It was a good speech. Very Che. The man spoke perfect English, but with a noticeable accent. He sounded like one of those Third World intellectuals who wins a scholarship to Cambridge and returns home years later, smoking a pipe and agitating for revolution. That would be good in the story. Otis made a mental note to ask about it. If he lived. He remembered that it was his turn to speak.

"I'm a reporter," he said. "I've come here to write a story about life on this island."

"There is no life on this island," said the rebel. "There is only crime. This island is run by criminals. They live in a tower rotten at its foundation. I intend to push it over."

"In the name of the people?" said Otis.

"In the name," said the man, rising dramatically, "of the truth. Write that story if you can."

The rebel turned on his heel and strode into the cluster of huts. By the time Otis had scrambled after him, he was gone. Otis looked down at the recorder in his hand and finally thumbed the stop button. That, he said to himself, was good shit.

Feeling pleased with his evening, Otis went back to his campfire, rolled himself into his blanket and, after a while, eased himself into sleep.

Two men were looking down at him when he awoke.

They were obviously native islanders. Brownish, fleshy, dark eyes, dark hair, ragged chinos, and faded work shirts. It was full daylight, the sun well up in the sky. He added an alarm clock to the list of equipment he really should have brought. Maybe some laser trip wires.

"Uh, hello," he said.

The men standing over him said nothing. They didn't look angry or violent, but they weren't exactly offering him breakfast either. Finally, one man pulled a small walkie-talkie from his pocket and spoke into it in the island's extremely foreign language. There was a crackle of static and an unintelligible reply.

"You've changed shirts again," said Otis.

The men grinned. Then they lifted Otis, blanket and all, and carried him into a hut.

"Uh, hey," said Otis. "What's going on?"

He struggled a bit for the sake of form, but while his captors showed no desire to harm him, their collective grip remained inflexible. They placed him on the cot, withdrew, and closed the door behind them.

Some unknown time later, Otis heard the hack of an outboard motor and a burst of incomprehensible conversation. The door opened. Three men looked in on him, grinning.

"Okay," said the new arrival. "You come. No problem."

Otis squinted at the man more closely. He was dressed like the other two, but carried himself with more confidence.

"Have we met before?"

Grin.

"No problem."

Otis gave an interior shrug and gave up the struggle. His new friends stowed him in the boat, a battered aluminum dingy with a tiny motor clamped to the back. Once everyone had climbed aboard, they began a surprisingly speedy putter across the placid water and back around the island.

It was getting dark again as Otis and his new friends puttered into the harbour of Pitouie City. They had said nothing to him through the long trip, muttering occasionally to each other in their own language. Otis had crouched there and nursed a secret relief that he wouldn't have to walk all the way back. Then his knees had cramped up.

Now, as they drifted up to a small dock near the beach from which his hike had begun, all three stepped smoothly out in silence, tied the lines and walked away into the night, leaving Otis where he sat.

"Are you just going to sit there?" said a woman's voice. Sarah and Garcia stood side by side on the dock, watching him like he was the most boring animal at the zoo.

"I didn't put myself into this boat," said Otis. "Why should I get myself out of it?" He was already making his perilous way upright and said this mainly to cover the sound his knees made as he straightened them.

"The president will see you now," said Garcia. He turned his back and marched up the dock, his hands clasped behind his back.

"Come on," said Sarah, helping Otis out of the boat with one hand. He got his feet on the dock eventually, but she didn't let go. He gave her hand a small squeeze and was rewarded with a small smile. He would have attempted a quick dance on the air, but his knees warned him against it. He opened his mouth to speak, but her expression changed, and he shut it again. She looked worried. She dropped his hand and began to follow Garcia.

"Come on," she said.

Garcia was waiting for them on the quay. As they approached, he turned again and led them on. The short procession threaded its way through the streets up the hill to the palace. The old woman with the tea somberly watched from her doorway as they passed, as if they were a funeral procession. It struck Otis for the first time that maybe he ought to be afraid. After all, he had stumbled on some kind of secret. He had been consorting with rebels. Well, a rebel. He was on a tiny island in the middle of a vast ocean, and if he disappeared into a dungeon or into the deep, he doubted very much that anyone would know or care.

It didn't help his mood when the palace gates clanged shut behind him like something out of a bad prison movie. Garcia and Sarah led him up stairs and down hallways toward the president's office. Otis reflected that he could have retrieved his recorder after all.

They stopped outside the plain wooden door. Garcia knocked. There was an answering grunt. Garcia swung the door open and stood back, as though he expected poison darts to come flying out. Sarah cast him a last, unreadable look as he stepped through, then the door closed behind him.

The room was much as he had last seen it. The desk was now scattered with books and papers. A merry fire was burning on the hearth at the other end of the room. Between the matched armchairs stood a small table bearing a bottle and two glasses.

Before all stood Don Roderigo Esquival Bolivar San Sierra Lopez, president of Federated Pitouie, chief executive officer of the Pitouie Development Corporation, general, commandant, and chieftain. He wore another impeccable charcoal suit. The medal on his chest gleamed in the firelight. The deep-set eyes also caught the light and flickered. They observed Otis with interest.

"Hi," said the maximum leader. "How's it going?"

"Um," said Otis, "Not too bad."

"I hear you've come to this island for a story."

"Well, yes."

"Have a seat, kid," said the president. "Have a drink. Have I got a story to tell you. It's all about a man named Lars."

Chapter 12

In the hierarchy of nuclear incident code phrases, Pinnacle Broken Arrow was almost, but not quite, as bad as it got. Pinnacle Nucflash was worse. That was the accidental or unauthorized detonation or launch of a nuclear weapon creating a risk of war. Pinnacle Broken Arrow covered accidents involving nuclear components that would not likely lead to war. The phrase was usually taken to mean accidental nuclear explosion, (which, as accidents go, is a pretty big one), but it also covered radioactive contamination and public hazard. It got somebody's attention.

Three hours later, planes began to land on the ice, one an hour. Not little bush planes like McMannus's, but massive three- and four-engined cargo planes with skis the size of bowling lanes. Each plane disgorged a crowd of very alert people, all wearing insulated space suits and waving Geiger counters. They swarmed through the village on snow shoes and snowmobiles, scanning everything that moved and everything that didn't. A knot of them quickly gathered around Big Joe. They bundled him onto a plane and flew him away. Another knot of them gathered around Lars where he sat brooding in Agatha's hut. The spacemen waved their devices over his plastic suit, and the air was filled with frightening clicks. They bundled him onto a different plane and flew him away too. As they walked him through the village and out onto the ice, Agatha kept trying to slip through the ring of white plastic suits that surrounded him, but they wouldn't let her. The last thing he saw as they shoved him up the stairs was her face turned up to him, small and sad, her hair whipped by the wind.

They took him back to the station. It was crawling with security grunts and unfamiliar officers. After all his time here with only Franks and the chief and the cook's insanity for company, seeing this little metal box crammed so full of people was more disturbing that being alone in the snow. Every module was standing room only. The air was filled with strange voices and sweat. Strange parkas were piled in every corner.

They hustled him through the throng to the chief's office. One of his babysitters knocked and opened the door. The other pushed him through and closed it behind him.

A major sat at Woolsey's desk, going through papers. He was a very sleek, very purposeful-looking major. He looked like the kind of major who woke every morning and thought first of how to become a colonel. He did not introduce himself.

"You are Lars Varick, radician. Report."

"Sir," said Lars. "May I ask if the chief has been located?"

"He has not," said the major. "Our first assumption was that he had gone to look for you. This does not seem to be the case. We have traced him as far as a civilian airfield in Inuvik. Once he got there, he seems to have melted into the mist. He is now officially absent without leave and in breach of contract. Do you know where he is?"

"No, sir." This was true.

"Do you know why he left?"

"No, sir." This was false, but he was still a technical snitching virgin, and he didn't feel emotionally ready to give it up yet. The major straightened the pile of papers in front of him.

"Mr. Varick, how did you come to call in a Broken Arrow from the village of Iglertok?"

Lars drew a deep breath.

"Sir, three days ago, the station chief informed me that he had discovered a toolbox full of radioactive material in one of the storage units. He said it had obviously been there for years. Someone from an earlier crew must have put it there and then forgotten about it.

"The chief was reluctant to inform PIN-MAIN, sir. He didn't want to cause trouble for any of his predecessors, he said. Also sir, I think that the nearness of his own retirement was on his mind. He didn't want to make any waves, sir. The chief asked me to take the toolbox by snowmobile a safe distance from the station and lose it in the ice."

"Did the station chief give you this order in writing?"

"No, sir."

"Even though this order was clearly in contravention of DEW Line standard operating procedure?"

"There's a procedure for this situation, sir? I was not aware of that," said Lars. He looked the major in the face for the first time. "I like the chief, sir. He taught me a lot. I wanted to help him out with a problem. A problem that someone else had left him."

"Go on," said the major.

"Well sir, halfway through the trip, my snowmobile broke down. I suffered hypothermia and frostbite, sir. Lost a toe."

The major raised one eyebrow, but said nothing.

"An Inuit hunter found me and brought me to Iglertok. I was unconscious for two days sir, due to slipping on the ice and injuring my head. When I woke up, I learned that the man who had rescued me was displaying symptoms of radiation sickness. He confirmed to me that he had been exposed to the contents of the toolbox. I did not know where the toolbox was, or how many other villagers might have been exposed, so I called in a Broken Arrow. Better safe than sorry, sir."

Well, there it was. It was a pretty thin story, but it was the best he could do on short notice. On the historical scale of military fuck-ups, a lost box of plutonium probably barely trembled the needle. He had piled a lot of shit on Woolsey's plate, but Lars doubted these guys would ever find him. Besides, he ran, so screw him.

The major leaned back in the chief's chair.

"My search team has located your snowmobile and secured the toolbox. Public exposure has been minimal."

"I'm relieved to hear it, sir."

"A significant amount of powdered plutonium seems to have been blown by the wind over quite a wide area. We're reading elevated radiation levels all over, but nothing dangerous."

"What about Big Joe, sir?"

"Who?"

"The Inuk with radiation sickness."

"He has been taken to Inuvik for treatment. I don't know any more than that."

Lars looked down. He didn't need to fake concern.

"Your snowmobile has a bullet hole in it," said the major. "How did that happen?"

"I did it myself, sir. It was frustration. Unprofessional of me, sir."

The major raised an eyebrow again. The corner of one lip twitched.

"My investigation is ongoing, Mr. Varick, but it primarily concerns the whereabouts of Station Chief Woolsey. His failure to report a dangerous substance on the base is a matter that will have to wait until he is located. Personally, I understand his concerns. Until such time as a formal enquiry is convened, you are not to discuss this matter with anyone. Is that clear?"

"Yes, sir." I solemnly swear not to make the military look bad, sir.

"Did you really lose a toe?"

"Yes, sir."

"I'll see what I can do about a citation. When we can't punish, we decorate. It's the next best thing."

"Thank you, sir."

"Dismissed."

The major and his swarm packed up and left the next morning, leaving a captain behind in temporary command of the station. Lars couldn't even be bothered to remember his name. The major had informed him that the investigation would continue from PIN-MAIN.

Days went by in blackness, but now a hint of something like light could be seen behind the horizon round about noon. He took to going outside every day to see it. The cold didn't seem to bother him as much as it used to.

On his first shift in the scope room, he got on the radio and tried to raise Iglertok. There was no answer. He remembered that they kept their radio switched off. He would have to try to catch someone in the shack. For the next three days, whenever he was on duty he would flick the radio on at random intervals and call out for Iglertok. It was like listening for a message from aliens in reverse.

On the fourth day, he got someone. A man with a low, guttural voice.

"Is that Iglertok?" he said.

"Yeah," said the voice. "Who's this?"

"DEW Line Station PIN-AA."

"Huh. What do you want?"

"Is Big Joe there?"

"No. He's gone."

"Do you know if he's okay?"

"He's dead. Soldiers took him away and he died."

Lars took a moment to examine the new thing he had just been handed. It was a warm thing in such a cold place, and it would get hotter the longer he held it. He decided he would have to hold it for a long time. He would have to take this thing and burn himself with it. But first he had one more question.

"Is Agatha there?"

"Sure."

"Can you get her for me? Tell her it's..."

He had never told Agatha his name.

"Tell her it's a friend."

"Okay," said the voice. There was silence. Lars sat and listened to the hum of the open channel until his shift ended, but Agatha never came to him.

The days dragged on, and Lars dragged himself through them. The guilt was so big and so intricate that he could only examine it a little piece at a time. He had never had anything so big in his life. He would go outside at noon into the barely-there light and pull out a tiny corner of the guilt to look at, to run his fingertips over. Then he would shove it back and ignore it as much as he could. He knew it would be a lifelong hobby for him from here on out, studying that guilt one little bit at a time. It would be a way to pass quiet, lonely evenings.

One day, as he stood by the end of the runway in the dim, a plane droned out of the sky and taxied up to a halt beside him. McMannus got out. He walked over to Lars without a word and put a baggie in his hand. Lars habitually reached for his wallet and fished out the cash he had.

"All I got," he said, handing it over. The pilot shrugged.

"You can owe me."

"Seen the chief lately?"

"Nope. I took him to Inuvik, and he turned into a ghost. I think you and me are never going to see him again."

"Did he give you any message to give to me?"

"Nope. Were you expecting one?" Lars shrugged.

Lars shrugged. "It doesn't matter. Have you met the new captain?"

"No."

"I'll introduce you," said Lars, and led him inside.

The dope was welcome, even if McMannus wasn't, exactly. The investigators had gone through his trunk and confiscated the last of his last stash. They hadn't said anything about it, but they took it.

Lars lifted the lid of the footlocker and dug out the April 1971 Playboy. He began to flip though the pages looking for rolling papers. He found a letter addressed to him.

He plucked the envelope from between the thighs of Miss April and looked at it in bafflement. It had his father's address in the top left corner and a cancelled stamp in the top right corner. It was baffling for three reasons. First, Lars had very deliberately forgotten to send the old bastard a change of address card. Second, he wasn't entirely sure his father knew how to read. Third, it hadn't been there the last time he checked.

He pulled the letter out. It was a single sheet of notepaper folded in precise thirds. It was handwritten in short, spiky lines. It read:

> Dear son,
> I very much hope this letter finds you well. You've been out of touch for so long. I hope, whatever challenges you have faced out there in the snow, that you return from your journey soon and find happier days. To that end, I'm pleased to be able to tell you that my recent

investments have paid off handsomely. I hope you won't be offended that a father wants to do a little good for his son. I know you'll be leaving the north soon, and you'll need a little something to give you a start in life. So I've set up a little trust fund for you at the family bank. I'm sure you once overheard me mention the name. The account number is 964321473. Use it well. I'm proud of you.

Your loving father

Lars put the letter back in its envelope. He put the envelope back between Miss April's thighs. He found the rolling papers, then he put the magazine back in the trunk. He put some weed inside one of the papers and twisted it shut. He put the joint between his lips and lit it. He inhaled. He exhaled. He put on a record.

He began to think.

Chapter 13

Otis put his glass down and Lars refilled it with single malt.

"How much was in the account?" said Otis.

"Exactly 500,000 US dollars," said Lars. Otis whistled. "Not a bad nest egg for '73. Of course, I didn't find out right away. The Union Bank of Switzerland didn't have a branch at the station."

"What did you do?"

"What would you have done?" said Lars. "I served out my time and went into a very comfortable retirement."

"What about Agatha?"

Lars looked into his glass.

"Didn't see her again. The new captain was keeping a pretty close eye on me that last month. Couldn't slip away. Couldn't get her on the radio." He shrugged. "Nothing I could do. In the end, I just left."

"You never went back?"

"No."

"Why not?"

"Thought it'd be better if I left the country for a while. Like twenty years or so."

"So you came here?" said Otis. "How did you become the leader of these people?"

Lars snorted.

"I'm not their leader. I'm just a guy who owes them a favour. A really big favour that I'll never be able to really pay off."

"How did you end up owing them a favour?"

"I just told you. They saved my life. In return, I brought them the gift of radiation poisoning. It was me that got them kicked off their land. So yeah, you could say I owe them."

Otis was buzzing from the Scotch and the sleeplessness and the strangeness.

"Wait," he said. "These people saved your life too?"

"No, idiot," said Lars. "These are the same people who saved my life the first time. Or their children. I brought them here with me."

Otis buzzed a bit more. He could almost see the shape of it, but not quite. He fiddled the knobs in his brain and tried to make the picture come into focus.

"Then all these people are..."

"The former residents of Iglertok, Northwest Territories," said Lars. "Inuit."

"I was living in Europe when I heard about what was happening," said Lars.

"When what was happening?" said Otis.

"I'm getting to that. Anyway, I was in Europe, out in the backwoods of France. The Europeans always enjoy it when the colonies do something nasty. Government and corporate power teaming up to obliterate a native village was bound to get some coverage over there. The story I saw was just a little news brief tut-tutting over the fate of these humble, naive little people and their simple way of life. I wouldn't have noticed it, except that it was so rare to get any news of my home and native land over there."

"When was this?" said Otis.

"About four years ago. I'm not even going to try to tell you how I felt when I realized what was about to go down and how much I was to blame. Suffice it to say, I felt like an asshole. When I found out a little more about the various happy companies involved I felt like even more of an asshole."

"What companies? What was the problem?"

Lars leaned forward in his armchair and pressed the tip of one finger into the table next to the half-empty bottle for emphasis.

"All those corporate wolves Woolsey fleeced, they didn't just slink away. They all had documents promising them exclusive mineral rights to about a hundred square miles of tundra. They had all forked out some pretty big money. I don't know exactly how much, but I can't picture the chief leaving me more than ten percent of the total score. Even split six ways, that's an investment no company wants to walk away from. Most of all, none of them wanted to admit that some old guy in a tin shack had out-played them. So they did what corporate wolves always do when they get embarrassed. They handed the mess over to the lawyers."

Lars swept his tumbler off the table and raised it in salute.

"Tenacious bastards, lawyers," he said. "Took 'em damn near thirty years, but they never gave up. Lots and lots of billable hours in a shit pile that deep. Just the kind of thing they thrive on. Not only is it so complex that nobody can really figure it out, it's also so embarrassing that nobody really wants to know the truth anyway. The whole thing was an exercise in saving face and coming up with an acceptable story.

"Six companies sat down at the negotiating table. Over the years two went bust, two merged into one, and another got a bunch of stock to shut up and go away. The two survivors eventually decided on a joint venture. They formed a new company, ownership split fifty-fifty, and both companies sold their mineral rights to this new thing. PerPok Exploration, they called it. Then they went north to claim their spoils."

"Uranium?" said Otis.

"Diamonds," said Lars. "All these guys had quietly sent survey parties up to the site, planning for the day they'd be able to go back in force. By this time they all knew there was no damn uranium up there. But their experts had come back all excited about Kimberlitic indicator minerals suggesting a massive diamond-rich pipe running right past the village of Iglertok. That's the other reason nobody was willing to cut their losses and walk away. They all had visions of pit mines dancing in their heads."

Lars tipped the Scotch down his throat and banged the glass back onto the table.

"When they had all their rocks in a row," he said, "they went to the Canadian government and got their 30-year-old mineral claim ratified."

"What," said Otis. "Just like that?"

"Well, not just like that, but the procedure is well documented in the literature. You find the one key politician and the one key civil servant and apply the standard techniques."

"What are those?"

"Thought you were a reporter. Don't you know anything about how the world works?"

"Pretend I don't."

Lars shrugged.

"Used to be you could just write some nice fat campaign contribution cheques, then you promise more when re-election time rolls around. It's a bit trickier now, especially in Canada. Public fat contributions are illegal, but you can finesse your way past that if you know what you're doing. The best approach is to set up a series of worthy conferences and fact-finding missions in the Bahamas or Paris or somewhere. You do it through a front organization, obviously. Something like the Foundation of Concerned Environmental Scientists and Puppy Owners. Then you invite your politician or your civil servant to contribute his wisdom, and you pay his way through the tour. First-class airline tickets, limousines, five-star hotels, fine food, theatre box seats for the wife, lots of golf, and very little actual work to do. Then, just when he's getting a real taste for the good life, you sidle up to him on the 18th green and say, 'You know, we'll have an open seat on our board of directors in about a year. Some people are saying you could be just the man we're looking for.' You casually bring up some unimportant formalities like the size of his signing bonus and stock option package. Then you slap him on the back and leave him to dream."

"That's all it takes?" said Otis.

"Well, you can't just throw all this together over the weekend," said Lars. "You've got to lay the groundwork years before you make your pitch. But that's okay, because our friends in the boardroom have had decades to pick out who they need to twist. They've hired specialists just for this."

"Then what?"

"When the moment is right, you spring the trap. You can even spring it on both suckers at once as they're standing side by side for maximum efficiency. In the spy game, they call this the burn. You tell your two good friends in government that you'd like their stamp of approval on a little mineral exploration agreement. You don't really think there's that much up there, but you'd like to go have a look. Just one thing. If by some miracle you should find something worth digging up, you may have to relocate a few Inuit. No problem, right?

"Your friends will hesitate. You can't build a successful career in government anymore by screwing over the natives. It doesn't look good. Your friends start to remember urgent appointments they need to get to. That's when you smile and regretfully inform them that if they can't come to a quiet agreement between friends, it'll have to be a messy and public court case. And oh, by the way, in court we might have to disclose how a Canadian army officer once sold bogus mineral rights to six different foreign companies simultaneously. Oh, and did we mention that he was responsible for stealing radioactive material from the US military and spilling it in an Inuit village causing at least one death and God knows how many tumours? Did we mention that the Canadian government knew this at the time and covered it up?"

"Wait," said Otis. "Did they?"

Lars shrugged again.

"Who knows? Wouldn't surprise me. Even if they didn't, no government wants to have to deny they covered up fraud and environmental catastrophe. Especially if the government is weak and under pressure from the opposition. Those bastards chose their moment well."

"So they signed."

"Yep," said Lars, refilling his glass. "A nice quiet backroom deal. No public announcement. No public hearing. Just get it over with quickly and hope no one sees you do it. No one would've either, if it hadn't been for Sarah."

Otis dropped his empty glass the last half-inch to the table.

"What about Sarah?"

"She was born in Iglertok," said Lars, twitching an eyebrow at his reaction. "But she was living in Montreal at the time. Somehow · she heard about what was going on back home, and she started a media campaign. Put out press releases, tried to get coverage, that kind of thing. Nobody in North America would touch it, apparently. Too far away. Too small fry. Too damn cold. Just business as usual. But like I said, some of the lefty European papers mentioned it, and that's how I found out.

"So there I was, living in fine style in the south of France on stolen money, and these people I had used to get it were about to pick up the tab for my endless vacation. If I were more like the chief, I probably wouldn't have cared."

"But you did," said Otis. Lars nodded.

"I felt, as I think I said, like an asshole. Sitting there in the Côte d'Azur with a cup of coffee and a neatly folded newspaper, copy of the Courrier International, I suddenly felt like a brand new person. Still an asshole, but at least a brand new asshole. What, I asked myself, have I been doing all these years? And I answered myself, nothing.

"I sat there for hours, re-reading the little article and thinking things through. By the time I got up, I had the start of an idea. I spent a couple of weeks in Paris doing research and getting certain necessaries lined up. By the time I left France, I had a plan. I would go back to Iglertok and get those people out of the shit I had dropped them in. I'd get them a whole new life."

"How much of the cash did you have left?" said Otis.

"Left?" repeated Lars. "What do you take me for? I was up to fourteen million by that time."

"Thought you were in retirement."

"Semi-retirement. I made a few investments along the way."

"Like what?"

"Look kid, I had half a million dollars in seed capital and all the stock markets in the world to screw around with. I don't know if you remember the eighties, but I would've had to work really hard to take a half-million and not turn it into three. Having three, I would have had to be aggressively stupid to not turn it into seven. And that's before the dot-com bubble. Do you have any idea what a man like me can do in an environment where serious, professional investors are just giving away money to any geek with a laptop?"

"You can turn seven million into fourteen?"

"Exactly. Listen. The main skill to have in life is the ability to convince other people to cover your expenses. That's my point. It's easy to save up a nest egg when you never have to pay for anything."

"Okay, fine," said Otis. "So you decide to become a white knight and ride to the rescue of Iglertok. How did you manage it?"

Lars waved a hand dismissively.

"I won't bore you with all the technical details. Rounding them all up took some time, but Sarah had kept track of them. We went by train to Vancouver, then hopped a ship to Santiago. There was more groundwork to do in Chile. I bought myself a civil servant. You can do that there. It makes things go so much more quickly. His job is to lose the paperwork if anyone ever asks about us. We also picked up Garcia while we were there."

"He was a government official too?"

"No, he was an actor. He was playing a corrupt police chief in some soap opera, but he got killed off by his mistress, and he was out of a job. I needed at least one person who could speak Spanish, so I offered him the role of security chief. I gather he was a very serious actor in his day. Still keeps a copy of Stanislavski in his office. Anyway, once I got those bases covered, we set sail for this lovely spot. That ship out in the harbour? That's the ship we picked up in Vancouver."

"You stole a ship?" said Otis. Lars looked offended.

"I convinced the previous owners to sell it to me. At a considerable discount, I'll admit. It's amazing what can be done with paperwork. The right form filed in the right place, and suddenly an asset is a liability. They were grateful to have me take the ship off their hands before the auditors showed up."

"Auditors?"

"They say you can't play an honest man. Of course, that's complete bullshit. You can play any man under the right circumstances. It's just a lot easier to play a dishonest man. That remains a truism. These shippers weren't exactly honest men."

"How did you find that out?" Lars shrugged.

"It's what I do. Find a weak spot and poke. At least, that's what I used to do. These days Sarah does the roping, and I strictly work the inside."

"Sorry," said Otis. "What?"

Lars gave him the kind of look a teacher gives a promising student who is having a sudden crisis of stupidity. He stood up.

"Come with me," he said. He walked to the door. Otis rose,

wobbled, and followed.

Lars led him through more passages and up more stairs until they passed out of the polished part of the palace and into a more utilitarian area. At the back corner of one barren concrete room was a barren concrete stairwell. It wound up through another floor and emerged into a small room that was all cracked windows and ancient electronics. It was the airstrip control tower. Lars was still moving. An iron ladder bolted to one wall led to a trapdoor in the ceiling. Lars climbed up, shoved the trapdoor open and disappeared. Otis followed.

They were on the roof of the tower. The moon was a high, small sliver. The stars were impossibly bright and seemed to take up much more sky than usual. A few lights winked in the city as it tumbled down the dark slope before them. Otis guessed that it must be after midnight. He felt very tired.

The roof was flat. Lars walked casually to the edge and stood there, arms crossed, like a pirate captain on the bridge of his ship. Otis more cautiously picked his way to the edge and sat down. Lars threw his arms wide as if to catch the island in his grasp.

"This island, Mr. Wilson," he said ceremoniously, "is one colossal confidence game. Our marks are large manufacturers with dirty laundry to hide. Sarah, as our public relations representative, finds prospective suckers and entices them in. That's what a roper does. She also works the media, setting bait in various business publications so that marks will come to her of their own free will. That's very helpful. Sarah studied you for months before inviting you here. Got to know you inside out to make sure you were the kind of person we were looking for. Told me on the phone that your girlfriend was about to dump you before it even happened. She's got real talent for this work. Couldn't ask for better."

Otis felt a chill in his bones. His stomach flinched. His shoulders tensed. So that explained that. All part of the service. So much for two against the world. He should have known. Lars continued his lecture.

"This island is our store. A store is a fake place of business where the inside man holds court. Classically, the store takes the form of a stock broker's office, but our game is a little larger in scale.

"I am the inside man. The man with secret knowledge and the means to make use of it. I tell the marks a story. I make them feel that I am the answer to all their hopes and dreams. I con the living shit out of them."

He crouched down next to Otis and began to murmur in his ear.

"Hey buddy, that's a lot of toxic waste you've got there. How would you like to just dump it in a hole and walk away? This island just happens to have a perfect hole. Got lots of guys here really eager to ram us in the hole, but for a small personal consideration, I could arrange for you to have exclusive access. Just put an eight-digit figure in this Swiss account. You can trust me. I'm the president of this shitty island."

Lars sat down on the roof next to Otis and kicked his legs over the edge.

"You know where I got the idea?" he said.

Otis shrugged.

"I was watching TV one night, and a news report comes on about this barge. It leaves New Jersey packed to the brim with incinerated garbage. Ashes, okay? Tons and tons of ashes. It's taking them to a landfill site in South Carolina somewhere. While it's out at sea, word gets around that the owner of the shipping company is in bed with the mob. The rumour is that the barge is loaded with medical waste. I don't know exactly what medical waste is, but it turns out you can't dump it just anywhere.

"The State of New Jersey cancels the contract and starts an investigation of the owner. When the barge gets to South Carolina, the port won't let them dock. The barge turns around and heads back to Jersey, but Jersey won't let them dock either. Now this poor schmuck of a barge captain, who sure as hell never asked for this, is sitting out in the Atlantic Ocean with six guys, 4,000 tons of garbage, and nowhere to go.

"So he heads south again along the east coast, calling in at every port he passes to see if they'd like to take some garbage off his hands. But word has got around about this toxic barge, and every single state slams the door in his face. Won't even let him land. He has to have food and fuel delivered to him at sea. Puts it on his credit card.

"So he keeps going. He pushes on to Mexico. The Mexicans tell him to take a hike. He tries the Bahamas, Jamaica, the Dominican Republic, Haiti. Everyone hides behind the sofa and pretends they're not home. He tries Belize, Honduras, Nicaragua, Costa Rica, Panama. No help. He tries his luck in South America. Colombia, Venezuela, Brazil, Argentina. Everybody tells him to get lost. He gets all the way to Cape Horn, then he gives up at last and turns the barge around.

"Eighteen months after leaving port, he finds himself back off the coast of New Jersey. By now the official investigation has cleared the shipping company of any wrongdoing. A health inspector rows out to the barge, pokes the ashes a bit and pronounces them perfectly kosher. Eventually the whole load gets dumped at a brand new landfill site that was built while they were away, about fifteen miles from where they started. Good story, huh?"

"Sure," said Otis. "But how did it give you your idea?"

"Well," said Lars, leaning in confidingly. "On their swing through the Caribbean, the barge did manage to dump a third of its load on a man-made island owned by this huge Malaysian shipping company. They paid through the nose to do it. Later the Malaysian company got cold feet about the potential liability, and they called the barge and made the captain come back and pick up his shit. But the idea stuck in my mind. A privately owned company that was also an independent nation. Cabinet and board of directors one and the same. Corporate mission statement and constitution written by the same people. The oceans of the world are full of ships just like that barge. Too risky to deal with, too valuable or visible to abandon. What they need, thought I, is a safe port of call. So, what I sell them is the idea of a safe port of call. All the rest is just detail and window dressing."

"And they believe you?" said Otis.

"Yes!" said Lars exuberantly. "Of course, we give them some convincing. We put on a bit of a show. That's what the fake village is for."

"So," said Otis. "You hit them all up for bribes, then...what? Take the best offer and send the others home?"

"Of course not. I take all the offers, best to worst. After I've spent a few days playing them off against each other, of course."

"And what do you do when the first six shipments of crud arrive? Pretend you're not home?"

"It never gets that far. We give them the blow-off."

"The blow-off."

"The last play in the game. Disaster strikes! Rebels attack! I am gunned down like the dog I am! All contracts null and void. Nothing to do but cut your losses and thank your deity that you at least got out alive."

"The rebels are fake too?"

"Yep. A well-timed explosion, some machine-gun fire in the distance, lots of smoke, lots of yelling. Garcia hustling our guests down to the airstrip in their pyjamas with a noble speech about fighting to the last man. He does it very well. Maybe you'll get to see it."

"So the ships never come?"

"But the bribes have been paid. After a year or so, we change the name of the island and start again."

"How often have you done this?"

"This is our third bite at the cherry. Our first was Asia, then we did Europe. Now we're on to North America. We don't like to do the same continent twice in a row. South America is too close to home and Africa really can't afford us, so realistically we've got Russia and the Middle East left to do. Then we'll start round again."

Otis was now very near to completely losing the thread. Between a long boat ride, half a bottle of Scotch and no sleep, he was feeling decidedly punchy.

"Sorry," he said. "I just don't believe it."

Lars looked at him and smiled.

"How'd you like to see for yourself?" he said. "Tomorrow, all will be revealed."

Lars ushered him down off the roof and bid him goodnight without further explanation. Otis wandered through the halls of the palace until he came to the dining hall. He let himself out into the garden to wait for Sarah. She slipped out of the palace a few minutes later and drew up behind him in the dark. He didn't turn around.

"So," he said. "This is a con game."

"Yes," she said. He thought she sounded a bit nervous, but wouldn't have bet his life on it.

"So. Sarah Vache. Not your real name, I guess?"

"The Sarah part is. Does the rest matter?"

"Lars said you're a roper. You picked me out months ago. You studied me and planned how to get me here."

"Yes. I did that."

"You needed a gullible hack reporter to pump this penny stock of an island for you."

"That was the plan."

"And I did it. I wrote a nice little story advertising your so-called business conference to a prime group of potential suckers."

"Yes."

"But then you invited me here. I don't understand that part. My job was done."

No answer.

"Now that I know what's really going on, what do you expect me to do?"

"Up to you."

"I was going to write a blistering account of an oppressed people, corporate irresponsibility, and potential environmental disaster. I was going to get it published it in a well-read and influential magazine. It would have been better advertising for you that two hundred puff pieces in an obscure trade rag."

"I know."

"Why did he even tell me?"

"Because I told him he should."

Otis shook his head.

"I just wish you hadn't made it so personal," he said.

"That part wasn't in the plan."

"All that smiling. All that attention. Walks on the beach and intimate conversation. Keeping me distracted."

He turned and stared at her. Her face was in darkness.

"You let me kiss you. How far were you willing to go?"

"What kind of person do you think I am?"

He shrugged.

"You're a con artist. Do you really expect me to believe you wouldn't use your body to keep a useful loser in the game?"

"You're not a loser."

"You didn't answer the question. 'I'll arrange something,' you said. Well, that sure was something all right. I should have pushed for more. Got something in return for my services."

"What do you mean by that?"

"I mean, you could have had the courtesy to fuck me after you fucked me over."

She looked at him for a moment more, then turned and walked away. Otis watched the stars.

Chapter 14

After a few hours of merciful sleep, Otis stood again on the quay in the harbour. It wasn't quite dawn. He was wearing an artfully ripped pair of khaki pants and the same faded work shirt as his island companions. The ensemble had come off of a rack of zip-lock bags and was accessorized with a pair of thick sandals that seemed to have been recycled from old tires, and a floppy straw hat pulled low over his face. He was on his way back to the fake plastic village. Lars stood beside him at the water's edge as a couple of dozen natives prepared to ship out.

"Look," said Otis. "I don't know if you've noticed, but I'm pretty damn white. What if the suits get suspicious?"

"They won't," said Lars.

"But I hit up every single one of them for an interview. Won't they recognize me?"

"No. You're one among the group. You're wearing the uniform. You're doing the work. To them, you'll belong just as much as anyone. Besides, these guys won't be all that eager to look you in the face."

"I just don't think I can pass for Polynesian."

"You're on an island full of Inuit who are all passing for Polynesian. Could you tell the difference?"

"Well, no. But I'm not Inuit either."

"You picked up a nice tan in the jungle. That'll be close enough for these guys."

Lars waved over an islander in a Hawaiian shirt and aviator sunglasses.

"This is the crew chief," he said. "He's in charge. Stick with him and do what he tells you. If you screw this up, he's liable to use you for whale bait."

Otis turned to see the man with the boat who had picked him up off the beach.

"Hi," he said. "Good to see you again. No hard feelings about yesterday I hope."

"Not really," said Otis, shaking his hand. "Your English has improved a lot since then."

"Had to stay in character," said the man. "Didn't know who you were or how much you had seen. Lars tells me you're in on the game now."

"I guess so," said Otis. He took a closer look at the man and mentally glued a pair of horn-rimmed glasses on his face. "So I'm going to assume you're not really Dr. Ernesto Sandoval, professor of vulcanology at the University of Chile."

"My friends call me Franklin."

"Funny. I never thought of Franklin as an Inuit name."

"You can call me Mr. Issumakattigeit if you want," said Franklin. "Relax. This'll be fun."

So he left the harbour in a train of little canoes to play a part in a grand deception. Sarah did not see him off.

When the boats hit the beach in front of the village, the islanders got out and set to work; men, women and children. They began stringing up laundry and spreading small personal trinkets around. Cooking fires began to flicker here and there, and the smell of lunch wafted between the huts. Two dogs Otis hadn't noticed on the boats began to chase each other energetically through the throng, pursued by a knot of yelling children.

"Setting the scene," said Franklin. "We have to make it look like we've been living here for generations."

"The dogs are a nice touch," said Otis. "Where did these huts come from?"

"Red Cross prototype emergency shelters. Adapted for our little play. Lars arranged it somehow. They just showed up one day a few months after we got here. Little white cubes you could sit through a cyclone in. Self-contained, with solar-powered batteries and everything. We built the outer layers ourselves, of course. What do you think?"

"Good tuna. Do you really need hurricane-proof emergency shelters just to use as window dressing?"

"No. But sometimes the kids like to camp out here."

"Mmm," said Otis. "What happens now?"

Franklin checked his watch.

"We've got a few hours to kill before the show starts. We'll eat. Then we'll relax."

Otis looked around. In small groups, the islanders were sitting in the sand and, yes, popping beers. Fried fish was passed around. Nobody seemed particularly worked up over what was about to happen. Just another day at the office.

"As you can see," said Sarah in her loud, cue card voice, "The cargo is brought into this remote village by barge from the client's ship, which remains offshore. In this way, public notice of a landing in Pitouie City harbour is avoided, and the ship's captain is excused from the necessity of recording such a landing in his log, if he so desires."

It was show time. Sarah was addressing the executive suitors, who stood in an awkward row just outside the village. They looked uncomfortable, either sweating in three-piece suits and wingtips, or trying for that business casual look in a variety of golf attire.

They made a great show of examining the village in every detail, but as Lars had predicted, they took pains not to get too close to the actual people. They all looked way, way out of their comfort zone.

Lars himself stood to one side, impressive and impassive in a suit that was not quite a uniform and a pair of mirrored sunglasses. He had not said anything. He simply stood and was observed. Garcia stood to one side and slightly behind him, occasionally barking an order in Spanish and brandishing a riding crop. Sarah was standing before the suits and making the sales pitch.

"We have arranged with our client to off-load this shipment during the day so that you may observe more clearly," she said. "We can just as easily manage a night shipment, giving you maximum flexibility, efficiency, and privacy."

Sarah's voice faded behind him as Otis walked in line down the beach behind Franklin to the waiting barge. With considerable effort, he had avoided staring at her as she, Lars, Garcia, and the suckers had arrived on a luxurious-looking houseboat half an hour earlier. None of them had spared so much as a glance at him.

Two islanders on the barge were heaving 50-gallon drums over the side to a waiting line wading in the knee-deep water. Each two-man team cradled its barrel in a rough stretcher made of poles and canvas, then turned and began to hump the load back to shore.

"Does this barge belong to the island?" said Otis in a low voice.

"Yes," said Franklin, equally low. "And the ship and the barrels. Now shut up."

Otis watched the barrels passing him on their way to the shore. They were ancient and rusty, festooned with biohazard stickers and the stencilled legend "MEDICAL WASTE." He wasn't sure how much a fully loaded 50-gallon drum weighed, but he wasn't exactly confident of his ability to carry one all the way up to the crater. If he collapsed, at least it would add verisimilitude to his impression of oppression.

Otis and Franklin spread their stretcher by the side of the barge. Otis braced himself, but when the barrel hit the canvas, it weighed almost nothing. Franklin turned his head to grin at him.

"Empty," he said. "But you were worried, weren't you? Now, make it look good for the crowd."

Franklin and Otis waded back to shore and made a modest show of load-bearing as they passed by the corporate assembly, through the village and into the trees. Otis could see the line of barrel jockeys threading before him along the trail. After a few hundred yards, each pair peeled off the trail and vanished into the woods. When they got to the spot, Franklin also turned off the track and Otis followed him, shoving their barrel through springy, slappy branches.

They came to a small clearing. A neat stack of barrels was piled to one side, and their former bearers were lounging in the shade, smoking cigarettes and talking quietly. Otis and Franklin added their barrel to the pile.

"There's no point in busting our asses all the way up the mountain," said Franklin. "We'll leave these here. After the game's over, we'll move them back into storage until next year."

"So now what?"

"We park ourselves here for about twenty minutes, then go back for another barrel. As far as our guests know, there's a relay of two hundred of us hauling these things all the way up to the top."

"What about the barrels I saw you throw in the crater?"

"We've got another set of drums stashed near the rim. There's a fishing net ten feet under the surface where we do the toss. After you left, we just pulled them out again and hid them in the brush."

"Wouldn't it be more logical to show the visitors the offloading first, then the crater?"

"Don't you have any sense of the dramatic? You arrive on

this island, a green jewel in the middle of the ocean. You eat an impressive state dinner with the president. The next day we truck you to the top of a mountain and show you an exquisite secret lake. Then we tell you that, for a price, you can piss in it. To a certain kind of mind, that's almost unbearably attractive. Inspecting the squalid native village can wait a few days until they're getting restless and need something new to look at."

It took five trips to get all the barrels from the barge to the clearing. As the last of the load was vanishing into the trees, the suits got back on their boat with Lars, Sarah, and Garcia and glided away back toward the city. As they moved out of sight beyond the next point, Franklin clapped his hands and called everyone together.

"Okay," he said loudly, once his troops had assembled. "Great show, everybody. Nice job. We'll camp here tonight, then tomorrow it's on to the next phase. Beer's on me."

There was a ragged cheer and the people began to drift away. The sun went down. Bonfires were lit. There was fried fish and baked potatoes and more beer. The night was clear and bright with stars.

Franklin told a story. A circle of rapt children watched him as he stood before the fire, miming the action with this arms and making faces. More than a few of the adults were listening in.

"A long time ago, when the land was new, there was a man named Kiviuq," he began. "He was the greatest of the people that ever lived. All the people are born equal, you know. It's what you do in life that makes you what you are. Kiviuq knew this. His heart was full of light and warmth, and so many spirits came to be near him. Kiviuq welcomed all of them that were not malicious, and so he became a great shaman.

"In the village where Kiviuq lived, there was an old woman who was also a powerful shaman. She had a grandson who was very clumsy, and all the people in the village mocked him except

Kiviuq, who was his friend.

"One day, the old woman decided to get even with all the villagers for mocking her grandson. She disguised the boy as a seal and told him to swim out in front of the village. Now, at that time, the hunting was poor and the village was hungry, so when the people saw the seal, all the hunters ran for their kayaks and paddled after him.

"The seal led them far out onto the sea. Just as the hunters were about to catch him, the old woman called upon the sea spirit, and a great storm swept over them all. All the kayaks were smashed and the hunters were drowned, except Kiviuq, who had been spared by the sea.

"And so Kiviuq drifted in his kayak, and after a long time he came to strange new lands where he met many new people and had many adventures.

"One day Kiviuq wandered into a small village. The people there welcomed him and invited him to stay for the night. An old woman invited him to come into her home. She told him that the villagers were so hungry they had become cannibals and that after dark they would kill him and eat him. She told him he must run away, but first he must sneak out and cut the bindings on all their sleds, or else they would catch him.

"So Kiviuq crept through the village and cut the bindings of all the sleds he could find. Then he started to run. The cannibals saw him and ran to their sleds to chase him down, but the sleds all fell apart when they stepped on them. Kiviuq laughed at them and ran on.

"But Kiviuq laughed too soon, for he had missed one sled, and one cannibal was still chasing him. His sled was pulled by a giant dog with two heads. Kiviuq took his bow and arrow and shot the dog through all four ears. In its pain, the dog ran right past Kiviuq. The cannibal yelled at the dog to stop, but the dog couldn't hear him because of the arrow through its ears. He ran all the way to the sea and pulled the sled into the water. The cannibal drowned, and Kiviuq escaped the starving village.

"Kiviuq wandered on across the land. One day he came to a small lake. Washing herself in the lake was the most beautiful woman Kiviuq had ever seen, and as he watched her, he fell in love with her. He went closer to the shore to see her better and saw her clothes piled on a rock. The clothes were all made of grey feathers, and Kiviuq realized she was a goose-woman.

"While the goose-woman was busy washing, Kiviuq gathered up her feathers and hid them. When the woman came out of the lake, Kiviuq said he would only give the feathers back if she married him. She agreed, and they were happy together for a time.

"One day Kiviuq and the goose-woman had an argument. She, being a bird, only wanted to eat grass and sand, but Kiviuq wanted her to eat meat like a human. After a long argument, the goose-woman flew away. Kiviuq was heartbroken and decided to look everywhere for her. This took a long time.

"Kiviuq wandered far and wide, searching for his missing wife. Eventually he came to the shore of a great sea. Standing by the shore was a giant, chopping a tree with a huge axe. Every chip of wood that fell into the water turned into a tiny fish and swam away. Kiviuq asked the giant if he knew any way to cross the sea. The giant swung his axe once more and felled the tree with a single blow. The tree rolled into the water and turned into a whale.

"Kiviuq climbed onto the whale's back, and the whale carried him across the sea to another strange land. There he found his wife in a new place where they could each be what they really were. And they lived happily together, for a while.

"Kiviuq has had many names and lived many lives. Some say he is on his last life now, but he is still wandering out there somewhere, on an adventure. They say that before he dies, he will return once again to be with his people. I would like to meet him, but I don't look for him. I want his story to go on."

"What's a kayak?" said one child.

"It's a kind of boat," said Franklin.

"Why not just call it a boat?"

"Because Kiviuq called it a kayak."

"What's a sled?" said another child.

"It's like a small cart with no wheels that's pulled by dogs."

"Doesn't it get stuck?"

"It only works on snow."

"What's snow?"

"Now you're just trying to be cute. Go tell your own stories if you don't like mine."

Otis sat on the sand around a fire with a group of islanders as they told dirty jokes and talked about nothing. He felt at home, even when he couldn't understand what they were saying. Franklin came and joined them.

"So," Otis ventured after a while. "You're all from Iglertok originally?"

There was general nodding around the circle.

"And now you live in the middle of the Pacific Ocean, pretending to be Polynesian and scamming international polluters?"

"More or less," said Franklin.

"How did Lars convince you all to do this?"

"How much convincing do you think it took? Most of us were looking forward to life in a shelter somewhere, or being a burden to some distant relative. Or starving to death. Besides, some of the old-timers remembered Lars from the seventies. They vouched for him."

"But weren't you, I don't know, sad to leave your ancestral lands?"

"Are you kidding? It's freezing up there. The nights go on for months at a time. Our young people fall into...bad habits."

"Like what?"

"Oh, solvent abuse and suicide, mainly."

"Mmm. And all your stories are about starving to death?"

"Only some of them."

Franklin took a swig of beer.

"This is a good place," he said. "There's whales here. Three different species. We go hunting once a year. Good fishing too. It's more like home than home ever was."

"I'm surprised you need to hunt," said Otis. "What with all the money you're bringing in."

"Oh, we don't need to. It's mostly just for recreation. Partly out of a sense of tradition."

"Um," said Otis, feeling his way out onto potentially thin ice. "About the money. I suppose you do trust Lars to hand it over when the time comes?"

"Well sure," said Franklin. "The elders vouched for him. Said he saved the town back in '73 when it just about got wiped out by some illness."

Otis sipped his beer.

"Besides," said Franklin cheerfully. "I've seen it on a computer. My name with a nice big number next to it."

"Mmm," said Otis. "What will you do when the time comes? Go back to Canada? What?"

Franklin's face puckered slightly.

"I don't think I'd ever go back. Too damn cold. But if I had to leave here, there's hundreds of nice islands around. We visit them sometimes when we're out hunting or fishing. Some of the guys already have wives and families on other islands. Only come back here to give us a hand with the show."

Otis had a sudden flash of the future. Some earnest anthropologist or genetic researcher was going to devote the rest of his career to figuring out how Inuit DNA got spread around a chain of Polynesian islands.

"How many people really live here?" he asked. "Not 1,500?"

"More like 150," said Franklin. "When we have guests on the

island, we all change clothes a lot and cluster around them to make the place look lively. The rest of the year, we put the city and this village into storage, and we all move into the palace. It's air-conditioned. I've got a great view of the harbour from my apartment."

"Are you happy here? Living like this? I guess that's what I really want to know."

Franklin laughed.

"Hey!" he yelled to the temporary population of the village, "The new guy wants to know if we're happy here!"

There was a murmur of Inuktitut as translations were made for the old-school. Then the murmur became laughter. The laughter spread from group to group until it coddled the entire village. Otis imagined them laughing back in Pitouie City. He imagined Sarah laughing, and the image pleased him. Most of all, he imagined Lars, standing on the roof of his stolen palace, holding out his arms and laughing with his tiny island of laughing people at the sad remainder of the world. Otis began to laugh as well. He laughed until his ribs cracked and his jaw ached. He laughed and laughed and laughed.

All right then. Fine.

When he finally stumbled into a hut to sleep, he slept deeply and awoke content.

Chapter 15

When they got back to Pitouie City the next day, Otis went to the palace and requested access to the presidential office.

"All right," he said. "I believe it. Now what am I supposed to do?"

Lars grinned and put a hand on his shoulder.

"Why don't you write a gripping first-person eyewitness account of revolution on a small Pacific island?" he said. "I'd enjoy reading that."

"What's the point? You're going to change the name of the place and then a story about the noble people of Pitouie will be no use to you."

"But next year, when we're making our first pass at a new list of marks, some of them will remember that they read something about a similar situation once. They'll remember that it sounded like a damn good idea, from a business point of view. And when it blows up in their faces, they'll remember that it's not the first time, and they won't feel so bad."

"Well, if you think it'll help, I'll write it."

Lars beamed at him.

"You won't regret this, kid. This is good and noble work. Few can carry it off with the proper wit and panache. You will be one of those people."

"A con artist? A criminal?"

"A free and autonomous individual beholden to no one. An artist of confidence? Yes. A criminal? We're not breaking any laws in this jurisdiction."

"But you are ripping people off."

"We're ripping corporations off, and I assure you, these particular corporations made the money by ripping other people off in far more heinous ways. No fortune is ever made with complete honesty. Standing at the base of every really big pile of money on this planet is a guy ripping people off. We just do it with more style, on a smaller scale and for a better cause."

"A better cause?" said Otis. "So a bunch of Inuit can lounge around on a tropical island?"

"Perfectly good cause," said Lars with equanimity. "Besides, we don't do any damage, and we didn't push anybody out to claim this spot. That's more than our guests can say."

"And what happens when I leave here? I just forget this ever happened and go back to covering garbage?"

"If that's what you want."

"You'd be happy with me running around back home, knowing what I know about this island?"

"What do you think we're going to do? Throw you in a dungeon?"

"There's probably lots of things you could do. Like you did with that ship in Vancouver and that civil servant in Santiago. I can't trust you. Everything you've told me, everything you've shown me could be complete and utter bullshit. You could be conning me right now."

"Could be, but I'm not," said Lars. His voice grew theatrical. "I am attempting to seduce you."

Otis twitched.

"I thought that was Sarah's job."

He regretted saying it before he had even closed his mouth. Lars cocked an eyebrow at him.

"No," he said. "That was never Sarah's job. She likes you, kid. If you find a way to fuck that up, you're dumber than I thought."

Otis did not twitch.

"Anyway, back to the seduction," said Lars. "The thing about all cons is that they don't last long. You can take as long as you like to find a good mark and nudge him into position. Ropers specialize in patience. But when the time comes to make the play, it all happens so fast. That's the key. You've got to get the mark into a state of mind where his shot at the big score looms so large in his mind that he literally feels giddy. That's the way it works if you're hustling some guy in a bar for his pocket money, and that's the way it works here. Our guests only stay for a week. When they leave the island the game is over, and they're already putting the experience out of their minds."

"Sure," said Otis. He wasn't really listening.

"If I were conning you right now," said Lars, "The same principle would apply. Quick turnover and a decisive endpoint. Let's leave aside the small matter that the professional only plays for money, and you don't have any. I could theoretically have some personal motive for stringing you along."

"I guess," said Otis.

"The point is, I wouldn't be able to keep you in play indefinitely. The longer the game goes on, the more likely you are to wise up."

"Maybe," said Otis.

"So here's an offer. Stick around for a while. This year's game is all over except for the blow-off. Watch it from behind the scenes. You'll enjoy it. The looks on their faces are always priceless. Then, after they're gone, hang out on the island for a while. Get to know the people. Judge for yourself whether or not this life is worth living. While you're doing that, I'll give you a crash course in the art of the big con. Then, next year, you can play along. We could add some really nice touches with an outside, independent journalist in our cast of characters. In the parlance of the trade, you'd be our shill."

Otis snorted. "Sounds great."

"Look," said Lars. "We didn't invite you here randomly. You're being headhunted. We looked at a lot of different scribblers before we got to you. We've read your stuff, you know. The contempt you have for your subject matter is awesome. So deadpan. These garbage guys. You spit in their faces in their own magazine, and none of them ever realize it. We were impressed."

"We?"

"Sarah and me. We wanted to get a look at you in person. We needed to see you in an environment that gave you some real scope for a change. If you had turned out to be just another hack willing to shrug your shoulders and swallow our story, we would have sent you home as dumb as you were when you got here. But you weren't. You chased those suits until you got every single one to talk. That was impressive all by itself. You wandered the city for hours all by yourself, looking for islanders to talk to. You even snuck off into the jungle alone to look for dangerous rebels. You got tossed into a boat by three large men and dragged in front of an absolute ruler for judgement, and you stood there and looked me right in the eye. We put you in the game to see how you would react, and you fit right in. We can make you this offer with confidence, so to speak."

Lars put both hands on Otis's shoulders and held him perfectly still as he spoke.

"You have more talent than you use, kid. Keeping it bottled up is practically making you sick. Your life is going to waste, and you know it. I can give you the chance to do amazing things and live an extraordinary life. Think of the biography you'll be able to write someday. I can save you from a 50-year wait for death."

Otis remembered the night he had decided to come to Pitouie. He remembered the pounding in his chest and the rising, unstoppable fear that climbed up his spine and scrambled his brain. He imagined what fifty years of that would be like. Fuck. He looked up into the craggy face of Lars Varick and found that he wanted to believe. But he didn't. Not yet.

"Why would you want to?" he said.

"Because I used to be just like you, and because I'll need someone to carry on after I'm gone."

Otis blinked and stared at him.

"What are you saying?" he said. "Is it...cancer or something?"

"What? No. I'm talking about someday in the distant future, when I get too old for this shit. I'll retire back to the south of France and watch the international news section for tiny stories about tiny islands with funny names, and know the one good thing I ever did with my life is still going strong. Or you could go home, blow the whistle on us and scatter us to the wind."

"I'm not going to blow the whistle on you," said Otis. "But joining you is a different thing."

"It pays really well. Just thought I'd mention that."

Otis laughed a bit.

"I've already talked to the elders," said Lars. "If you want to stay, you'll be welcome. They'll make you part of the tribe, like they did with me."

"Wow," said Otis. "I've never been part of a tribe."

Lars showed him to the door and opened it for him.

"I know. It's the main reason your life is so sad. Think it over. There's no rush."

Garcia shot to his feet so fast that his blood couldn't keep pace with his brain. Lightheaded, he clutched for the arms of his office chair and eased himself back down. When the spots before his eyes faded away, he reached a slow hand for the walkie-talkie on his desk and snapped it off. Its twin was stashed under a bookcase in the presidential study with a rubber band around the talk button. It had been well worth the risk to plant it there.

Garcia gave himself over to total incredulity. Could Varick possibly contemplate setting up this hack as the inside man? Garcia had never considered the possibility that Varick might step down, but now that he was considering it, he couldn't help feeling he had just been quietly passed over for a promotion richly deserved. Who else could take over the big chair? Who knew the game as well as he? There was Sarah, but Sarah was the roper and was never on the island anyway. There was Franklin, but Franklin was soft. No backbone. Neither of them had the bearing to play the part of a tropical dictator. Only he himself could be trusted with that role. This raw recruit, this rank outsider, flush with his first taste of secret knowledge, had no training and no skill. What could Varick possibly see in him?

The game was changing direction. It was only a question of which way, and who would do the pushing. Garcia sat and pondered.

There was a knock at the door. Otis had been sitting in his room for several hours, looking out the window at the night and poking his laptop out of sleep mode. He hadn't written anything yet, but if he was going to stay awake, he expected the damn computer to keep him company.

Sarah was at the door. He knew it as soon as he put his hand on the doorknob. He pulled the door open, and there she stood, looking officious.

"Lars asked me to check if you need any details about how our coup will work. For the story you're writing."

"Oh," said Otis. "Okay, great. Actually, I, uh, haven't really started yet. I'm not exactly sure where to start."

They stood there for a moment and regarded each other through the doorframe.

"You're really going to do this?" she said. "You're going to fabricate a story and run it under your own name in a major magazine?"

"Well, you couldn't really call it a major magazine. But otherwise that's about right."

"Why?" she asked. He could tell she had an acceptable answer in mind, and he knew what it was. Even so, he wasn't going to just come out and say it, mostly because he knew he would fuck it up. He stalled.

"Why not?" he said, utterly failing to make it sound like light banter. Her face folded. There was no denying it: he really sucked at this.

"Well," she said, "If there's anything you need to know about the coup..."

"I'm sorry about what I said the other night," he blurted. He paused just long enough to register what he was about to do, then plunged on regardless. "I didn't mean to imply that you were being nice to me just to manipulate me. I mean, I did mean to imply that then, but I don't believe it now. I know you're not...you know. The thing is, I was off balance and a little freaked out. I'm sorry if I hurt your feelings or anything."

He quickly scanned over the words as they floated in the air between them. A bit weak. Not exactly a passionate cry from the heart. Still, could've been worse.

Her eyes closed, then opened. She looked at him. She sighed. The tension eased out of her posture.

"It's okay," she said. "I'm the one who put you in this position. It's just that I wasn't expecting this."

"Expecting what?" he said.

She stepped through the doorway, closed the door behind her, laced her arms around his neck and kissed him very hard.

They didn't talk much about the coup.

"How the hell did you get into this?" he asked her.

"I was born into it," she said. "In Iglertok."

"Right. Lars mentioned that. All these people are your family?"

"Only in a sense. My parents died when I was a baby. Car crash. They were visiting Montreal at the time, so my dad's parents took me in."

She said this without any particular emotion, like she was relating the life of a distant ancestor.

"I can't complain," she said. "They were good people. Made sure I did well in school and all that. Gave me a nice dull life in the big city. I guess it mostly stuck because I never felt any desire to go back to Iglertok. Not for years."

She stretched under the sheet. Otis made a little more room for her.

"But you did go back eventually," he said. She nodded.

"I finished school. I got a job at a public relations agency. Looking back, it was great training for all this. You know what PR is like."

"Oh I do. But you don't seem like the PR type. Most of the flacks I've met can barely scrape together enough proper English to fill a press release, never mind pull off something like this island."

"Who wastes their time writing press releases? That's what interns are for. What I'm talking about is the amazing moral flexibility you have to develop. You become something close to a clinical sociopath. Necessary precondition before you can really rise in the field. You learn to compartmentalize your life so completely that you revert into an entirely different person when you clock off for the day."

She brushed a strand of hair out of her face and looked over at him.

"I once read a thing about French collaborators during the Second World War who were assigned to interrogate suspected resistance members," she said. "They would spend all day torturing their fellow countrymen with electrodes, but they would still give up their seats to little old ladies on the bus ride home. I've done sort of the same thing. Someone hands you a cheque, and you spend six months putting a sunny face on the fact that your client's new drug is killing people. Then you go home and watch the news like it's something real."

"Pretty extreme example," said Otis, trying to be helpful. "How often does that happen?"

"Often enough to have a name. They call it crisis management."

Otis snorted. She went back to staring at the ceiling.

"But most of the time, you're just trying to convince some brain-dead hack of a reporter that your client's trivial little story is more worthy of sacred media coverage than the other three hundred stories being chucked at his head that day," she said

"The shameless selling the useless to the clueless," said Otis. "The indifferent selling the unimportant to the unconscious. Story of my life."

"I know. Well, you can guess how that would wear you down after a few years. I felt like a total waste of space."

"It's not any better from the news side. Trust me."

She shrugged. He kissed her shoulder. Then she said, "Anyway, about then was when I read about PerPok winning the Iglertok diamond concession. I made a few calls and found out the whole village was about to be bulldozed to make way for the pit. It wasn't even really in the way. They were doing it just to demonstrate their absolute sway over their fiefdom. Or maybe they were just being spiteful. Either way, there was no coverage of the displacement of Iglertok cluttering up the business section. So I moved back home and started issuing press releases. Do you know how hard it is to send press releases from a place that doesn't even have phone service? I had to bring in a satellite dish and do everything over the Internet."

"Was it hard for you to go back?"

"It wasn't exactly easy. I didn't know anybody there, and they only remembered me as an infant. I don't even speak Inuktitut. I'm really only half Inuit. My dad was a white-bread climatologist from McGill doing research on ancient pollen counts or something. I don't think anyone really understood what I was trying to do. The only media you can get up there is the CBC, and nobody bothers to listen to it. Not like they were picking up my stuff anyway.

"I did get some coverage in Europe, but practically nothing closer to home. Later I found out how messy the situation was, and how no one in the government or the company wanted any light on the deal. They moved so fast, PerPok didn't even have to call out its crisis management team. They just showed up with a couple of cargo planes and a bunch of rent-a-goons and herded us all to the next village. Then they turned around and flew away, leaving each of us with a cheque for $2,500, which we couldn't cash because there was no bank for 1,600 kilometres."

"Twenty-five hundred?"

"Independently verified fair market value for a 200-square-foot shack in Iglertok. To be honest, they overpaid."

She rolled over and stretched herself again.

"Have you ever seen an open pit mine?" she said.

"No. Not in person."

"They're huge. I mean, the pit at Iglertok isn't even that big compared to some of the really legendary ones, but you stand on the edge, and your brain just can't take in the scale of it. You see these dump trucks driving down the access road, round and round in a spiral all the way to the bottom, and you think that gives you a pretty good idea. Then you see those trucks when they come back up, and you realize each one is bigger than a house. Just one wheel stands three times taller than the driver. Then you look at your watch and see that it took them three hours just to drive to the bottom and back."

"Wow."

"In Russia, there's a pit mine so big, aircraft aren't allowed to fly over it. The change in air pressure just sucks them right in. It holds the record for biggest hole in the ground ever dug, and it eats airplanes."

"Huh."

"Iglertok isn't anywhere near that size, but PerPok is doing what it can. They blast sections of the pit face in nice precise curves, widening the hole and making more access roads as they go. They fill up those giant dump trucks with rocks and send them off to a secure facility in Yellowknife. Fifty million years these rocks sat there, not bothering anyone, and they end up in Yellowknife in a building that's built like a prison. Each truckload of rocks contains enough raw diamond to maybe cover the palm of your hand, so they can't afford to let any of it escape."

"So what do they do with all the leftover rock? There must be mountains of it."

"There is. They make road surfaces out of some of it, but that doesn't really make a dent. The rest just piles up. For a while, they were dumping it in the ocean. I thought we'd really be able to nail them on that. Altering the ecosystem, destroying the fish population, that angle."

"Sounds good."

"Then they got bids from three different companies to reclaim the tailings."

"What's that mean?"

"They sift through the leftover rock looking for tiny little crumbs of diamond that slipped through the cracks of the primary process. By the time they're done, all that's left is dust. So now PerPok just saves up the tailings in a nice pile and charges admission to play in them."

"Guys know how to make a buck."

"Five hundred million a year for the next twenty-five years."

"Impressive."

"It is impressive, in a way. I mean, as a testament to the power of humans to change the planet. There's even beauty in it, if you subtract the function of the thing. If an artist said his next work would be a big spiral hole in the ground, way out in the middle of nowhere, dug over a span of twenty-five years, he would be hailed as a creator of breathtaking audacity and vision."

"You sounded very PR just then."

"More publicist, but anyway. My point is it would be beautiful if not for the side effects."

"Which are?"

"You mean, besides the wholesale removal of a group of people who had lived there for a thousand years?"

"Okay, yes."

"That's the really annoying part. Environmentally, it's not all that awful. Kimberlite tailings just aren't very toxic. Not compared to the crap that comes out of gold mines or coal mines or uranium mines. That's where you find the real poisons. Cyanide. Alkakides. Lead. Evil shit. I could have done so much with some of that."

"Too bad."

"I can't even make a moral argument against them. They train and employ tons of Inuit, and at least these diamonds aren't being dug with slave labour to buy mercenaries for some warlord."

"So that leaves you with the wholesale removal of a group of people who had lived there for a thousand years."

"Yeah. Problem is, there's not that many of them, and the rest of the world seems to think it's a small price to pay for some nice shiny stones. Even they don't care much. They like it here."

"But you're still holding a grudge?"

"Yes."

"Why?"

"I'm not really sure. It just seems like someone should. Even if there's nothing I can do to change it, at least I can be pissed off about it. I am the designated holder of the grudge."

"I'll get you a T-shirt."

"Thank you."

"So the media campaign didn't work out."

"Nope."

"Then what happened?"

"Lars showed up."

"Ah."

Otis snapped straight up in bed an hour later, tingling with revelation.

"His heart gave out," he said to the room. "It wasn't his fault. I can't tell him. He doesn't talk to me. Holy shit!"

Sarah turned on the bedside lamp and stared at him.

"What?" she said.

He threw his arms around her and kissed her until she broke away, gasping.

"What?" she said, more urgently.

"You've got some kind of phone here, right?"

"We have a satellite phone," she said dubiously.

"Can you show me where it is? I need to make a call. It's important."

Chapter 16

"*B*uenos días, Colonel. Good to see you."

Garcia looked up from his afternoon tea. It was Wilson, looking chipper and unsubversive. Be calm.

"Yes, Mr. Wilson," he said. "A very fine day."

"Do you mind if I join you?"

Calmly, calmly, Garcia motioned the reporter to a chair. Wilson set a cup of coffee on the small table in the great hall and sat down.

"Lars has explained to me what you do here," he said.

"Ah," said Garcia.

"In fact, he's invited me to stay here. Help out with the next one. Be a part of the tribe."

"Ah," said Garcia. Part of the tribe? The man pronounced the words with great warmth and satisfaction. Why? Being part of the tribe was just part of the role. Wilson sipped his coffee.

"He wants me to learn the business. I wanted to ask your advice on where to start. I know how important you are to the game here."

"Ah," said Garcia. He was marshalling his thoughts to say more when Sarah seated herself at their table, coffee cup in hand. She and the young man exchanged bland greetings, but the look that passed between them was so physical he could practically taste the sweat. So, Wilson had another ally. Garcia suddenly felt himself out in the cold.

Sarah and Wilson fell into remarkably easy conversation. Garcia sat and sipped his coffee and contemplated the future. It was some time later that he noticed he had once again been addressed.

"And the rebel guy out in the jungle was brilliant," the man was saying. "Do you think I could meet him?"

Garcia mentally rewound the conversation and played back the parts he had missed.

"You saw a rebel in the jungle?" he said.

"Yeah," said Wilson. "A man in a camouflage suit with a bandana tied across his face. His speech was a little melodramatic, but his delivery was perfect."

"I see. Where did you meet him?"

"On the beach by the village. He said he had been watching me and trusted me to take the truth to the outside world. Great stuff. I totally bought it."

Garcia stood up.

"You must come with me," he said. "There are no rebels in the jungle. Someone else is on the island."

Wilson's smile faltered, then faded.

They were back in the dented aluminum boat, skimming over the gentle waves at top speed.

"What do you mean there are no rebels?" said Otis. "I thought you used a fake rebel attack at the end of every game."

"We do," said Garcia. "But we don't make them live out in the jungle the whole time. Our rebels are just regular islanders dressed in silly hats and firing machine guns into the air. The guests only get a glimpse. The rebels don't have speaking parts, and there is no romantic leader character. Sarah has gone to speak with the elders. It's possible that one of the islanders is clowning around in the woods without clearance, but I doubt it. We usually encourage improvisation, but not to this extent."

Garcia sat at the stern with his hand on the throttle of the outboard. Otis sat in the middle. In the prow sat the same two men that had tailed him through the city.

"Who are these guys?" said Otis.

"They work for me," said Garcia. "They are field agents."

"So they were following me."

"On the president's orders, yes. He noticed your habit of wandering off. He wanted an eye kept on you."

The light was fading by the time they ground to a gravelly halt on the sand before the village. Garcia swung out and stalked up the beach. Otis followed.

"You met this man on the beach?" said Garcia. "Where, exactly?"

Otis walked to the spot and turned to Garcia with an inquiring look.

"And when he walked away, which way did he go?"

Otis pointed. Garcia walked to the tree line, staring up into the leaves. Otis watched in puzzlement as Garcia walked from tree to tree, looking intently up into each one.

At last he called out to the security men. One trotted over to the tree and, with minimal grace, began to shinny up the trunk. Otis walked over.

"What," he said. "You think he's hiding up a tree?"

"No," said Garcia. "We have a number of video cameras concealed around the village. We use the recordings to improve our performances. The cameras are activated by motion. Your rebel walked quite close to this one. We may be able to recover his image."

"Why do I need to be here?"

"You are the only one who has seen him. You talked to him. He even seems to like you. When we find this man, he may respond better if you are there."

This was untrue, but Garcia was pleased with his menacing

delivery. It was more likely that the boy and the intruder were partners, in which case neither of them could be allowed to roam unsupervised. Even more likely was that the rebel in the jungle was a fabrication, and this was an effort by Wilson's little cabal to keep him distracted. If so, the reporter might be due for a closer inspection of the bottom of the lake.

He rolled that thought back and played it through again. It was unexpectedly cruel. He shrugged internally and accepted it. His thoughts had been much darker and more ruthless lately. That was The System of the Book at work.

At last the security ape descended from his tree, sliding down the trunk into a heap at its base. Clamped under one arm was a coconut with a lens sticking out of it.

"Let's go," said Garcia.

The coconut lay on the security chief's desk with a slender black cable plugged into it. The cable looped across the desk and plugged into a laptop computer. Garcia and Otis huddled in front of the screen, squinting at the grainy footage as it flickered frame by frame in front of them.

"I think this is the best one we're going to get," said Garcia, freezing the playback. The screen showed a man-sized shadow moving against some other shadows. Garcia rubbed his eyes and checked his watch. It had been close to midnight by the time they got back to the palace. Now it was not far from four, and they were no nearer to identifying the intruder.

"Can you clean up the image?" said Wilson. "Run some filters? Increase the resolution? Something like that?"

"No," said Garcia. "This isn't a television show. Nothing can come from nothing, and this recording shows nothing. Waste of time."

He snapped the laptop closed and unplugged the coconut.

"I need more information. Are you sure you have told me everything he said?"

"Listen for yourself," said Wilson. He pulled a small electronic device from his pocket. "I've got our whole conversation right here."

Garcia was going to open with, "Why didn't you mention that before," but the reporter prodded the device with his thumb and a familiar voice came out of it.

"No," said the voice. "In the name of the truth."

"Play it again," said Garcia. Wilson did so. Garcia plucked the tiny recorder out of Wilson's hand and held it up to his own ear.

"I know who this is," he said. His brain scampered to retrieve the right nut and found it. "It's fucking Bridgewell. What the hell is he doing back here?" Garcia ripped open a desk drawer and began to yank out file folders.

"Who?" said Wilson.

"Clement Bridgewell. He's not a guerrilla fighter. He's upper management at a British chemical company. We performed for him last year. He went off after the show as quiet as a mouse. No suspicions. But now he's back, lurking in the jungle and talking about truth. He must know. Somehow he's found out. But what does he plan to do? What does he think he can do? We need to find him."

Garcia rifled through the folders and began tossing large glossy photographs onto the desk; headshots of executives in stark black and white. He threw the folders on the floor and arranged the photos in two rows of six.

"This year," he said, pointing at the upper row. "Last year." He pointed to the bottom row. "Who looks familiar?"

Garcia and Wilson stood and banged their eyeballs back and forth between the images. The reporter shrugged.

"All of this year looks familiar. None of last year. Actually, they all look pretty much the same."

Garcia sat down, closed his eyes and drew a long, deep breath. Method. Detail. Concentration. He exhaled and looked again. He selected one picture from the bottom row.

"This is Bridgewell as he appeared last year."

Slowly he slid the picture across the desktop below the more recent photos. Detail. The key would be in the detail.

There, second from the right.

Garcia snatched up a pen and began scratching at the second face. The reporter leaned over his shoulder with interest as a rough beard was etched into the glossy paper.

"No way," said Wilson.

Garcia whipped a walkie-talkie from his belt and began flicking through the frequencies.

"Any agent, report," he said. "Any agent, acknowledge this transmission."

"Agent Rose here sir," came a voice from the speaker.

"Rose, where are you?"

"Outside your office door, sir."

Garcia passed a hand over his eyes.

"Assemble all available agents. Search the city, the beach, the airstrip, and the surrounding jungle. Locate Christopher Trace and bring him to me. Alert the palace guards to keep watch for him. Send someone to search his room and bring me his passport. Is that understood?"

"Yes, sir."

Lumbering footsteps receded down the hallway outside the door.

"You're telling me Trace was here last year?" said Wilson.

"No, Mr. Wilson. I'm telling you Bridgewell is here this year."

Wilson shook his head gazed into a corner.

"Bridgewell. Clement Bridgewell. Why does that sound familiar?"

The reporter's head snapped back up.

"I need to go get my laptop. I need to check something."

"Stay here," said Garcia. He spoke into the radio again. "Any agent in the palace, respond."

"Agent Stern here, sir," said a man's voice.

"Go to Mr. Wilson's room and bring his computer to my office."

"Yes, sir."

Garcia and Wilson sat and studied the photographs in silence until the sound of running feet in the hall disturbed their meditation. A woman burst into the room.

"Trace's passport, sir," she said.

"Good work, Agent Stern. Report to Agent Rose. Assist with the search."

The woman saluted and ran out. A man rushed in.

"Wilson's computer, sir,"

"Thank you. Return to the search."

Salute. Exit.

"How many agents do you have?" said Wilson.

"Not enough." Garcia flipped open the passport. "British, but with an American address. Palm Beach. Issued in the name of Clement Bridgewell. Most recently stamped in Santiago. Trace is our man."

The reporter rattled his fingers across the keyboard of his machine.

"I knew it," he said. "I keep a complete backup of all the stories I've ever written for *Waste Insight* on here. Item 11,623: 'Bridgewell steps down at IntraChem. Clement Bridgewell has retired from the position of senior vice president of operations at London-based IntraChem Holding Group Plc to spend more time with his family. No replacement has yet been appointed.' Filed about eight months ago."

Garcia shuffled the files on the floor and leafed through one of them. He shook his head.

"Bridgewell has no family. They pushed him out. Now he has returned to push us. Come with me, Wilson. We need every able body for the search."

"Shouldn't we tell Lars and Sarah?" said the reporter.

Garcia's eyes narrowed.

"Very well," he said. "Let us go report in."

They banged on the door of the presidential bedroom, but got no answer. Lars was up and doing in the wee small hours, thought Otis. They wandered the halls, Garcia keeping up a stream of conversation with his radio.

"No sign of Trace in the city or the palace," he said at last.

"What if he's still out in the jungle?" said Otis.

"Then he can stay there as long as he likes. Our guests will be departing today. When they are gone, we can hunt him at our leisure. But I doubt he came here for a camping holiday."

They finally found Lars standing on a small balcony at the end of the second-floor hallway. He was smoking a cigar in the cool night air and looking out over the city.

"We have a problem," said Garcia. "We need to talk."

"My study," said Lars, motioning them back down the hall. He led them in procession to the door and let them in.

"Now," he said, "What problem?"

"There is an intruder on the island," said Garcia. "One of our guests from last year has found his way back."

"Who?" said Lars.

"That would be me," said a voice. They all turned to the far end of the room where the cold fireplace stood, flanked by its two easy chairs. Sitting comfortably in one of them was Christopher Trace. He was wearing camouflage pants and a matching jacket. A checkered bandana hung loosely around his neck. A small automatic pistol was held loosely in one hand. The gun was pointed in the vague direction of the other chair. In the second chair sat

Sarah, looking annoyed.

"My name is Clement Bridgewell," he said. He spoke now in an English public school accent that Otis recognized. "Good to see you again, Mr. President."

Otis felt his body clench. Without thinking, he took a step toward Bridgewell's chair. The gun snapped up precisely to the level of Sarah's forehead. He stopped.

"Stay where you are please," said Bridgewell. He lifted his other hand to display a small round object. "I have a hand grenade here. The pin is out. In this enclosed space, I think it would certainly kill us all were I to drop it."

"You," said Otis. "You're the guy I met at the village. 'I intend to push this tower over.' You weren't sick. You were running around out in the woods. Why didn't you tell me who you were?"

"Why would I?" said Bridgewell. "I hadn't quite decided how to handle you, Mr. Wilson. At the time, I thought it might be better to remain Trace to you. Also, in the end it was simply too much fun not to do it this way. You must forgive the theatrics."

"Mr. Bridgewell," said Lars. "I don't normally permit guests to enter my private study without an invitation."

"Please excuse the imposition," said Bridgewell, the barest edge in his voice. "I happened to meet Ms. LaMarche in the garden. She was kind enough to show me in. We've been waiting here for some time."

"So," said Lars. "What do you want?"

"I want you, Mr. President. I want the man who took from me five million pounds sterling one year ago."

"Did you come to ask for the money back?" said Lars. "Because you should know, bribes paid to dictators are invariably non-refundable."

Bridgewell smiled blandly.

"I don't care about the money. It didn't come out of my pocket. I'm here for my own satisfaction. To reclaim my personal honour, one might say."

"With a gun and a young woman as a hostage?"

"No," said Bridgewell, waving the gun in the direction of Otis's lower intestine. "With him. I'm going to give this reporter the story of his life. I'm going to blow this operation wide open, as they say. I'll be a hero, and you'll be in prison somewhere where I can come laugh at you from time to time."

Otis opened his mouth to speak defiance, but Lars poked him in the back, and he said nothing. Bridgewell turned to him.

"You came here looking for a story about corporate malfeasance and poor exploited natives, didn't you?"

"Well, yes," said Otis.

"I can give you a story even better than that. I can give you a criminal mastermind. He is standing directly behind you. Are you interested in what I have to tell?"

Lars poked him again.

"Okay," he said. "Sure."

"I have nothing to hide," said Lars. "I don't care who hears your ridiculous story. Tell it to everybody on the island if you want. I guarantee they won't believe you."

"Won't they?" said Bridgewell. He pursed his lip as if an intriguing wager had just been proposed. "Perhaps the first telling of my tale does deserve a wider audience."

"Send the girl to gather them," said Lars. "I don't care."

Bridgewell tilted his head to one side.

"No," he said. "Ms. LaMarche stays with me." He gestured with the gun at Garcia, who stood uncertain by the door.

"You," he said. "Go get this year's plane-load of fools. Bring them to the dining hall. We shall meet you there."

Lars turned, as if noticing Garcia for the first time.

"Colonel," he said. "Why are you not wearing your dress uniform? Have you forgotten that today is Pitouie Independence Day?"

Garcia's eyes flickered wildly between Lars and Bridgewell for a moment, then he straightened his spine.

"Sir," he said, clipping the syllable down to an expletive.

"Carry out your orders, Colonel," said Lars.

Garcia's eyes flickered again, then he clicked his heels and marched out of the room.

"Well," said Bridgewell. "Shall we go down?"

He stood up and prodded Sarah in the shoulder with the barrel of the gun. She stood up and slapped him in the face. In the second it took Bridgewell to recompose himself, Lars bent his head to Otis's ear.

"Keep him talking," he muttered, then straightened and gazed at Bridgewell with disinterest.

"Ready whenever you are," he said.

They walked though the halls and downstairs to the great hall in silence. Lars walked in front, erect and calm, as if he were on his way to a state banquet. Sarah walked to one side, eyes pointed straight ahead at nothing, still looking annoyed. Otis was a step behind them, trying not to stare at Sarah. Bridgewell herded them along from behind.

Otis tried to think like a con artist. The con was short for confidence, and the art lay in keeping the mark's confidence long enough to get your hands on his money. Otis had Bridgewell's confidence for now. To Bridgewell, he was an impartial observer and a potential ally, or at least not an enemy. But what could he do? If he were a fully trained con artist, he could probably use this situation to get into the man's bank account, but all he really wanted was for Sarah to be under a cast-iron bathtub on the next island over. It made it hard to concentrate on devious ploys.

They arrived at the dining hall. It was empty and dark. Bridgewell flipped the light switch with the tip of his pistol and waited while the fluorescents plinked into light. He gestured Lars into a chair, then swept away the other nearby furniture with his feet. Lars sat alone in the middle of the linoleum. Sarah and Otis stood slightly to one side. Bridgewell backed up a few paces and perched himself on the edge of the breakfast buffet.

Keep him talking, thought Otis.

"So," he said. "The Christopher Trace thing. What is that? An alter ego?"

"In a sense," said Bridgewell. "Do you know the saying, 'You can't step into the same river twice?' Well, it seems the same can be said about this island. I knew I would need to be somebody else if I were ever to set foot here again."

"You knew? How?"

"Thereby hangs a tale, Mr. Wilson."

"I'd like to hear it," said Otis. He took the voice recorder out of his pocket. "For the story."

"Very well," said Bridgewell. "It seems we do have a little time."

He wiggled his ample hips into a more comfortable position and scratched the back of his head with the end of the grenade.

"There I was back home in England, happy to have escaped a violent revolution in a foreign land with my skin intact. But after losing five million in a puff of smoke, my career at IntraChem was quite dead. I had had my eye on a seat on the board, but after a debacle like that the best I could hope for would be managing director of some invisible subsidiary. That was not for me. I chose early retirement instead. My golden parachute was very generous, so I abandoned England and embarked upon an opulent retirement in Florida.

"Now, every retired man needs a hobby, and mine became this island. I wanted to know how things were getting along here. I scanned the newspapers avidly, but there was no news. Hardly surprising that events in a tiny, far-off place should go unnoticed by the American press, so I took to haunting the local library, scanning back issues of papers from New Zealand, Australia, Hawaii, Chile, anyone who might consider a coup in their general neighbourhood to be newsworthy. I found nothing. I was astonished. I mean, what kind of revolutionary in this day and age doesn't even know enough to issue a simple press release?

"I began to put my back into it. I made enquiries at the Chilean embassy in London, but no one there had ever heard of Puerto Ombligo. I contacted certain old school friends who had gone into the intelligence game, but they couldn't tell me anything either. I even tried going to my fellow guests here on this island, my rivals for the use of this volcano. None of them would even admit to having been here. It seemed I was all alone in my quest. No one in the wide world cared what had happened to Puerto Ombligo, except me. I confess, I began to feel proprietary about this island, as if I had a right to its secrets. I might even go so far as to admit to a slight obsession. Call it an eccentricity. I'm English. It is permitted me.

"Sadly, my efforts were all in vain. I had to console myself with my other hobby, which was keeping abreast of developments in my former industry. I subscribed to any number of technical journals and business magazines, and somehow I got added to the subscription list of an insignificant little publication called *Waste Insight*."

"Wait," said Otis. "You actually read it?"

"Oh yes," said Bridgewell. "When there was nothing else around. And what should I see in its pages several months ago but a tiny article about a South Pacific island offering itself up as a chemical dump site. It all looked very familiar, I must say. I visited the island's website and found a potted history that exactly paralleled that of Puerto Ombligo. Honestly, I think someone merely performed a search-and-replace on the name."

He looked at Sarah pleasantly.

"Was that part of your job, my dear? Naturally, I was curious about this remarkable coincidence, so I invented a false name and a suitably shady company to represent, and I contacted the island's public relations representative. It took only a few moments' conversation to satisfy myself that the Ms. Vache of today was the Ms. LaMarche of yesterday, and that by extension, Puerto Ombligo and Pitouie must be one and the same. A moderate payment to a certain official in the Chilean Ministry of the Interior confirmed my conclusion."

He shook his head in wonderment and smiled fondly at Lars.

"Truly," he said. "A part of me is deeply impressed by the audacity of your achievement here. It is an unrivalled masterpiece of deceit. Nevertheless, for making me the butt of your secret joke, I will smash your masterpiece utterly to dust."

Lars made no reply.

"Naturally," Bridgewell continued, "I booked a reservation for the conference immediately. I shaved my beard, dyed my hair and adopted an American accent. And so I arrived here, courteously invited by the very people who had eluded me for so long."

"What about all that stuff you told me about the lawyer in Gibraltar and the consortium of secret interests?" said Otis.

"Oh, I took that from a spy novel I once read," said Bridgewell.

"And what were you doing out in the jungle in a camouflage suit?"

"Like you, I was looking for rebels. Had they been real, they would have been natural allies in my efforts to rid this island of the squatters who now claim it. But like you, I found no one. You and I will have to crush this nest of vipers on our own."

"Mmm," said Otis.

The door to the great hall burst open, and Garcia strode in, looking harried and wearing his dress uniform jacket unbuttoned and hanging open. Straggling in behind him came a line of sleepy executives. Bridgewell eased the grenade and pistol into his jacket pockets and left his hands there.

"Gentlemen, good morning," he said. "Sorry to disturb you so early, but I have important business intelligence that you must hear before you leave this island."

"What the hell is this, Trace?" said Coombs. "Some kind of late-breaking bargaining tactic? I'm not interested in any kind of joint usage scheme. My company is satisfied with the arrangement we've already reached."

"The arrangement you've already reached?" said Penner. "What are you talking about? My firm has secured the exclusive rights to this island's services."

"What the hell are you wearing?" said Laurier.

The collective executives were awake now, talking over top of each other and pointing executive fingers. Bridgewell was trying to regain their attention, but the disadvantage of keeping his hands in his pockets and his butt on the table hampered his efforts.

Lars caught Otis's eye.

"We need a few more minutes," he muttered.

"Wait," said Otis loudly. "I'd like to say something." He glanced at Bridgewell, who shrugged and nodded. Otis walked to a spot on the floor halfway between Lars and the unshaven, baggy-eyed and generally rumpled corporate campers. He turned very slowly to face the single chair alone in the middle of the room.

"As you all know, I'm a reporter," he said. "I have information about this man that none of you has. Information that has lain undiscovered and unknown for thirty years."

He swept the businessmen with a meaningful look. There was silence. He turned back to Lars. His eyes urged caution. Who's worried now?

"A few days ago, I went for a stroll through the city. I met a woman who offered me tea. She asked if I was staying at the palace, and I said yes. Then she said something I didn't understand. But there are lots of things I don't understand, so I didn't worry about it too much."

Lars's eyes went dark with warning. Otis ignored them.

"Well, the days went by, and I picked up a piece of information here and a piece of information there, and the other night my brain finally put all the pieces together for me. Yesterday morning I had a telephone conversation with a very nice man at the coroner's office in Inuvik, Northwest Territories, Canada. It took a while to find the records. I only had a partial name and date to go by, and they're not computerized. Fortunately, this very nice man has worked there for decades and can put his hands on anything. Eventually he found the record I wanted."

Now Lars's eyes were dark and blank and disbelieving. Otis went on.

"Joseph Takiyok. Admitted to Inuvik General Hospital on February 3, 1973, with pneumonia. Died on February 5, of heart failure."

Otis watched as the disbelief in Lars's eyes changed shape. He knelt beside the chair and spoke in a clear, calm voice.

"He didn't die of radiation poisoning. It wasn't your fault."

Lars slowly turned his head to Otis.

"I don't believe you," he said.

"Then believe Agatha," said Otis. He pressed a button on the voice recorder.

"Tell him, if you can," said a sad female voice. "He didn't know. His heart was always weak. It was the strain of the journey. The strangeness of the place. His heart gave out. It wasn't his fault. I can't tell him. He doesn't talk to me. No one will talk to me about him. They think it is a kindness, but they don't know. Only I know."

"She's been waiting all this time to explain it to you, but you never talk to her," said Otis. "You should."

"Maybe I will."

"What was the point of that story?" said Bridgewell.

Lars looked up and laughed. It wasn't a laugh for effect. It was a good, real laugh, if Otis was any judge. The suits looked at each other awkwardly. Coombs rolled his eyes.

"Sorry," said Otis. "I just thought it was interesting." Behind him, Lars let out a whoop.

"The point is," said Bridgewell, "this man is corrupt, and this island is a mockery of standard business practices."

He swivelled a few degrees on the buffet table to better pose for his audience.

"There was supposed to be a fair and open bidding process for the contract to make use of this island, wasn't there? But then our friend the president here took you aside one by one and told you that he could arrange for your bid to win, as long as you showed him a little personal consideration."

None of the suits bothered to look embarrassed. Laurier shrugged. Coombs studied his fingernails. The rest continued looking blankly from Bridgewell to Lars.

"Of course, that is a perfectly acceptable business practice," said Bridgewell. "Especially in certain parts of the world. But this man does not seem to feel himself bound by traditional best practices. He apparently feels himself to be above the basic standards of trust that allow commerce to take place."

Bridgewell had reached his grand finale. He stood up and turned to the knot of guests, spreading his arms wide to them.

"He took bribes from all of you, and he intends to give you nothing!"

There was a gasp. Every head in the room turned. It had come from Garcia.

"Bribes?" he shouted at Lars. "You have been taking bribes? Without telling me? Then it is as I have long suspected."

His hand snaked inside his open jacket and emerged holding a chromed revolver. He extended it toward Lars in an unhurried manner and shot him in the chest with formal precision. Lars toppled backward over his chair and onto the floor, his eyes staring at the ceiling, his shirt a mass of blood. Otis could smell the gunpowder and feel the ringing in his ears. Bridgewell and the executives stared at Garcia with open mouths.

There was a moment of silence, then there was an explosion. Dust fell from the cracks in the ceiling, and the lights went out. A dim orange emergency bulb flickered on over the doorway. Outside the palace walls, Otis could hear machine gun fire and people yelling. There was a thunder of running boots in the hall, then the door flew open, and eight islanders charged in. They took up positions around the room and levelled a battered collection of automatic rifles at the executives.

"Ah," said Garcia. "My guerrillas. Viva la revolucion." He turned to the suits. "You," he barked. "Get off my island. I want to see you run to the airstrip."

He placed one hand on his hip, feet spread wide, held the revolver above his head and fired a shot into the ceiling. The guerrillas began to close in. The suits hustled toward the door.

"Go!" shouted Garcia at their fleeing backs. "Go back to your soft and empty lives. And tell the world. Tell them Pitouie is dead."

He led the guerrillas after them, still firing, and was gone.

Bridgewell stood alone in the middle of the room, his arms still outstretched, looking like a child who has just watched his birthday party rush off without him.

"Excuse me," said Sarah.

Bridgewell turned to her. She swatted him neatly across the temple with a steel coffee pot. He fell to the floor, not so neatly.

"The grenade!" said Otis. "Get down!"

Sarah put the pot back on the breakfast buffet. Then she went to Otis and kissed him.

"Relax," she said. "Didn't you notice the missing kaboom when he took his hands out of his pockets? It's fake. But the gun is real."

She knelt down, reached into the unconscious man's pockets and extracted the grenade and the pistol. She tossed the grenade to Otis. It was plastic. One side was stamped with the words The Really Fun Toy Manufacturing Company of China Inc.

"Nice speech," she said.

"Nice swing," said Otis. He looked down at the recumbent pseudo-rebel. "What the hell do we do with him now?"

"Oh, I've got that all planned out already," said a voice from the floor behind them. They turned. Lars was getting stiffly to his feet, wiping the blood off his face with the corner of a tablecloth. He stopped when he saw Otis staring at him, then looked down at his mess of a chest.

"Exploding dye pack," he said. "I use one every year to fake my own death. The trigger is in the ring." He held up the hand with the diamond ring on it. "All I have to do is squeeze my fist in a certain way. Garcia knew I would be wearing it once I reminded him that today is coup day. That's why he had to be the one to round up the guests." He said this to Sarah, half-apologetically. "I needed to give him a chance to get his gun. That's why we had to wait around so long. The coup was scheduled for 5:15 AM. We needed that distraction to get the suits out in a convincing manner."

He took a cigar from his jacket pocket, tried to wipe the fake blood off of it, then gave up and put it back in his pocket.

"All in all, I'd say that went well," he said.

"Don't tell me you planned for all this," said Otis. "Because I will not believe you."

"Well, it wasn't our usual endgame, to be sure," said Lars. "But the result is the same. The suits think I'm dead. They are, as we speak, escaping a bloody revolution by a hair. They know something strange was going on, but they don't know what, and they can't find out. Most importantly, we keep the money, and we're still good to play again next year. Improv, you see. Garcia was always good at improv. Nice touch, claiming the island for himself."

"So," said Sarah, poking Bridgewell in the ribs with her toe, "What do we do with this guy?"

"Under other circumstances, I might offer him a job," said Lars. "He showed natural talent. But since he seems to hate our guts, we'll just keep him tranquilized until the plane gets back. Then we ship him air freight to Thailand or somewhere. Leave him to wake up naked on a public beach. The local authorities will assume he's just another Western tourist who got too much sun and opium. They won't believe anything he says, especially about living in the jungle on a secret island full of criminal masterminds. With no papers, no money and no identity, he'll bounce between the bureaucracies of the world for a year maybe. Eventually he'll get home okay."

"But what if he comes back again?" said Otis.

"Why would he?" said Lars. "He thinks I'm dead."

"He thought you were dead the last time too."

Lars frowned slightly.

"What do you want me to do, kill him? If he ever does come back, we'll think of something. Improv, you know. In the meantime, I'm going to have to take a trip to Santiago and have a little chat with a certain civil servant. When I buy a man, I expect him to stay bought."

"The standard business practice in certain parts of the world?" said Otis.

"Just so," said Lars. He looked Otis hard in the eye, then held out his hand. Otis shook it.

They stood there, the three of them, and listened to the machine gun fire heralding the dawn.

Epilogue

Bloodshed in Paradise - *Not That Magazine*, Vol. 23, No. 2
By Otis Wilson

The guerrillas attacked at dawn, creeping down from the jungle and through the streets of Pitouie Island as the residents slept. At exactly 5:15 AM, they blasted a hole in the palace wall with explosives and stormed the seat of government, bent on revolution. But their job was already done. President Roderigo Esquival Bolivar San Sierra Lopez was dead, gunned down in the grand hall of his own sanctuary by his second in command, Colonel Juan Cortez Garcia, head of security on Pitouie.

Everyone on the island had heard the stories about the rebels on the mountain. Nobody paid them much heed. A tiny handful of malcontents, it was said, with no supplies and no real backbone. Their leader, a man known only as Claudius, wanted to free the island from the rule of President Lopez, who, it was whispered, had fallen into corruption.

But when the rebels entered the great hall of the palace that morning and beheld the cooling body of their former foe, it was Garcia they acclaimed to take his place. Garcia and Claudius, it turned out, were one and the same.

For months, the security chief had led a dangerous double life. By day, he was the loyal, some would say brutal, functionary of the president. By night, he secretly recruited a band of followers and trained them deep in the jungle for their mission of liberation.

Pitouie is a minute island lost in the vast expanse of the Pacific Ocean. A former territory of Chile, it gained independence two years ago with the negotiation of a treaty of free association. At the same time, a corporation known as Pitouie Development LLC was established. This corporate entity was the landlord of the entire island and its only commercial interest. The company was controlled by President Lopez.

The residents of Pitouie lead simple, isolated lives. Most are fishermen. There is no television or radio on the island. There is only one satellite telephone, located in the palace. There is an airstrip, but no airlines make regular flights. There is no industry and only one natural resource on the island. President Lopez, upon assuming leadership of the civil government and control of Pitouie Development, set out to convert that resource into money in the most direct way possible.

The resource in question is a hole in the ground: Lake Pitouie, the crater of the dormant volcano to which the island owes its existence. The president's plan was as audacious as it was dangerous. He would auction exclusive access to the crater to some rich foreign company to use as a toxic waste disposal site. Some of the most hazardous substances known to chemistry would be poured down this geological drain, and the company would sail away with a certificate saying that the waste had been disposed of according to all applicable laws and safety regulations. As president of Pitouie Development, Lopez had the power to make such a contract for the use of the volcano. As head of state for Pitouie Island, he had the power to make sure there would be no such laws or regulations. The money this reckless scheme would bring to the island would buy a lot more than fish.

At first, Colonel Garcia showed no sign of opposition to the plan. The colonel may be many things, but he is not an environmentalist.

However, he is, by reputation, stoically loyal. If his president said this plan was the best way to bring prosperity to the island, he would see it done without comment.

It was only with the passage of time, as the process of finding a suitable client advanced, that Garcia found cause for concern. It came to his attention that the president was soliciting personal bribes to sway the course of the auction. The colonel is unwilling to go into detail regarding how he obtained this information, but it is not difficult to speculate that the security chief had both official and unofficial access to the president's private communications.

For the first time, Garcia told this magazine in an exclusive interview, he began to have doubts. If the president were willing to institute this dangerous plan and sell the health of the islanders to a foreign company merely to line his own pockets, the colonel concluded that his friend and mentor was no longer fit to hold power. He began to make plans.

Finding islanders willing to support his cause was not difficult. The president was a cold, aloof man at the best of times. He was obeyed by his people, but not beloved of them. When Garcia laid the evidence of corruption before a potential recruit, the result was always the same: another partisan for the struggle.

The difficulty was maintaining secrecy. He would need time to prepare his strike. One word to the president about his disloyalty before then, and Garcia would find himself at the bottom of Lake Pitouie.

He adopted the codename Claudius. He never revealed his face to his followers, always wearing a checkered bandana across his mouth and nose. He even cultivated the habit of standing in the shadows as he supervised their training in small arms and explosives. It seems incredible that on an island of only fifty square kilometres with barely 1,500 residents that such a secret could be kept. Yet his survival and success prove that long shots sometimes strike home. When death came to President Lopez that morning, it came as an utter surprise.

And what will the new president do with his authority? How will he pay the bills now that the island's best hope for instant wealth has been abandoned? Will he follow in his predecessor's absolutist footsteps, or will he chart a more populist course? Not That Magazine recently sat down with President Garcia for an exclusive interview to discuss these and other questions.

NTM: Mr. President, what are your future plans for Pitouie?

PG: First, we shall change the name. Pitouie is a name that was forced on us by the tyrant as a branding decision. It means nothing to us. We will choose a new name that reflects who we are as a people. This will show the world that the old regime is truly gone and now we stand on our own feet.

NTM: And after that?

PG: There will need to be a recovery operation to track down and retrieve the money that was embezzled by the tyrant. This may take some time. Who knows in what corners of the banking world he has hidden his plunder? But as the funds become available, some will be redistributed to the citizens directly, and some will be held in trust to pay for infrastructure improvements.

NTM: Such as?

PG: Paved roads, medical supplies, school books, electrical generators. Simple things to improve the quality of life for our citizens.

NTM: Sir, your predecessor was known for his autocratic and authoritarian leadership. Will this island know democracy under your administration?

PG: This island is a tribal society with long-established customs for reaching decisions. There are so few of us, it is easily possible for the entire population to debate a range of options and come to a consensus. This process is managed by a small group of elders who are held in high respect by all. This was how the island was governed for centuries before colonization. Even our late tyrant habitually left day-to-day decisions to the council of elders while he concentrated on looting the public purse.

NTM: If the former president was so disliked, how did he manage to stay in power in the face of this parallel source of authority?

PG: He ruled through secrecy and fear. Most islanders had no idea of his plans to sell the crater to the highest bidder. He never went among the people. He lurked in this palace and confided in no one.

NTM: Except you.

PG: Even I received the least amount of information possible. He always held back each detail until the very last possible moment. Longer, if he could get away with it. And those who did know his plans were unlikely to raise a fuss over them.

NTM: Why not?

PG: For fear of reprisals. The tyrant had two personal bodyguards who were not under my command. They reported to the tyrant directly and were paid highly for their loyalty. They were mere hired thugs, used to intimidate or even kill any threats to his power.

NTM: You yourself, I understand, are not a native islander.

PG: True. I, like the former tyrant, am a leftover remnant from colonial times. But I have lived here so long that I could never think of calling another place home. I love these people, and I am honoured to call myself one of their tribe.

NTM: How will the island find its way in the world now

that the waste dumping scheme has been scrapped?

PG: It is true that we cannot remain simple fishermen forever. After a transition period, this island will again make its voice heard in the world. We do not plan to be isolationist. We will invite foreign partners to invest with us in a sustainable, ecologically responsible, and ethnocentrically sensitive manner that will be transparent and mutually beneficial. My advisors and I are considering a number of options, but it would be premature to discuss them now.

NTM: Can you estimate how long it will take to put these plans into action?

PG: Look for us to be back in the game in a year's time.

NTM: Mr. President, thank you. And good luck.

PG: The honour has been mine.

"Merle?"

"Otis? Is that you? I can barely hear you."

"Sorry. It's a satellite phone."

"No shit? What's up?"

"I quit."

"Is this because of that story you wrote? I saw that. I told you, serious journalism is a scam. Is that what you're doing now?"

"Not exactly. But I am going to hang out here in the South Pacific for a while. Lots of interesting stuff going on. Lots to learn."

"You know, technically you're supposed to give us a month's notice."

"Do I have to bring up the three and a half months of vacation time you still owe me?"

"Okay, okay. Where do you want your last paycheque sent?"

"Get the boss to cash it and buy yourself a case of decent Scotch on me."

"What the hell happened to you out there, man?"

"I met this girl."

"Say no more. What if I need to reach you?"

"Put a note in a bottle and throw it in the ocean."

"She must be quite a girl."

"Yeah."

"Okay, kid. Good luck."

"Thanks. Hey, Merle?"

"Yeah?"

"Get the fuck out of there while you've still got some life in you. Go do something."

"Maybe I will."

The two thickset men panted and sweated and cursed in the darkness as they shoved the steel drum up the narrow path to the rim of the crater. The beams of light from their headlamps jumped erratically as they stumbled over shadowy rocks.

Unlike every other steel drum that had made this trip, this one was not empty. The straining men were not acting. The drum was full of concrete. Inside the concrete was Clement Bridgewell, former senior vice president of operations (retired (deceased)), IntraChem Holding Group Plc. Strapped around his dead head were a matching blindfold and ball-gag.

The two men got the drum to the lip of the crater, then paused for breath. Both men reached to wipe their brows. As their hands came off the barrel, it teetered for a heartbeat, then began to roll down the inner slope of the crater.

The two men shouted to each other and reached for the drum, but its metal surface was slick and offered no purchase. After a few yards, it had picked up enough momentum that the men wouldn't have been able to stop it anyway. The barrel rolled smoothly into the darkness, gathering speed.

The men looked at each other in the light of their headlamps.

There was the sound of a heavy object crashing through undergrowth, then a distant splash, then silence. The men shrugged at each other and started back down the trail.

Garcia emerged from the shadow of a boulder and watched the bobbing lights make their way down the slope. Well, that was that done. Imagine Varick thinking he could just let the man go wandering through the world after all that he had seen. Better to tie up the loose ends. Varick would never suspect that the plane had left for Thailand short one passenger. He was so trusting. Maybe he didn't have what it took to play this part after all. Maybe he should retire. Maybe it should happen sooner rather than later. The elders wouldn't like it, but the elders listened to the voice of the people. And he had people now. People could get him everything he needed. In return, he could give them a paradise.

He headed back down the mountain.

Otis stood on the beach watching the sunrise. He held the garbage can voice recorder in his hand. His thumb slid back and forth over the buttons, pausing now and then to play back a few seconds of conversation or interview. It was solid gold. It was a hell of a story. If he wrote it up, it would be worth a book deal at least. Maybe even a movie. He considered. He sighed. He slid his thumb over the buttons until the words "ERASE ALL?" appeared on the tiny screen. It would only take the slightest pressure of his finger.

Footsteps crunched behind him. He shoved the recorder back in his pocket.

"Here you are," said Sarah. She was holding a bottle in one hand and a pair of glasses in the other.

"Champagne," she said, hoisting the bottle. "A tradition at the end of every game. Hold these." She passed him the glasses and set to work on the cork.

"Three times makes a tradition?" said Otis.

"It does if we say so," she said. The cork popped out of the bottle and came to rest in a small pool of water between a stand of rocks. Foam overflowed the neck and splattered the sand at their feet. She poured out two glasses, then wedged the bottle into the sand. She raised her glass to him.

"To Pitouie," she said. "Now, no more."

Otis raised his glass in return. They drank.

"What do you think it'll be called next year?" he said.

"Doesn't really matter."

They drank again.

Derek Winkler is the editor of an obscure trade publication that you have almost certainly never heard of. He also performs any number of dark and arcane tasks for *Broken Pencil* magazine. He has done just enough freelance journalism to be able to make the claim with a straight face.

His two most prized possessions are a broken motorcycle and his grandfather's 1926 edition of The Complete Works of Shakespeare.